Amy Bloom is the author of two collections of stories, *Come to Me* and *A Blind Man Can See How Much I love You*, a novel, *Love Invents Us*, and a non-fiction book, *Normal*. She teaches at Yale University.

ALSO BY AMY BLOOM

Normal

A Blind Man Can See How Much I Love You

Love Invents Us

Come to Me

Away

AMY BLOOM

Away

Granta Books
London

Granta Publications, 2/3 Hanover Yard, Noel Road, London N1 8BE

First published in Great Britain by Granta Books, 2007
This edition published by arrangement with Random House, an imprint of
Random House Publishing Group, a division of Random House, Inc.

A CIP catalogue record for this book is available from the British Library.

1 3 5 7 9 10 8 6 4 2

ISBN 978-1-86207-970-0

Printed and bound in Great Britain by William Clowes Ltd, Beccles, Suffolk

For my family

Contents

July 3, 1924

    And Lost There, a Golden Feather in a Foreign, Foreign Land 3

    Apples and Pears 17

    The Song of Love 27

    I've Lost My Youth, Like a Gambler with Bad Cards 39

    If I Had Chains, I Would Pull You to Me 63

    Orphan Road 95

September 3, 1925

    Ain't It Fierce to Be So Beautiful, Beautiful? 109

    What Folks Are Made Of 141

October 5, 1925

    Hard Times, Hard Times 155

    O Beautiful City 169

    Bread of the World 181

May 19, 1926

    I Hope We'll Meet on Canaan's Shore 193

    Our Brief Life 203

    Author's Note 237

    Acknowledgments 239

July 3, 1924

And Lost There, a Golden Feather
in a Foreign, Foreign Land

IT IS ALWAYS LIKE THIS: THE BEST PARTIES ARE MADE BY PEOPLE in trouble.

There are one hundred and fifty girls lining the sidewalk outside the Goldfadn Theatre. They spill into the street and down to the corners and Lillian Leyb, who has spent her first thirty-five days in this country ripping stitches out of navy silk flowers until her hands were dyed blue, thinks that it is like an all-girl Ellis Island: American-looking girls chewing gum, kicking their high heels against the broken pavement, and girls so green they're still wearing fringed brown shawls over their braided hair. The street is like her village on market day, times a million. A boy playing a harp; a man with an accordion and a terrible, patchy little animal; a woman selling straw brooms from a basket strapped to her back, making a giant fan behind her head; a colored man singing in a pink suit and black shoes with pink spats; and tired women who look like women Lillian would have known at home in Turov, smiling at the song, or the singer. Some of the girls hold red sparklers in their hands and swing one another around the waist. A big girl with black braids plays the tambourine. A few American-looking girls make a bonfire on the corner, poking potatoes in and out of it. Two older women, pale and dark-eyed, are pulling along their pale, dark-eyed children. That's a mistake, Lillian thinks. They should ask a neighbor to watch the children. Or just leave the children in Gallagher's Bar and Grille at this point and hope for the best, but that's the kind of thing you say when you have no child. Lillian makes herself smile at the children as she walks past the women; they reek of bad luck.

Lillian is lucky. Her father had told her so; he told everyone after she fell in the Pripiat twice and didn't drown and didn't die of pneumonia. He said that smart was good (and Lillian was smart, he said) and pretty was useful (and Lillian was pretty enough) but lucky was better than both of them put together. He had hoped she'd be lucky her whole life, he said, and she had been, at the time.

He also said, You make your own luck, and Lillian takes Judith, the only girl she knows, by the hand and they push their way through the middle of the crowd and then to the front. They are pushed themselves, then, into the place they want to be, the sewing room of the Goldfadn Theatre. They find themselves inches away from a dark, angry woman with a tight black bun ("Litvak," Judith says immediately; her mother was a Litvak).

Suddenly, there are two men right in front of them, who, even the greenest girls can see, are stars in the firmament of life, visitors from a brighter, more beautiful planet. Mr. Reuben Burstein, owner of the Goldfadn and the Bartelstone theaters, the Impresario of Second Avenue, with his barrel chest and black silk vest and gray hair brushed back like Beethoven's. And his son, Mr. Meyer Burstein, the Matinee Idol, the man whose Yankl in *The Child of Nature* was so tragically handsome, so forceful a dancer, so sweet a tenor, that when he romanced the gentile Russian girl Natasha, women in the audience wept as if their husbands had abandoned them, and when Yankl killed himself, unwilling to marry poor pregnant Natasha and live as a Christian, everyone wept, not unhappily, at his beautiful, tortured death. Meyer Burstein is taller than his father, with a smart black fedora, a cigarette, and no vest over his silk shirt.

The two men move through the crowd like gardeners inspecting the flower beds of English estates, like plantation owners on market day. Whatever it is like, Lillian doesn't care. She will be the flower, the slave, the pretty thing or the despised and necessary thing, as long as she is the thing chosen from among the other things.

Mr. Burstein the elder stands close to Lillian and makes an announcement. His voice is such a pleasure to listen to that the girls stand there like fools, some of them with tears in their eyes at its gathering, thunderous quality, even as he is merely telling them that Miss Morris (the Litvak) will pass around a clipboard and they are to write down their names and their skills, or have someone write this down for them, and then Miss Morris will interview them all and indicate who should return tomorrow evening for more interviewing. There is a murmur at this; it was not so easy to get away for even one night, and Lillian thinks that the bad-luck mothers and the women who look as if they've walked from Brooklyn will not be back.

Miss Morris approaches Lillian. Judith and Lillian have rehearsed for this moment. "Very well, thank you," if the question seems to be about her health; "I am a seamstress—my father was a tailor," if the question contains the words *sew, costume,* or *work;* "I attend night classes," said with a dazzling smile in response to any question she doesn't understand. Judith will get the job. Things being what they are, Lillian knows that a girl who can sew and speak English is a better choice than a girl who just got here and can barely do either.

Lillian studies the profile of Reuben Burstein; the impresario looks like a man from home. She heard his big, burnished voice, and like a small mark on a cheek, like a tilt in the little finger of a hand injured a long time ago, the tilt and the injury both forgotten, underneath she heard Yiddish.

Lillian moves. She presses close to Reuben Burstein and says, "My name is Lillian Leyb. I speak Yiddish very well, as you can hear, and I also speak Russian very well." She digs her nails into her palms and switches into Russian. "If you prefer it. My English is coming along." She adds in Yiddish, *"Az me muz, ken men,"* which is When one must, one can. When Reuben Burstein smiles, she adds, "And I am fluent in sewing of every kind."

The Bursteins look at her. Miss Morris, who did have a Lithuanian mother but was born right here on the Lower East Side and graduated from the eighth grade and speaks standard Brooklyn English, also looks at Lillian, without enthusiasm. The crowd of women look at her as if she has just hoisted up her skirt to her waist and shown her bare bottom to the world; it is just that vulgar, that embarrassing, that effective.

The elder Mr. Burstein moves closer to Lillian. "Bold," he says and he holds her chin in his hand like he will kiss her on the mouth. "Bold. Bold is good." He waves his other hand toward Miss Morris, who tells all the women to form groups of four, to make it easier for her to speak to them. There are immediately fifteen groups of four. Lillian loses sight of Judith. She feels like a dog leaping over the garden wall. She smiles up at Reuben Burstein; she smiles at Meyer Burstein; she smiles, for good measure, at Miss Morris. Lillian has endured the murder of her family, the loss of her daughter, Sophie, an ocean crossing like a death march, intimate life with strangers in her cousin Frieda's two rooms, smelling of men and urine and fried food and uncertainty and need. Just so, she thinks, and she smiles at these three people, the new king and queen and prince of her life, as if she has just risen from a soft, high feather bed to enjoy an especially pretty morning.

Reuben Burstein says in Yiddish, "Come back tomorrow morning, clever pussycat." Meyer Burstein says, "Really, miss, how is your English?" And Lillian says, very carefully, "I attend night classes." She pauses and adds, "And they go very well, thank you."

IT HAD TAKEN EIGHT HOURS for Lillian to get from Ellis Island to the Battery Park of Manhattan and another four to find Cousin Frieda's apartment building. She had read Cousin Frieda's letter and the directions to Great Jones Street while she stood on three different lines in the Registry Room, while the doctor watched them all climb the stairs, looking for signs of lameness or bad hearts or feeblemindedness. ("You step lively," a man had said to her on the crossing. "They don't want no idiots in America. Also," and he showed Lillian a card with writing on it, "if you see something that looks like this, scratch your right ear." Lillian tried to memorize the shape of the letters. "What does it say?" "What do you think? It says 'Scratch your right ear.' You do that, they think you can read English. My brother sent me this," the man said and he put the card back in his pocket, like a man with money.)

They had room, Cousin Frieda's letter had said, for family or dear friends. They had a little sewing business and could provide employment while people got on their feet. It was a great country, she wrote. Anyone could buy anything—you didn't have to be gentry. There was a list of things Frieda had bought recently: a sewing machine (on installment, but she had it already), white flour in paper sacks, condensed milk, sweet as cream and didn't go bad, Nestlé's powdered cocoa for a treat in the evening, hairpins that matched her hair color exactly, very good stockings, only ten cents. They had things here that people in Turov couldn't even imagine.

Lillian had walked through the last door, marked PUSH TO NEW YORK, and showed her letter to a man moving luggage onto the ferry.

He smiled and shrugged. She held up the letter and the block-printed address a dozen times to faces that were blank or, worse than blank, knowing and dubious; she held it up, without much hope, to people who could not themselves read and pushed her aside as if she'd insulted them. She hadn't imagined that in front of her new home, in her new country—after the trolley cars and the men with signs on their fronts and their backs, the women in short skirts, the colored boys with chairs on their backs and pictures of shiny shoes around their necks, and a team, an old man in red pants working with a young girl with a red hat, selling shoelaces, fans, pencils, and salted twists of dough, which smelled so good, Lillian had to cover her mouth and swallow hard—the first thing she would see when she finally got to Great Jones Street was a woman in her nightgown and a man's overcoat, weeping. Lillian watched the woman open a folding chair and take a china plate from her pocket and hold it on her lap. People passed by and put a few coins in the plate.

Cousin Frieda had run down the stairs and hugged Lillian. "Dear little Lillian," she said. "My home is your home." Frieda was thirty. Lillian remembered her from a family wedding when Frieda took her into the woods and they picked wild raspberries until it was dark. Lillian watched the woman across the street, sitting stock-still in the chair, tears flowing down her face onto her large, loose breasts, dripping onto the plate with the coins.

"Eviction," Frieda said. "You can't pay, you can't stay." She said in Yiddish, *"Es iz shver tzu makhen a leben."* It's hard to make a living.

She wanted to make sure Lillian understood. She didn't want Lillian to be frightened, she said, everything would work out fine between them, but Lillian should see, right away, how it's nothing to go from having a home, which Lillian does now, with her cousin Frieda, to having no home at all, like the woman over there who was thrown out this morning. Lillian did see.

Frieda took Lillian by the hand and crossed the street. She put a penny in the plate and said, "I'm sorry, Mrs. Lipkin." Taking Lillian up the stairs to her apartment, Frieda said to Lillian, "Poor thing," and she gestured over her shoulder to a small room filled with a bed and two wooden crates. "You share with Judith."

The lesson of Mrs. Lipkin was not lost on Lillian, still holding everything she had in Yitzak Nirenberg's leather satchel.

IT'S ALWAYS THE SAME DREAM. She's dead. She's blind, too. All she can see is a bursting red inside her eyelids, as if she's on her back in Turov's farthest field on the brightest day in June, closing her eyes to the midday sun. The entire world, the trees, the birds, the chimneys, has disappeared; there's nothing but a gently falling white sky, which becomes her bedsheet. A straw pokes through to her cheek and she brushes it away and feels dried blood on her face. She rubs her eyes and feels the strings of blood that were closing her lids. They roll down her cheeks and into her mouth, solid bits of blood, hard as peppercorns, softening on her tongue, and she spits them into her hand and her hands turn red.

She sees everything now, in all directions. The red floor. Her husband lying in the doorway, covered in blood so thick his night-shirt is black and stiff with it. There are things on the floor between them: her grandmother's teapot in four pieces, the bucket, standing on its mouth, the cloth they hung for privacy. A hand. Her mother is lying on the floor, too, gutted like a chicken through her apron, which falls like a rough curtain on either side of her. Lillian stands naked in the red room and the color recedes, like the tide.

Her father lies at the front door, facedown, still holding his cleaver against the intruders. His own ax is deep in the back of his neck. Her daughter's little bed is empty. Another hand is on the floor beside it, and she can see the thin gold line of Osip's wedding band.

Lillian screams herself awake.

Judith says, "Bad dreams."

Lillian nods her head and Judith says, sensibly and not unkindly, "You don't have to tell me."

And Lillian doesn't tell her that she'd heard the men whisper beneath their bedroom window, that the walls of the house had been so thin in places, she heard a man cough on the other side of the wall and another man sigh and it seems to Lillian that she had stopped breathing. Little Sophie lay on her stomach, dreaming, sucking on the corner of the quilt. The men put their shoulders to the door, hard, and Lillian reached for Sophie. The walls rocked violently, holding on to the door, but it was an old house, old wood, old mud, all pitted with holes as long and thick as pencils, and plaster began to fall from around the door. The wall would give way in just a minute.

Lillian put her hand over Sophie's mouth. Sophie's eyes opened wide in the dark and Lillian felt Sophie pressing her lips against Lillian's damp palm, to make little kisses in the dark. Lillian whispered into Sophie's ear, "Not a sound, *ketzele*." In the outer room, a man none of the Leybs had ever seen drove an ax blade into her father's neck and Lillian held Sophie tighter. Osip stood up in the dark room and the moon edged out briefly and Lillian's last glimpse of her husband was of a tall thin knight in an ivory nightshirt, fumbling for his glasses.

A man whose father's cattle grazed not far from the Leybs' barley stabbed Osip as he entered the outer room, and Osip's body fell in front of the privacy curtain. He crawled toward the front door.

Lillian wrapped her blue wool scarf around Sophie's neck and shoulders, tucking the ends into her little nightgown. Osip cried out. Lillian slid the small window open and lifted Sophie up. She kissed her on the forehead. "Run to the chicken coop," Lillian said. "Hide behind the chickens. Quiet. Quick. I love you."

She pushed Sophie up and out, holding her until the last possible second, so the drop would not be too hard. She may have said I love you too softly, she wonders about that all the time, but she couldn't say it again, she couldn't call out across the yard. She heard the thud of Sophie's solid little body, she did hear her say *Oh, oh*, very bravely. She heard Sophie's footsteps, hesitant, heading for the chicken coop.

Lillian shoved the little pallet and Sophie's doll under her bed and looked up to see a man coming in, pushing back the curtain. He stared at Lillian, weighing his options, or perhaps regretting the evening already (These dead people will not bring back his father's cattle; this may not be the Jew who cursed his father, after all). There was a long moment, the only noise in the other room the sound of two men dropping valuables (the kiddush cup, a small silver picture frame, a copper pan—there was nothing more) into a pillowcase; it took no time at all and beyond that, she heard the thin, persistent whistling of the constable as he ran his stick along the fence. The man came toward Lillian with his knife and Lillian, too, weighed her options. She stood up and faced the man, thinking that a long fight and a slow death would give Sophie her best chance. She flung herself toward him with the slowed, rippling clarity of physical disaster. The man swiped at Lillian's nightgown, cutting it from her underarm to nearly the hem, and it flew out around her.

Lying beside Judith in this warm, narrow bed, her skin tightens with the shock of that cold night air, when she had been sweating just seconds before. She had made her hands into claws, to go for his blue eyes, bloodshot but sky-blue even so, and he reached back to cut Lillian in earnest, and the constable called the men by name this time. He raised his voice in a friendly, firm way, as if he had caught boys smashing bottles behind a barn or bothering a girl in the market. "Go on home, comrades. Big night for everyone—go on home now. Enough." And the man slashed Lillian once across the chest, from her shoulder to her hip, and then shook his head, as if she had wasted his time. The constable called again. The men stretched their legs to walk over the bodies of Lillian's parents and her husband and one man knocked a teacup onto the floor; it might just have been an accident, a moment's carelessness as he wiped his knife on her mother's tablecloth. Then the three men walked out over the front door and outside and were gone, down the front path, away from the chicken coop.

LILLIAN UNDERSTANDS COMPLETELY the cool space Judith left between them after the evening at the Goldfadn. She is sorry. That is, she plans to apologize to Judith if Judith doesn't get a job, too. She plans to put in a good word for Judith, if it seems that putting in a good word is the kind of thing—showing generosity, loyalty, fairmindedness—that is rewarded by the Bursteins of the Goldfadn Theatre.

Lillian had washed out her cami-knickers and her hose and laid them on the radiator, which goes stone-cold in the night. At dawn, her stockings are still damp. Lillian slips out past Judith and walks to Second Avenue in her cold underthings and damp stockings.

Judith moves into the warm space Lillian has left. Lillian climbed into the lifeboat, and she didn't put down a ladder for Judith. Didn't even think of it. Didn't put down a ladder, she didn't put down so much as a bit of rope for Judith, without whom she would not even have known about the Goldfadn. Judith's been sleeping next to Lillian for five weeks, since Lillian's first day in America, and for five weeks, Lillian has been screaming into the pillow and grabbing Judith's petticoat with both hands, like it's a blanket or a body, and Judith has had to pull it back and shake off Lillian and her bad dream. Every morning it goes like this: Lillian screams, the teakettle whistles, and the three other night sleepers, the men in the parlor, get up and drink tea and eat bread in the kitchen until Lillian and Judith have dressed. There'd been four night sleepers, Judith and three men, which was not too bad, and now Lillian makes five, plus two more men, day sleepers who Judith sees only when they come in and lie down in the bed Judith and Lillian have just left. One lost a sock under the bed, and Judith thought about him, that he must have gone all day with one sock, bleeding at the back of the heel.

After they eat, the men go out and Judith and Lillian and Frieda spread the sewing out on the big table. Lillian is a learner, is what Frieda says. Lillian does the idiot jobs Judith used to do: pulling out basting, separating silk flower petals for the hats, pinning pink feathers to pink felt, removing buttons. Their fingertips are covered with small blackened holes where they have pricked themselves a hundred times and the dye has seeped in. Judith and Frieda speak in Yiddish and Russian, and a little English for things for which there are only English words (*movies, subway, pizza pie*), and Lillian tries.

Even if Lillian had stayed home on July Fourth, it would be just Frieda and Judith having a cup of tea. It would be Lillian's turn to buy thread and pick up the sheaf of patterns. Frieda ("Call me Fritzi," she tells everyone) pays them both a dollar a day, minus the rent, of course, and minus money for the breakfast she makes ("I wouldn't let you go hungry," she tells Judith).

Frieda sleeps in the kitchen on two chairs pushed together. It hurts her back, all right, and she would not ask to have boarders, a tragic cousin and six other people, living with her. She would not ask to bargain every month with Italians for the privilege of doing piece-work in her apartment, but she sees it all as part of the great ladder upward. She feels the smooth, pale wood under her hands, she sees her feet settled firmly beneath her; she dreams almost every night of her spiritual home, Fifth Avenue, and she is strolling with her friends, well-dressed women flashing silk ankles and strapped shoes, accepting compliments from handsome, prosperous, cigar-smoking men (clean-shaven, well-spoken men), climbing the polished marble steps to her brownstone, in which Frieda waltzes from room to room,

skirt flaring as she catches a glimpse of the gleaming porcelain fix-
tures in her modern bathroom with its black-and-white tile floor, the
whole place gas heat only, silver platters on marble counters, spilling
grapes, bananas, mangoes, and tangerines, and there are white sheets
and a dozen white pillows on her damask-canopied bed.

In the fifty-seven blocks of the Lower East Side, just that day in
July 1924, there are a hundred and twelve candy shops, ninety-three
butchers, seventy saloons, forty-three bakeries, and five hundred
thousand Jews. When Frieda looks out the kitchen window, the only
window, she sees Opportunity.

Lillian wants to see Opportunity, too. She waits at the door
of the theater, trying to feel a warm sun beating down on her, drying
her knickers. If she gets this job, she'll buy Judith a little something.

The first time Judith ever really spoke to Lillian was a week ago.
Two pins dangled in the corner of her mouth. They bobbed up and
down as Judith worked, moving only a little when she whispered to
Lillian that they were hiring seamstresses the next Sunday at the
Goldfadn Theatre. Every girl in the city from Delancey to Fourteenth Street would go. Judith was on her way to being an American
girl. She gave away her shawl—she told Lillian she *gave* it away, she
wanted so bad to be rid of it—and bought a little blue jacket at
Kresge's. Judith has the American shoes and the green blouse she
bought from the vendor, irregular but very good, and she is learning
English very fast. To Lillian, Judith's English is good already; it's like
something you hear on the radio.

On the way to the Goldfadn, Judith had steered them past piles
of horse shit and crying children and men selling fireworks, and they
stopped for hot dogs and mustard and sauerkraut, and the man gave
them extra because Judith has a way about her. That's what she said
to Lillian, I have a way about me, as one might say, I am right-

handed. Lillian might have a way about her, too. Back in Turov, there were people who thought she had a way about her, but not here. In English, she is the ugly stepchild; people are not inspired to give her things; they don't even want her to be where they are looking.

THAT'S WHAT IT'S LIKE. She dreams of the murder of her family. She wakes to the sound of her own screaming and to Judith's warm body. She eats bread and cabbage with strangers in a small, dirty room. She puts in and takes out stitches to make cheap hats, puts together blue petals and takes apart flawed silk flowers, and she does it all badly. She learns the language of a country that terrifies her so that she can dig deeper into it and make a safe hole for herself, because she has no other home. She walks with Judith down Essex Street Saturday nights at eight o'clock, to watch the modern world, to move like an ox, among Americans.

She bangs on the Goldfadn door again.

She imagines herself doing whatever either Mr. Burstein wishes her to do. She doesn't know much, but perhaps not knowing will appeal to them even more than something else, something Lillian imagines prostitutes do, and if she knew what it was she would be rehearsing it right now.

Miss Morris opens the door. Oh, she says, you're on time. In here, she says, and Lillian does not find herself unzipping the younger Mr. Burstein's pants and does not find herself sitting on the lap of Mr. Reuben Burstein; she finds herself putting on a neat black smock and taking her seat next to a fat, pretty girl named Pearl, with brown curls and a pink, friendly smile. Miss Morris hands her a gold velvet tunic and tells her to take in the waist two inches—Lady Macbeth has lost a little weight.

She has gone on, she has traveled through a terrible darkness and come upon Jerusalem surrounded, Jerusalem saved.

Apples and Pears

L ILLIAN DOESN'T LIKE TO THINK OF IT AS A HABIT, AND SHE doesn't like to think of it as stealing. She borrows, is what she says to herself—she just borrows like crazy from the other boarders. Pennies that have rolled out of Joe's pocket when he's drunk on the couch, never more than two every few days, to save up for decent stockings, for a wide leather belt to keep her dress closed. She eats the extra slice of bread Joachim leaves behind. Every day at the Goldfadn Theatre is an Opportunity, and you can't wait for Opportunity to find you. Frieda says that all the time; she talks nonstop about Opportunity as if it is a handsome man riding by and you have to toss your hair and pinch your cheeks and leap into the middle of the path, whistling, to make him stop. Frieda is such a big believer in Opportunity and Getting Ahead that she doesn't yell at Lillian for taking the job at the Goldfadn and leaving her shorthanded with the hats. Frieda contemplates and moves on to Joe, encouraging his interest in Judith, who got nothing at the Goldfadn and would not now pour dishwater on Lillian if Lillian was on fire. Frieda encourages Judith to consider Joe's good qualities (he's honest, Frieda says, and he wouldn't drink if he had a woman). Frieda has offered Lillian the couch if she wants to sleep alone; not next to Judith, who would like to cut her throat while she sleeps, is what Frieda means, but Lillian would rather sleep next to a woman who hates her, who lets an elbow slide out sharply into Lillian's kidneys, who lays a heavy arm on Lillian's hair when she turns over, than give up another nickel for the couch. If everyone would cooperate, Frieda could move Joe and Judith onto the bed as a couple and Lillian onto the couch, charging her a little more than she charges Joe, who is a man and brings coal and city wood to them on his way home every day, but she can see how Lillian figures it.

Frieda leans out the window to watch Lillian on her way to the Goldfadn. She's not too surprised little Lillian is carrying on and she's not sorry, either. She's heard things and it can't hurt to have her own cousin the mistress of someone at the Goldfadn Theatre.

Lillian is not anyone's mistress; she would be Meyer Burstein's if he wanted—every girl in the costume room would, and the actresses, too, and the women who gather around after his performances, even married women, their husbands standing by shyly, like peasants offering their wives to the duke, lucky if their lives are touched by his interest.

Meyer Burstein may be having sex with someone, but it's not Lillian and since it's not Lillian, and there's no reason to think that he's angling for it to be Lillian, how has it come to pass that Meyer Burstein asks her out for tea and cakes at the Royale? Lillian has stood in the wings and watched *Macbeth* followed by *Flowers Among the Thorns;* she has seen *The Queen of the Moon* (which Meyer says was originally about a king, not a queen, and his two ungrateful daughters and the one good one); and she has seen seventeen plays about New York, New Jersey, and Odessa (also some make-believe kingdoms and the Catskills, as well), and prodigal returns and assimilation and the persecution of Jews, and now she watches for the dropped line, the lost prop, the missed cue, like a stagehand. But Meyer's performance always takes her the way it did the first time she saw him. He is Romeo to the Juliet of Ida Liptzin, whom Lillian could do without, batting her thick lashes like a spaniel and sweeping about the stage, brusque and bossy, as if she were Mrs. Montague getting ready for a dinner party instead of a young, lovesick girl. Meyer is a wonderful Romeo, impetuous, tender, burning with passion, and there is even a wry café wit that Lillian is sure is Burstein, not Shakespeare (about which she is correct; the Bursteins have taken the best of Shakespeare, skipped over some dull pieces of business, given a lot more lines to the Nurse, a role clearly written for the Yiddish theater, and made a few judicious cuts that have transformed Romeo from a boy in love—by its nature a joke to the Goldfadn audience—into a passionate, full-grown man torn between duty and love, which everyone understands). Women throw white roses, which are the Meyer Burstein flowers, and men cheer.

Meyer has told Lillian to come right to his dressing room after. He wants her to watch his transformation; when he dips his hand into the thick cold cream, wiping off greasepaint and powder, wiping away the darkened eyebrows, the blue dots at the corners of his eyes, the white triangles at their edges, the pink slashes across his cheeks, it is like undressing. Lillian stands in the doorway, her hands clasped. Meyer steps behind a screen and comes out slowly with a navy-blue paisley dressing gown over his dark trousers and a stained white towel around his neck. "Come in," he says. "Have a seat. I'll be done in a jiffy." He scrubs his face clean, and then, as if he has just noticed the water dripping onto his dressing gown, he tosses the robe over the chair and stands in front of Lillian in just his undershirt and dress pants. Osip did not look like this. This is a beautiful man, like a beautiful chestnut horse.

He puts on a clean shirt, so sharply ironed the breast shines like ice, and tucks it in, and when he puts on his jacket, he leaves the collar turned up. Lillian puts her hand out and then takes it back. Meyer smiles. "Do I need fixing?" Lillian nods, and, her heart beating loudly, she smooths the lapels of Meyer Burstein, the Matinee Idol, and feels the muscles of his chest. He offers his arm, and they walk to the Royale, and the three blocks are like a dream.

Meyer's father is already at a small table in the corner of the crowded room, sitting with a thin, dark man as shabby as the Bursteins are elegant. Meyer kisses his father and nods to the other man. Lillian has no idea what the appropriate behavior is; she has never been out with rich men; she has never been on what anyone here would recognize as a date (kisses behind the barn, an interminable evening with Osip's mute, glowering parents and his whey-faced sisters). She has never been in a café like this, theater people, women wearing makeup and spangled hats and waving cigarette holders, blowing bright-red kisses and smoke at men in velvet capes who are laughing as if they've heard something fresh and funny and possibly obscene, and all of it apparently swirling about the Burstein table.

Reuben Burstein kisses her hand, and Meyer helps her into a slippery, curvy chair. Lillian bangs her knee on the wrought-iron leg of the table. Reuben Burstein says in English, "We're so glad to have you join us," and in Yiddish, "You've become a big favorite with my son." Meyer orders food for both of them and puts his hand on the back of her chair. He says he has to circulate for just a minute.

The thin man looks from Lillian's breasts to Meyer's handsome back, disappearing into the crowd. He winks at her, horribly, as if he has seen the depths of her desire and despair and her calculation, as if every stolen penny and pinch of powder and pocketed button has been totted up and entered. She looks away to Reuben. She will start a conversation with Reuben Burstein if it kills her; she's not going to look again at the thin man with the dark, dark hair and sharp black eyes and skin as white and smooth and bloodless as candle wax.

Reuben Burstein introduces the man. "My dearest friend—"

"Your only friend," the man says. "The rest schnorrers, slaves, and four-flushers."

The last word is in English and Lillian doesn't know it. She is sure the man wants to make her aware of how much she doesn't know.

"Yaakov Shimmelman," Reuben says.

The man bows and hands Lillian his card.

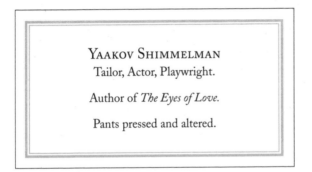

YAAKOV SHIMMELMAN
Tailor, Actor, Playwright.

Author of *The Eyes of Love.*

Pants pressed and altered.

Lillian laughs when she reads the card.

"It's funny?" Yaakov says coolly.

"No, no, it's not funny," Lillian says. There is no way to pretend she hasn't laughed.

Yaakov turns to Reuben Burstein.

"She laughed at my card," he says. "She found it funny. You saw that she laughed."

It may be that he's crazy and everyone knows it, but that does Lillian no good; he's Reuben Burstein's old friend, she just heard, the best friend of Reuben Burstein. She has ruined her life by laughing.

"It's not funny," Lillian says. "I was surprised. I was—"

Yaakov puts his hand on Lillian's.

"I was just teasing you, *ketzele*. Of course it's funny. It's true, it's absolutely tragic"—and he adds, in English, "abso-tive-ly, pos-a-lootly"—"but that does not make it any less funny. For people like us," and he looks at her closely, to see if she is people like him, and he seems satisfied, "that makes it even a little bit funnier."

Lillian notices that Reuben Burstein is rubbing her back, while he tells her that Yaakov Shimmelman is harmless, just high-strung, no one to be afraid of.

Yaakov pushes a plate of herring and a basket of rye bread toward her. "For God's sake, eat, girlie. The Bursteins are paying, and for a tailor and a seamstress, for people like us, that means time to eat." Reuben tells his friend to calm down, not to frighten the child.

Meyer comes back to his father and his father's best friend enjoying Lillian, fixing her little herring sandwiches and pouring slivovitz from Yaakov's flask. Meyer doesn't drink Yaakov's Old World rotten-fruit booze; Yaakov has nothing to offer, as far as Meyer is concerned.

Meyer looks at Lillian's pricked, dyed, callused hands. "You ought to get some gloves," he says. "Everyone's wearing gloves these days to go with their outfits."

He doesn't want to embarrass her, and he's not ashamed that she's a seamstress. He *is* ashamed that she's a seamstress, but she's a good-looking girl and not stupid, and her poverty, her seamstress-ness, is appealing; he is the kind of guy, he thinks, who wants a real woman, not just some painted doll or society girl.

Lillian smiles at Meyer and she tucks her hands into her pockets, and Yaakov grabs Meyer by the lapels like he's just kidding, pretending to be a tough guy when he's half Meyer's size and a nobody, and he says, in English, so it will mostly pass Lillian by, "You want her to have gloves, you big six, you buy her some gloves. You want gloves to match the outfit, get her the outfit. What she can get is that ribbon in her hair, on what she makes."

Meyer says, "It so happens it's a pretty good job. She's working for Hattie, and we treat the girls fair."

Reuben Burstein is above the fray. He watches everyone who comes in. He is kissed and hugged, in the Russian manner, in the less exuberant French manner, and a dozen more times in the universal and eternal theatrical manner. Pretty pink hands are laid on his thick forearm; older hands, still beautifully shaped but spotted, even trembling, smooth his shoulders, remind him of who they once were; men who remember when the Goldfadn was a room over a luncheonette come by to see if that memory matters to Reuben Burstein anymore. Reuben watches Meyer to see how he handles Yaakov, to see how the girl handles Meyer, to see what use might be made of clever Lillushka with the ruined hands.

Yaakov winks at Lillian and says in Yiddish, "Two things: a dictionary, you can get Russian-English; and what I like better than a dictionary, a thesaurus. Tells you all the words that are like the word you are looking up."

Lillian nods. A thesaurus.

"Also, listen to me."

Lillian has turned to watch Meyer moving through the crowd like the sun.

"If it so happens it doesn't work out, you call me, if you are not liking being Meyer's protégée," and he then adds, as if translating from the French, "his *kallehniu*," which does not mean protégée; it means little bride. Lillian understands that Yaakov is telling her, with some kind of tact, that her real job is being Meyer's mistress, even if the man himself has not mentioned it.

MEYER FINALLY SAYS, after three weeks of walks in the park and two nights at the movies and lots of hand-holding and kissing, "I'd like to spend more time with you."

Lillian has been waiting for this. He can skip the courting; he knows where she lives, he knows how she lives; he doesn't ask the details, but even Jews who live in nice brownstones in Brooklyn know how other Jews live on Great Jones Street. It's possible he took her for a decent girl who would be shocked and heartbroken at such an offer, but Lillian has done her best to let Meyer know that it isn't so, that she welcomes his advances (she brushes her breasts against his arm every time he moves, like a gentleman, to the street side as they walk), and that although she is not opposed to matrimony, she has no political beliefs about it at all and she is not bothered by the idea that two people might exist very happily in an arrangement that does not include a marriage license or a big party at the Concourse Plaza Hotel with white gown, rented carriages, a lousy five-piece band playing "If You Knew Susie" when the party gets going, and all of it costing serious money that Lillian can imagine much better spent on things a person really needs (requires, demands, claims, and also covets, craves, desires; Lillian's thesaurus is now her constant companion). The bookman sold her Webster's dictionary, fine and useful for what it is, and Roget's thesaurus, which has a little story for every word. This is like this, Roget tells her; this is related to this other; people on the street might say this like so; and then there is the antonym, introduced in 1867 by Mr. C. J. Smith, which is, sharply, exactly, and also completely not anything like that first word. Comfort: gladden, brighten, relieve, refresh, renew; idiomatically: to give a lift to. On the other hand: distress, perturb, bother, agitate, grieve. Her dictionary, and especially her thesaurus and the prospect of becoming Meyer Burstein's concubine, comfort her like a mother's hand.

Lillian has made all of this as clear as she can to Meyer, and he has said several times while they walked, and once when they were eating hot dogs, "You're a very sensible girl." Lillian loves hot dogs; she is a connoisseur of hot dogs now, and she knows to point to the one she wants, not the ones at the back, and she would choose a Nathan's hot dog over a Shabbat brisket anytime. Lillian nods and smiles. This is exactly what she has been telling herself. She is not dead, she is not what Yaakov likes to call "corpsy." She is just sensible.

The Song of Love

Meyer Burstein has made his move. He gets a little apartment for himself and for Lillian on Second Avenue, a block from the theater. He has prepared what he'll say to his parents at dinner—It's good to be able to stay the night after I do two shows; this way I don't disturb Ma when I come home late; what I save on cab fare will pay for the place; just a room, really, on Second Avenue—and his mother looks at him and says, "That makes sense, darling," and his father, who knows the landlord, who knows the locksmith, who knows the number one importer of mattresses, box springs, and bed frames on the Lower East Side, and who has spoken to all of them on Meyer's behalf, nods as if resigned to his son's independence.

Meyer buys Lillian an ice cream cone and they walk to Second Avenue.

"Come on up," he says. "I got a surprise for you."

If she were another girl she would be wrapping her arms around his neck, taking the starch out of his collar with her good fortune, admiring everything and begging to decorate, put tiebacks on the curtains, add some little favorite thing that will make the place hers. Lillian drops her book. She looks around. Very nice, she says. She looks at the icebox happily, she looks into the bathroom and sees the tub. She sits on the edge of the tub and looks up at Meyer like a cat who has just discovered where the sunlight falls. Meyer puts a key and five dollars into her hand. Tonight'll be our night, our night of nights, he says. I'm back by eleven.

There may be Romance, Lillian thinks. Sighing. Eating while looking into each other's eyes. She finds nice napkins and a pretty oilcloth for the table. If there are going to be big gestures, if there's going to be chicken thrown on the floor for passion's sake, she wants to have things ready. She loves the getting ready, she loves the shopping, she loves the bold walk through the fresh fruit and the Italian man watching her, judging her, then smiling, then offering, snipping a sprig of grapes from the stem with a beautiful bird-shaped pair of very small scissors. She puts the grapes in her mouth and wants nothing more than to sit on the barrel in front of the greengrocer's and contemplate the sweet, glassy crunch of grapes, and silver scissors just for cutting them, and her new life as a woman with five dollars and a rich lover.

She sets the capon on the sideboard with little plates leading up to it and away, Polish-style: cold potatoes with dill, herring and sliced onions in cream sauce, herring salad, carrot salad, white rolls, softening butter, two bunches of those green grapes, which she arranges and rearranges in the silver-plate bowl from Copeland and Perlmutter that Meyer bought last week, just like his mother's, he said, a little present to make our house a home. She pokes the grapes a final time, to copy the silver grapes that twist along the rim and drip thickly down to the base. She lays out in a fan shape the square American cookies with pink frosting that Meyer likes and cannot get at home. At home it is still *rugelach*, and *taiglach* so crusted with honey it makes his teeth hurt, Meyer says, forcing him to disappoint his mother. Lillian knows this because Meyer tells her the whole story of last Friday night, every detail, as if there is a greater point being made, as if now, when the truth about the too-sweet balls of dough and his aching teeth and his firm but not unkind refusal and his mother's frozen silence is revealed, she will see how it is. Lillian sees two things: Meyer shouldn't complain about the *taiglach*, and it will be some little while before Lillian the seamstress is invited to dine *en famille* with the Bursteins. Esther Burstein still makes her own *rugelach* on Friday mornings, and Lillian would come just for that. She wouldn't waste her spit on the pink cookies.

Lillian paces the red-and-pink flowered carpeting, she stretches out on the green damask settee. She fluffs up the wine-red silk cushion that Meyer has borrowed from the theater to hide a small hole in the seat of the rattan chair. The lights on the wall are low. Lillian puts a pink scarf over one, then covers them both. It looks like the walls are weeping pink tears. She puts the scarves back in the drawer.

Lillian looks at the room. It's like a stage set for a romantic comedy. *The Spring Flowers*, she thinks. *The Maiden and the Mensch*. There had been days, days in a row, when she woke up and watched herself yawn in the tragicomedy of Frieda's apartment. She'd stood across the room and watched herself at the basin. She'd told herself, A young woman in America would have breakfast now. She would have tea. A young woman hoping to see her boyfriend (her swain, her young man, and also her sheik, her crush) would wear this, would say that, would put her lipstick on like so. Lillian's life in Turov hadn't been a performance. She was a daughter, she was a wife, she was a mother. She was not acting like an anything then.

This is not strictly true. She playacted the dutiful daughter, wanting to knock her father's pipe out of his mouth for making such a poor deal for their wheat that it was as if they had worked for nothing. She pretended her husband was smart as well as gentle so people would not take advantage of him. ("I leave it to Osip," she told everyone. "He has the head for business. I just leave it to him," she said every market day, and thought, May God not strike me where I stand.) Like every mother, she feigned patience and goodness twenty times a day from November to April so she wouldn't lash out at Sophie, wouldn't wish to smack her just one time for spilling ashes on the rug and drawing in them when it was nothing more than winter fever, for both of them. None of this seems like pretending now; it seems like the warm opaque inside of being alive and with Sophie.

Lillian struggles into the peignoir set Meyer has left draped over the bedroom door. It is ridiculous. Irritating tight lace across the breasts, filmy green chiffon foaming down to her ankles. Cheap stuff, Lillian can tell—it warms too fast when she rubs it between her fingers. She can see the dark of her nipples and between her legs in the mirror, three stones at the bottom of a murky ditch.

It is ten. It is eleven. The show ends at eleven; it's midnight. Lillian takes a chicken leg and a bottle of wine and puts her feet up on the table. He might not come after all. It's not nice to be so late, but it's not terrible that he doesn't come. It is rude (crass, inelegant, uncouth, and also lacking in social refinement). She has bought the food he likes and put on the insane nightgown and spent the evening waiting for him, only flipping through her dictionary, prepared to have sex, willing to say to anyone who might want to know that Meyer is her lover, willing to be his lover (beloved, flame, inamorata, sweetheart) if that's what he wants.

Lillian picks up the other chicken leg. It's not so bad, the chicken and the wine, and the room is warm enough (she never, ever, minds being warm; only the cold frightens her), and she has the dictionary with her and the *Forverts*, in which she has begun reading a letter in the Bintel Brief section from a decent young girl—and they are all decent girls, Lillian thinks, you couldn't fill a section with Letters from Smart Girls with Their Legs Wide Open for Business. The writer of the letter is worried about her fiancé, the Talmudic Scholar, who has not come to Shabbat dinner with the Decent Girl and Her Expectant Family the last two Fridays. Someone—and Lillian can picture the someone, a nosy, hurtful bitch from the third floor, herself abandoned—has seen the Talmudic Scholar at the dance hall, bringing in Shabbat with a tango.

This is how Meyer's father finds her, bare feet on the table, green nightgown halfway up her white thighs, laughing out loud at the suffering of a decent girl.

"Oh, *gottenyu*, Mr. Burstein," she says, standing up, pulling down the nightgown, looking around the room like a woman trapped in a fire.

"I got a key," Reuben Burstein says. "Don't get up—finish your chicken."

"I am up—I get my robe," Lillian says. She is blushing so hard her ears hurt from the inside.

"You looked fine the way you were." His eyes are gleaming.

Lillian says, to understand a little better what is happening here, at midnight in Meyer's apartment, "It would be for propriety for you and me, I should get my wrapper."

Reuben Burstein shrugs. He seems to wink at her. Oh, Lillian thinks, and sits down again, without the robe. She sets her legs back up on the table. Her feet rest against the bowl that is like Mrs. Burstein's, her toes brushing the silver grapes. They both watch the hem of the nightgown slide up and stop at her knees.

He sits down across from her like she was waiting for him, like she's made him this lovely meal and he is right on time. He eats a grape.

"If you're comfortable," he says, "I'm comfortable." He takes off his hat and his jacket and puts them on the rattan chair with the burgundy cushion. He looks at the chair and laughs.

"Someone owes me for that cushion, Lillushka."

"All right," Lillian says. "I owe you."

Reuben Burstein walks past her and opens a little closet Lillian hasn't even looked into and takes out a towel. He pulls back the mint-green bedspread and the forest-green blanket, and he pushes the small, square mint-and-forest-green decorative pillows, the ones Meyer just bought, onto the floor, rolling his eyes.

Lillian looks at him. "Meyer bought that bed," she says.

Reuben stops what he's doing.

"Yes," he says, "and the pillows, I'm sure, and these are Meyer's sheets, too." He holds up the towel, waiting.

It's a contest now. If she'd said nothing, Reuben would have taken it on himself. They would have played the gentleman and the milkmaid, Reuben Burstein and the seamstress, he moved by her innocent beauty, she awed by his imposing presence. But they can't do that if she's going to say things like This is your son's bed you're planning on fucking me in, if she's going to make Reuben out to be—not that they don't both know but why make a point of it— a man who fucks his son's mistress while she's wearing a special nightgown his son picked out for a special evening.

"A towel you throw in the wash. You've had your bath, a few baths, you need a clean towel. Towels are no trouble."

Reuben smooths out the towel in the middle of the bed, and when he comes, although they've been all over the mattress meanwhile, he will have managed to position them both, to have them back on the towel when they need to be.

MEYER IS WALKING, not so slowly you would remark on it, not so fast you couldn't get a good look at his green suit, his dark-brown suede shoes. He couldn't bring himself to wear a red necktie, not even with a black suit; he is astonished at the nerve of men who wear their red neckties around the city on Saturday nights, men who don't seem to mind the dago brats and even his own people, their boys, sticking their fingers in their mouths, sucking hard, and yelling, "Hey, mister! Hey, Ethel!" at the red neckties. It is a long quarter-mile from the southeast edge of the park to the mall. Vaseline Alley, Bitches' Walk. It couldn't be Via della this or that or Rue de something nice. Filthy words, he can hear them in his father's big, rolling voice. His "I am Reuben Burstein, and let me introduce my humble assistant, God" voice. Lillian says that Meyer has the modern voice, the voice that goes with movie-star looks. Your father is Old World, she says.

If Lillian were here—well, Lillian wouldn't be here, but if this were another walkway—he could put his arm through hers and be at ease. They could walk through the park, for nothing, for a Sunday afternoon, he would show her places, they would have an ice cream. The first thing he did, one of their first dates, was buy her ice cream; something about ice cream every greenie loves. She had coconut and her eyes flew open with surprise, she had pineapple and laughed, and when he put a spoonful of double chocolate on her tongue, she closed her eyes and moaned and Meyer thought that it might be possible to be aroused by Lillian in bed if it involved ice cream. With Lillian, he would be Meyer Burstein, the Matinee Idol of Second Avenue, hilarious comedy one night, heartbreaking tragedy the next, women with flowers, and not just flowers, at the door after every single show, and he would not be this.

When he was twenty-two, Reuben had said to him, Let's go uptown. They went to Times Square, where his father tipped his hat to the prettiest prostitutes and smiled a little at the *faygeles* strolling by and looked sorry for the punks selling themselves in Herald Square. "Hard life for them," he said. "Maybe someone gives you money, maybe they give you a hit on the head. No one helps them, and so they in return, they are not so nice. Maybe they take a fella's money, maybe worse. The girls, too." They ate in Thompson's Lunch Room, and Meyer watched a man with blue eye shadow reach over and adjust the bow tie of the man he was sitting with. After the tie was straightened, the man with blue eye shadow patted the other man's cheek. In the corner booth, two good-looking men in elegant suits sat side by side. Meyer could see they were holding hands under the table.

"Fairies," Reuben said, and ordered lunch.

Meyer made what he thought was a sound of disgust.

Reuben shrugged. "Who do they hurt?"

His father steered him back downtown, walked him past the Everard Baths, and said, "Men go there. It's clean." Reuben nodded at a fancy set of bronze doors across the street, and touched the brim of his hat to the big colored doorman in brown overcoat and gold epaulets. The doorman nodded and raised his hand to his gold-trimmed cap. "You want a great whorehouse," Reuben said, "you gotta go French." They took the train again and Reuben lifted an eyebrow toward the public restroom on the platform.

"Dangerous," he said. "Any minute, could be the police. It could even be a cop that's saying to the poor schmuck, 'Come on over here,' you know."

Meyer's father had given him a five-hour world tour of Poofs on Parade, without asking him a thing.

MEYER IS ALMOST THROUGH the park. The man on the end of the bench at the corner, sitting next to the tough in tight pants, black curls, and a sailor's peacoat, who is next to an old queen batting violet eyelids and playing with the fringed ends of a white silk muffler exactly like Reuben Burstein's, a thought Meyer hopes will pass quickly—that man on the end looks up. He could be any man in a gray suit, any gentile businessman, blond as a hussar, of course, so Meyer's shame can be complete. The man lifts his brilliantined head like a snake and watches Meyer walk.

Meyer has a good walk; he has been crossing the stage since he was two. He can stroll, he can swagger, he can muse, lost in tragic thought, he can stumble like blind Oedipus. He can skip like Heidi of Switzerland if he has to. Meyer allows himself to look backward toward the man without seeming to, and to slow down half a beat. He breathes in, as if a baby-pink spotlight is on him. He breathes deeply into his diaphragm and lowers his shoulders so they look even broader, squared under his jacket. "The shoulders," his father likes to say, "are like breasts on a woman. They signal. They persuade." Meyer pulls his chin in a little to stretch his spine. He is as tall and long as Nature will allow him to be.

The man stands up. They walk along, side by side, and Meyer watches their feet on the gravel path. He cannot stop thinking about the incident in the park last month. A man was set upon by hoodlums—they held him down and gagged him with his own tie and tore branches off the maple trees and shoved them up the poor bastard's ass, and worse. He died, Meyer heard, and the newspaper wrote in its awful, leering way that the "Fruited Plain" had been blighted.

The rain's finally stopped, the man says. It has, Meyer says. I like your suit, the man says. Oh, Macy's, Meyer says. I have one just like it, the man says. Oh, yes, Meyer says.

There are huge shrubs, as tall as a two-story building, some of them; a few bent by years of wind make green brambled canopies. These are very popular. Meyer and the blond man look around, for police, for thieves, for harassers, for other couples. This is what it is to be this way; desire rises in you like a fountain of champagne, your blood is bubbling, and you're trying to smooth a place on the dirt so that gravel will not tear the knees of your green suit, and you're pushing the spiky black branches of the bush away from the back of your neck, and instead of perfume and the faint trail of musk or vanilla or cinnamon you get off a woman, it's the scent of his new leather belt and his cotton drawers and the smell of him and there you have it. It is the thing that ruins Meyer's life; it is like a lion stalking his mother's house, that smell. Warm skin and grass and that close, thick scent, onion, salt, animal. The air shimmers a little as the man pulls out his cock. Meyer would like just to breathe for a moment, but you don't kneel and breathe like a boy in a bakery when you're on your knees in front of a stranger, and Meyer closes his eyes and opens his mouth, and thinks, This.

IN BED, UNDER THE BLANKETS, Lillian puts her head on Reuben's thick freckled shoulder and her hand in the field of gray hair on his chest. She has never seen so old a man naked—she wants to look; it might be better not to look, but what she has seen clearly in the last hour, the big chest, the big belly, the arms like a blacksmith's, is fine.

Reuben's eyes are closed, so Lillian closes her eyes, too. They have more time, somehow, than she thought, and she relaxes. Drowsy, unmindful, at ease, adrift in Meyer's bed with Meyer's father, she feels herself fall through the sheets, the mattress, the linoleum floor, through the New York rain that has been falling for two days, through the pocked asphalt street, through the ocean and the sand beneath, through the splitting rocks and burning lava in the middle of the earth, to life before everyone was killed.

She opens her eyes. It is extremely painful, although not something you would choose to stop. It is like giving birth or making love the first time; you want it for what it brings, for what becomes of your life when the pain passes. In Yiddish, the word for blackberry, *ozhene*, is darker and sweeter. The word for rain, a fierce rain, *mablen*, is more troubling, and colder and more serious. What falls in Turov in November is like steel; it could take your house, drown your animals, cut your throat. Bed talk is not Oh, you doll, aren't you the berries, but words that feel like the tongue itself, little songs from the heart to the mouth, My beauty, my dearest desire, my sweet soul.

Reuben says, as if he has heard her, *"Zeiskeit."* Sweet thing. In Yiddish, in English, in Russian, and even in his dime-store French, he has calibrated exactly the distance from the present to the future, from possible losses to estimated gains, from Esther, his wife, to Gloria, his mistress, one of each, twenty years apart in age, Brooklyn and Brownsville, Wednesday night and one weekend a year, for the trip to Pittsburgh that Esther refuses to make. "You want to see second-rate actors in third-rate plays in a fourth-rate city?" Esther Burstein says. "Who's stopping you?" But Reuben can bring Lillian some books, at least. Why not? She's burning up to learn English. He can get her some decent clothes; she doesn't have to look like a Fourteenth Street whore. He can take her to lunch with Yaakov, who adores her. And if he keeps in mind that he doesn't love her, that he is too old to start over, that he is who he is, that love is not the reason people act like fools—it is the excuse they use to act like fools—this will be a nice little nothing. A fling.

Reuben doesn't ask himself why, if it's a nothing, he's already deciding which shows he might skip next week—no law says he has to watch every goddamned performance that takes place in his theater—and also there is the matter of shopping, of which books to buy her, and of the tone he plans to take—gruff, faintly disapproving, with a certain paternal fondness emerging—when he and his wife discuss Meyer's new girlfriend. And Meyer, Reuben thinks, can kiss his ass.

And Lillian, who can also chart the distance between Sweet Thing and My Heart's Dearest Desire, is returned, through the heat and the cooling earth, through the fields of Turov, up through the gray, charred rain of New York, to her dead American self.

I've Lost My Youth,
Like a Gambler with Bad Cards

THURSDAY AFTERNOONS, IT'S QUIET AT THE CAFÉ ROYALE. Manny the Hunchback knows to bring a tea for Lillian and a coffee for Reuben. Reuben sends Manny back for petits fours and leans against the wall, the favorite position for gangsters and royalty; he likes to see who comes in: the pretty women, news from Vilna, actors in rival companies (if they look discouraged or angry, he offers them coffee and cake and says, frankly, that it is painful for him to watch great talent go unappreciated).

WHEN PEOPLE SEE Reuben and Lillian sitting together, Reuben says, "It's the English lesson for Meyer's girl. Yaakov teaches, I buy the cakes, everyone goes home happy." Sometimes, to gild the lily, he says, "My Esther is more modern than you think—she wants Lillian to speak English at home." If there is any doubt—if the listener raises an eyebrow or looks at Reuben and then away, wanting to say, wanting to hear some brave soul say, "Esther Burstein wants Lillian to speak English in whose home? And why the hell should Esther care what language the girl calls out in?"—Reuben's face closes and he becomes Mr. Burstein, the Impresario of Second Avenue.

When people are difficult, he nods to Lillian, to show her she should sip her tea and take a bite of cookie. He sips his coffee. He adjusts his white silk muffler. He says, with great, menacing charm, So good to see you, darling—regards to your lucky husband. We miss you at the theater, old man. Come by this weekend for tickets. People smile back, a little frightened. And he nods to Lillian again—she should put down the cookie and touch the corners of her pretty mouth with her napkin, and then she should say, How nice to meet you, as politely, as nonchalantly (and he demonstrates nonchalance for her, tossing his imaginary blond hair, gazing off into a corner), as possible. It is a great comfort to Lillian when he does this. Step on their filthy necks, she thinks. Make them tremble. Make them weep with terror.

YAAKOV COMES IN with *The New York Times* and throws it on the table, piece-of-shit *farkokteh* right-wing anti-Semit' excuse for a newspaper, and he picks up a little cake. He eats it and then another, and points out to Lillian that in the despicable *New York Times*, unlike the *Forverts*—and he doesn't wish to offend her, a devoted reader, or everyone's hero, Mr. Burstein, that divine light, that golden sunbeam of the Yiddish theater—sentences are sentences. Yaakov eats another cake ("I'm saving you from yourself," he says to Reuben) and shoves *The Beautiful and Damned* at Lillian (modern American you can learn on, he says, plus insight into the moneyed classes). Gently he lays an English copy of *A Tale of Two Cities* next to his own seat. He lets Lillian plod through a few sentences of Fitzgerald, maybe a whole page of beautiful language she knows she is grinding in her teeth and spitting out like paste until she's ill with it, and then Yaakov takes it back and reads a chapter to himself while Reuben plays the professor with Lillian.

Reuben is the worst teacher in the world. He picks up the *Times* and reads a few headlines aloud, nodding editorially. He hands the paper to Lillian, and her damp fingers leave long black streaks on the front page. Reuben invites her to read—he commands her to read each article until the jump. He hounds her on diction and inflection: "You're not with the goats now, Lillian." He corrects every word. Most of the time he doesn't so much correct as allow his palm to drop sharply on the table as he says loudly, "Not like that—who speaks like that?" Sometimes he says, "You're a smart girl. You don't hear the difference between a *v* and a *w*?" And then he recites half of Hamlet's soliloquy, managing to roll not only his *r*'s, which is not easy for Lillian, but also his *w*'s, which is not easy for anyone.

When Yaakov has had enough of Reuben's bullying, he takes over. *"Neshomeleh,"* he says, "it's fine. Relax. The rest of the lesson is English only, but you'll see, easy-peasy. I'm going to show you some tricks." Reuben shakes his head. "Mister, it won't help." And Yaakov smiles and says, "Lillian, you know the joke?"

A great actor is performing in the middle of William Shakespeare's great play *Hamlet,* and in the middle of Hamlet's soliloquy *"Tsu zayn, nisht tsu zayn,"* the actor turns red in the face and keels over. A doctor runs onto the stage and listens to his heart. He turns to the audience. "Ladies and gentlemen, I regret to inform you that our star, the great Minskovich, has died." A member of the audience yells out, "Give him an enema! Give him an enema!" The doctor says, "Perhaps you didn't hear me. The man is dead." The same voice yells back, "Give him an enema!" "Sir," the doctor says, "the man is dead! It won't help." And the Jewish know-it-all calls back, "It couldn't hurt!"

Reuben and Yaakov laugh until they cry, and Lillian tells herself the joke at night until she has it from beginning to end, and it is the only joke she ever tells.

Lillian sighs. She reads aloud a short article (she looks for the shortest ones) about a gang of bicycle thieves on the East Side. She struggles with the sound that *cycle* makes. Reuben bangs his big hand on the marble tabletop, the cups jump in their saucers, and Yaakov pulls Lillian to her feet and begins to waltz her through the Royale, singing in his rough baritone, "It won't be a stylish marriage (*won't*, not *von't*), I can't afford a carriage, but you'll look sweet (*sweet*, not *sveet*) upon the seat (*seat*, not *sit*) of a bicycle built for two. Daisy, Daisy, give me your answer do." Reuben applauds, Manny the Hunchback refills their cups without being asked, which is like a standing ovation, and Lillian, who has just now been taught to waltz by Yaakov Shimmelman, thinks that if he was this kind, this buoyant, this insistently generous and gentle when his wife and children were alive, they must have been the happiest family on earth. She knows better; Yaakov has told her several times that he was not. "Before," he says, "when I was alive, I was a schmuck. Now I am the beautiful corpse. I am a waltzing cadaver. You know." And she does.

Reuben nods. If it were anyone else, he would change the subject—there's no need to talk about death in the middle of tea and cakes. But it's not only that Rivka and the twin boys died of TB and Yaakov did not, which is bad enough; it's that Reuben knows what bar Yaakov was in the night Rivka collapsed and what bar Reuben had to pull him out of when the boys died two days later. After he paid for the three funerals, and tore Yaakov's suit lapels and his own, Reuben woke up at two A.M. for no reason anyone could think of, took a cab from Brooklyn back to Second Avenue, pulled Yaakov out of the hot red bathwater, ripped up the thin sheets to make tourniquets, tied them around Yaakov's wrists, and rocked the man in his lap like a baby. Yaakov slept for fourteen hours while Reuben paced and smoked furiously and watched over him. When Yaakov woke

up, ashamed to be alive, Reuben left the room and didn't talk to him
for two weeks, sending a dull, homely girl to cook and change his
bandages. ("He should stir in you compassion," Esther said. "He
did," Reuben said and then he called Yaakov every name for a
worthless, cowardly, irresponsible piece of shit that you can find in
Yiddish. Reuben still likes to tell this story when people complain
about life.) Yaakov and Reuben both understand that Yaakov's life is
Reuben's now; that when you save the golden fish, the turbaned
djinn, the talking cat, he is yours forever.

Yaakov is pleased that his friend is pleased. The girl does something nice for him. She doesn't bring him back to the man Yaakov
knew thirty years ago (God forbid—who needs that arrogant, mer-
ciless, blind sonofabitch); she brings the man he is now closer to
who he might have been. When Reuben sees her coming, he frowns
as if she is late or badly dressed. (And she has been both, but she
takes her cues now from Reuben and Yaakov, and she doesn't wear
the things Meyer bought for her, the gay clothes that made her look
like a pony in a hoopskirt. She doesn't dress like Gloria the Mistress,
platinum blond and frankly piss-elegant, not that Yaakov would say
so to Reuben, and she doesn't dress like Esther, either, Madame
Burstein, very Grand Old New York with her pearls and black
cameos and elegant little gray suede pumps, which he happens to
know are a size too small. Now Lillian wears the clothes, they don't
wear her, Yaakov thinks, and she could shorten the front of that skirt
a half-inch and he'll tell her so. If Yaakov had been born in France,
he could have been in Chanel's atelier; he could have been Coco
Chanel, for that matter, since they are as one on the subject of mix-
ing costume jewelry with real, the appeal of the suntan, pants for
women, and above all, the need for insouciance.) Reuben frowns
when Lillian approaches because if he didn't, the smile would break
across his face like dawn, color would flood his high, lined cheeks,
and the whole world would know what so far only Yaakov knows.

Lillian has told Yaakov that Reuben feels like home to her. He himself would rather sleep in Battery Park than live under and on and within the confines of Reuben Burstein, but he knows—you need a roof, you need food, Look, you say to yourself, there's a nice fire going, you take what you need and then you sleep, safe for the first time in weeks. Lillian is a tramp stopping through for the night. Yaakov has told her so. Eat that last little bite, he says to her, warm your hands one more time, my dear, and go find your own house before the weather turns. When the owners come back, they won't let you stay.

EVERYONE HAS TWO MEMORIES. The one you can tell and the one that is stuck to the underside of that, the dark, tarry smear of what happened.

The scar across Lillian's chest is a dull red line.

The scar on her shoulder is a fat little oval of rough, ridged purple with a thin curdled edge of whiter skin, made by the hot underside of a steel soup spoon. She has been asked about it a few times, by an interested man, an interested woman. The interests are not the same. There is the curious caress, the soft cluck of the tongue from a man who might break your heart the way he ignores you during dinner but when he comes to the scar later he walks his fingers around and across it to the white buttons on your camisole, like you are a sweet, quivering bird, Sh-sh-sh.

Women say, Pox? Scarlet fever? A man? Oh, I have one like that on my thigh, twice that size, you should see, like a wild animal bit me.

Reuben has seen plenty of scars. He has plenty of scars: the blue cleft in his shin, long and wide as a butter knife, from the train he jumped out of near Uman; the tip of the finger lost to the ax in Lutsk; two toes gone to frostbite, and his feet ache even now in winter, as if crying for their lost parts; the thick ribbon of white braided skin around his neck, a bad night in Odessa. Czar Alexander II is killed, so what must they do but chase Jewish actors down the street with a wire noose. You ask people about scars, they tell you a terrible story, a story they want to tell more than they know. You could stop a man as he's about to put it into the prettiest girl in town and say, Hey, Yossel, that scar on your back, tell me how you got it, and he will ease away from the girl, pull up his pants, and say, That? That's an interesting story. Reuben was the same way until he turned sixty; then he didn't want to tell the story or hear it, either: terrible suffering, undeserved tragedy, unexpected luck. More often than not, someone dies, but not the person with the scar, of course, and so again and again they tell it, guilt and pleasure pushing their fingers over the mark, again and again.

"So, what's this?" Reuben says, touching the purple mark.

Lillian presses her shoulder against Reuben's hand and says nothing. It would be nice if he asked one more time, as if he really wanted to hear. She could even talk about her childhood, which is probably not so different from his. It's not Meyer's childhood, of course, which Meyer describes as a festival of sledding in Central Park, shopping at Bloomingdale's, and Sunday lunches at Ratner's.

"My mother was not a patient woman."

Lillian is working on the *w* sound. Reuben says she'll speak English like a real American, not a greenie. He's sure she will.

"My mother endured . . . she endured many things but she did not have . . . she had no equanimity and composure."

Everything Lillian says right now takes a few extra minutes so that she can weigh and choose the words. Reuben doesn't mind. His hand has fallen on her behind, kneading her a little bit through the nightgown, which feels like it will open up under his fingers, it's so thin. He'll tell Meyer to buy her silk drawers—why shouldn't she have silk and why shouldn't it be Meyer who buys them? It is only ten o'clock, there's a nice little fire going, he has a glass of vodka, some herring on a plate, very thoughtful of Lillian. Esther doesn't expect him home until midnight. It is by no means the worst scar he has ever seen, even among women.

"Go on," he says. "Go on, *ketzele*, tell me the story."

Lillian tells the story she can tell.

"When I was a little girl, I was helping . . . I thought that I was helping my mother to cook. She was making barley soup. A little chicken, cups of barley. I chop the onions, give her the bowl of onions. I stay standing there, I want to see, I want to stir, I want to help more. I am in her way, she bumps into me when she goes to get the chicken. She picks up the hot spoon from out of the soup, and *ssst*, into my shoulder, to teach me a lesson. That's the story."

Reuben kisses the scar. This ugly little patch of rough skin, he can see now, looking at it closely, he can see it has the tiny nicks and grooves that must have been in the metal when that woman pressed it into her child's arm twenty years ago, and still it is newer and fresher in the world than the sweetest, smoothest part of him. He traces the other scar, a thin red cut from her shoulder to her hip. Lillian moves his hand to her breast.

She says, "So, where's Meyer tonight?"

Reuben says he didn't know last week and he doesn't know this week.

"You could guess."

"I won't guess," Reuben says. "I don't mix in his business."

Lillian looks at him coldly, and then she laughs. Reuben laughs, too, but that is what he thinks. Where Meyer goes that Lillian doesn't know is Meyer's business. What Lillian does is now Reuben's business. He pats her on the behind. Lillian falls asleep and it seems that there is no reason, right then, for him to resist her. He puts his arms around her, as if they have been doing this for years.

Reuben holds her but not too long. It seems likely to him, suddenly, that Meyer may come here straight from the theater tonight, that what happened last week (home to Brooklyn by cab at two A.M., gone in the morning with a foolish note for his mother left on the breakfast table) won't happen again. Whatever Meyer's doing or done, sooner or later he'll come to Lillian.

Reuben gets up and Lillian opens her eyes, and together they re-make the bed. He picks up the foolish little pillows and arranges them as they were, and Lillian kisses him on the cheek for helping. Reuben is pleased by the kiss, pleased to be the kind of man who makes the small domestic gesture, which he is not, as a rule. He wonders why, knowing that Meyer will have to show up sooner or later, he made love to Lillian slowly, like it was summertime in a meadow, and they lay in the bed after, like nothing bad could happen. Like it was impossible to imagine Meyer bursting in on them in the middle of the act or while they drowsed on Meyer's sheets or were in the middle of pulling the sheets tight on Meyer's bed. It is not impossible to imagine, it is easy to imagine, because it is what any sane person would expect. Reuben gets dressed.

"Put on your robe," he says. "About that scar—that's not such a story to tell men."

It's not a story for seduction, he means. He means no man wants to marry a tough little doxy who tells a story about her mother deliberately hurting her. It's not encouraging.

"What should I tell?"

"Me, you can tell anything. But you know what women tell men. You know what men expect."

"Oh, this happened to the baby, that happened to the goat, this happened when I went to get a loaf of bread."

"That's right. Men like that. It's like a little melody in the background. The calliope music."

Reuben picks up Lillian's hairbrush. "Let me help."

"Men like to hear, 'Oh, you are a magnificent lover.' "

"Sure," Reuben says, smiling at her in the mirror, brushing her hair to the ends and curling them around his fingers. "You don't have to tell me—it's not necessary."

If she knew him better, she would ask, Not necessary because you are so confident, or not necessary because you know the truth and do not need to be lied to? It's fine with her that it was not magnificent (grand, majestic, lordly, glorious). It was pleasant, some tender kissing she hadn't expected, nothing to lose her head over. She prefers it this way, and Reuben does, too. She can tell.

Even as Lillian leans her head back and feels his thick fingers delicately unraveling a little knot in her hair, even as Reuben gathers her dark hair in one hand and pulls it up so that he can see and smell the white skin at the nape of her neck, they pretend they are not doing what they are doing. It may not even be right to say they pretend; they believe they are engaged in a sensible transaction, an exchange of goods and services, for which they have each done a fair and accurate assessment of who has what and how much might be ventured for how much greater return on what now seems to be a promising investment. They have no idea what they're doing.

MEYER SKINS THE BACK of his right hand pushing through the trees, hurrying home, and his knuckles are still sore and seeping red when he climbs into bed with Lillian. He walks past the food Lillian has left out, and he gets the message: You can eat, you can let it rot; it's nothing to me. The bottle of wine is almost empty. The ruined food tells him more about Lillian than he knew before; he thought she was a sweet girl, just a little greenie with big eyes and grateful for everything. You gave her a sandwich, she was happy, you gave her a piece of cake, she would kiss your feet. The actual Lillian would probably let vermin crawl over the table, let the grapes rot and the wine turn, before she would clear a single plate.

Meyer pours himself a brandy and washes his hands. He drops

his cuff links and pocket watch in the ceramic dish on top of the dresser. Lillian lies there in the uncomfortable nightgown. Reuben said he'd get her a nicer one to tuck away in the bottom drawer for when he comes to visit. It would be much better—better made, better lace—than what Meyer gave her, he said, and Lillian believes him. You cannot admire Reuben for his integrity (forthrightness, honesty, purity, honorableness), and a good man would not enjoy knowing his gift was hidden in the apartment his son pays for, but Lillian thinks that Reuben is better than honest and better than good; he is strong.

Meyer sips his brandy and watches Lillian sleep from the doorway. Lillian makes herself breathe in and out deeply, the way she used to pretend to sleep when Osip wanted her and she didn't want to, the way she has pretended to sleep every night in America, even and comfortable, as if there is nothing to be afraid of.

Meyer lies down on top of the bedspread, sliding on the sateen. He stinks; he can smell the dirt he knelt in and the other man's sweat, like malt and iron, and his own aftershave and the two beers he had coming home (as if this is home, as if beer would help) and the Sen-Sen he popped into his mouth coming up the stairs. He pulls himself up against Lillian's smooth back, and she lets him.

"Your shoes," she says, and he kicks them off.

Meyer rests his heavy green-gabardined arm around her waist, and Lillian lets him.

JUST AS THE STAGE-DOOR LADIES and *patriotn* imagine, even at seven o'clock in the morning, cheeks creased by his pillowcase, Meyer is a handsome man. Brown curls frame his white forehead, his lashes lie long and thick on his smooth cheekbones, and his nose is the nose of Yiddish theater, Roman, hawklike, balanced by the big Burstein chin (known elsewhere as the Barrymore chin, and the first time Lillian sees John Barrymore, eight feet high on the silver screen, teeth gleaming and a dimple as big as a hatbox, she will think, with happy surprise, of Reuben's chin). Meyer's mouth is full and red but not too red, and he is snoring a little, not unpleasantly.

She thinks about Reuben in his undershirt and loose suspenders, helping make the bed, smoothing the sheets, plumping the pillows, pulling the sateen bedspread tight over the corners so that the corded edges lined up with the mattress, quick and natural as a housewife. She liked him very much then, and she liked him most of all when she pressed her body against his and he said her name in English, and she stretched out on top of him so they were one from chest to hip, and he moaned at last, in Yiddish, that he couldn't resist her.

Lillian sighs. Meyer opens his eyes and smiles at her. A man stays out all night, sleeps in his clothes, wakes up stinking like a barnyard, and then he smiles, generous and sure, like the angel telling Abraham to be of good cheer. Without apologizing, something the Burstein men do not do, Meyer offers her dinner tonight at Ye Olde Chop House at 118 Cedar Street.

DINNER AT YE OLDE CHOP HOUSE is pretty much what it has been for the last hundred years: faded velvet banquettes, gilt-trimmed pink lights to flatter the faces, grilled veal and rabbit and terrapin and sizzling steaks the size of plates, on plates the size of royal chargers, and the customers are happy, hungry Christian men and their wives or their colleagues. This is not to say that they do not serve Jews ("Sure," Yaakov says, "baked or broiled?"), but Lillian can tell, anyone can tell, gentiles set the tone, which is ruddy and cheerful in some corners and swanky and gluttonous in others. She watches a man feed oysters to a beautiful red-haired woman whose white powdered breasts move up and down as she swallows, and Lillian stops watching only when Meyer kicks her. She has never seen oysters, never seen a man feed a woman, never seen that shade of red in nature. Meyer orders for them both: steak and potatoes and creamed spinach, which Lillian loves, she would order a bucket of it to take home if she could, and silver coupes of vanilla ice cream with hot cherry sauce, and after a little discussion the waiter brings two sodas to the table, which are really brandy made in Canada and poured into two Coca-Cola bottles and Meyer says, "Here's to President Harding," and the waiter smiles.

Meyer and Lillian laugh all the way home in the cab. Lillian rests her head against his shoulder, and Meyer gives her a squeeze.

"I won't look," the cabbie says genially, and Meyer kisses Lillian on the tip of the nose and then, deeply, on the mouth.

In the apartment, Lillian and Meyer undress. That's the thing that Lillian notices, they each undress. There is no frenzied tearing at belts and zippers, there are no buttons flying to the corners of the room. Meyer undresses down to his shorts and undershirt and lies down on the bed, his hands folded under his head, as if he is taking a little nap. Lillian takes the time to hang up her dress, put her hat on the top shelf, put her shoes side by side in the closet. She stands in front of the mirror in only her lace-trimmed cotton underpants, unpinning her hair, and Meyer watches her from the bed. She is a nicely made woman, solid as a little rock, with long ropy muscles along her spine. If he looks at her from the back, the square shoulders, the high white ass, the sturdy legs, he might be able to do something with her. The front, when she turns to him, is not his terrain. He knows what happens when he touches a soft breast, the warm fur between a woman's legs.

Lillian comes toward him uncertainly. She lies down beside him and puts her hand on his chest, sliding her fingers beneath the edge of his undershirt. Everything about him looks good, the broad chest, the flat stomach, the ribs high and wide like a ship's hull under his smooth skin, the strong arms that are not as thick as his father's, but prettier, of course. Even his long feet are pretty. He is the best-looking man Lillian has ever seen, and the most attractive, and lying next to him, seeing that he is unaroused (he is worse than unaroused, she knows, but she cannot bring herself to believe that the man who kissed her so warmly in the taxicab is actually repulsed by her near-naked body), she thinks that for him she is like wax fruit, beautiful at a distance but impossible to have the way God intended.

Meyer rolls toward her and puts his arms around her, and it doesn't feel like an imitation; his heart is beating fast, like hers, his skin is hot, like hers. He puts his hands on her breasts and with-draws them. He puts both hands around her waist and flips her over like a fish and spreads her legs. He puts his hands on her ass and pulls her farther apart. She can hear him thinking, as if he is whis-pering in her ear, All right then, this? You want this? He spits on his hand and rubs his spit into her, it makes her cringe but it is neces-sary, she is dry as a summer stream, and then, as if she has some lit-tle deformity that he is careful of, some small difficulty he must mind, he tucks a pillow under her stomach, and then another, and then he pats her twice, for warning or for comfort. He pulls her close with one strong arm and enters her so neatly that there may be only three or four inches of them that touch at all, and he bangs against her backside like a heavy wood door in a storm, and then the storm passes and the door swings out and quietly away.

LILLIAN WAKES UP with Meyer's hands on her, shaking her hard.

"You're screaming," he says.

"A bad dream," Lillian says, and rolls away from him.

"Tell me," he says in a soft voice, and she tells him, not the ac-tual dream—to speak those words would make her sick for Sophie for the rest of the day—but she tells him what Reuben would say is the kind of dream a man can stand to hear. She tells him she is walk-ing down a snowy hill and she comes to a grave. It is her husband's grave. He was very handsome, she says, and Meyer nods. She feels very sad in the dream because she has brought no flowers, and she starts to cry. Each tear becomes a flower, and soon the grave is covered in beautiful flowers.

Meyer loves the dream. It moves him. He pictures Lillian's handsome husband, slim with long dark hair, tragic-looking. He imagines them making love, Lillian's husband holding her pressed to his flat stomach, his strong, graceful hand knotted in her hair. Meyer looks at Lillian tenderly and rolls her over onto her stomach.

"You poor kid," he says into her shoulder. "That's terrible."

"Terrible," Lillian agrees, and lifts herself up for Meyer to put the pillows under her.

Afterward, they have tea in bed, naked. Meyer is eating the pink cookies he likes so much, and Lillian is eating a pumpernickel roll, and they are having a nice morning.

"Listen to me," Meyer says. "I'm not a romantic."

"You are kind," Lillian says. Romantic is not something she's looking for.

"I'm a regular guy. There are worse, I know—you read about it all the time. But I'm not . . . I'm not ready for marriage."

Lillian laughs and sips her tea.

"I just wanted you to know."

"Believe me," Lillian says, not wanting to insult him, but between the father and the son, she gets a little tired of what can't be said, "it is okay. I know."

There is nothing in it for Meyer to ask her what she knows, and even as he's thinking that he might just tell her, that she would be a safe person to tell, that they are not really so different, both of them trying to make their way in a hard world, that they could really help each other, Lillian gets up and washes herself in a very businesslike way. She does not wash herself with regret or longing or love, and although Meyer would not want to see any of that, although it would make him feel terrible to have brought any of that about, a woman who doesn't feel at least one of those things in these circumstances is as dangerous as dynamite.

Lillian looks at him, washcloth halfway down her thigh, waiting.

"So," Meyer says, "we understand each other?"

"Oh, yes," Lillian says. "Sure we do."

MEYER FINDS LILLIAN so accommodating (Lillian? Reuben would say. Anything but, even in her second language, but the two men rarely talk about her) and Lillian finds Meyer's body such a bland comfort, after the unexpected disturbances with Reuben, that she has fallen into a routine with both of them. Father and son are equally unpredictable about condoms and Lillian is sure her body will never hold another baby. It should not surprise her when her breasts begin to ache and swell and fresh coffee smells like skunk spray and the taste of red meat sickens her. But her time of month comes and goes, and it does surprise her.

Lillian's body repeats everything from her pregnancy with Sophie. She is as hot in the morning and as cold at night as she was four years ago. Her breasts are tender and swollen, and her nipples darken and chafe under her camisole. There is a metallic taste in her mouth most of the day, and bread and cookies and pastry fill her with a craving so deep it verges on sorrow.

And Lillian remembers every odd little thing about the day Sophie was born. Standing in the yard, chickens scattering at her approach and then coming up to her bare, swollen feet as if they were some new animal. Standing with one hand rubbing the small of her back, belly stretching a housedress let out three times. She had just thrown a bedsheet over the line when she felt a snake of pain from her back to her groin to her rib cage, circling her body, biting as it went. She must have fallen in the yard, because there was dirt on her arms and hands as she clutched the wooden bedposts, but her legs were white and wetly clean and her mother was holding them, and Tante Liesl, who assisted with all the babies, was massaging Lillian's inner thighs and saying encouraging things that Lillian could not quite hear over her own cries. Lillian pushed and fell asleep, screamed with pain and fell asleep again.

Much later, her father had pulled up a chair a few feet away from the bed, smiling behind his pipe, and Osip sat on the floor, holding Lillian's hand and saying her name. Sophie was round and red, muttering in disbelief, and, when she realized that the cold and the light and vastness of the world was not a passing unpleasantness, she squalled in outrage. She had a shock of black hair like a paintbrush and her eyes were midnight blue, and although Tante Liesl said they would change in a few months and they all watched for the change, none came. Sophie was born red-cheeked and blue-eyed, filled with understanding and opinion, and she stayed that way.

Sophie's happiness was Lillian's. Even Lillian's mother, who had nothing to spare for anyone, could always find two scraps of cloth to make a clothespin doll for Sophie, or a crescent of cinnamon dough to drop in a little oil. When her mother gave to Sophie, Lillian forgave her, and when Lillian dried Sophie after her bath and the two women watched her grabbing her toes, singing to each one, it was as if the house had only ever held happy children and loving mothers.

This new clump of cells (handful, bulge, ball) will never be Sophie. Lillian imagines another baby, a girl, dimpled like the Bursteins, and it makes her sick. She asks around, as one does; carefully, obliquely, she turns conversation in the direction of Dr. Tolman's Monthly Regulator and what it might or might not do. Slippery elm, one of the Goldfadn seamstresses says, and another says, Slippery elm—what are you, an Indian? And another girl puts her arm around Lillian's waist in the cloakroom and says, Lye. You put it right up you, as much as you can stand for as long as you can stand it; you don't want to let it run out too fast. The same girl comes back the next day, rushing to Lillian like someone who's got an even better tip on the big race. You gotta throw yourself down a flight of stairs, she says—that'll do it. I'm sure it will, Lillian says, and thinks that while she is hesitating to poison, burn, and maim herself, she should talk to the putative fathers.

LILLIAN CATCHES THE N TRAIN, right near the adult-education classes that she used to go to, when she wasn't too tired, when she couldn't get Joseph, who made more money than anyone else in Frieda's apartment and stammered badly and smelled like smoke and rotting leather and was therefore desperate for company, to take her to the movies, which for Lillian was also an education. Lillian looks high and low for Reuben. When she does find him at the Blue Bonnet, Reuben puts down his sandwich and says, "A grandfather. *Keine hora.*"

"Grandfather," Lillian says, and thinks that there is a way in which men are not like human beings at all. "It's more likely yours than Meyer's," she says.

Reuben shrugs. Meyer looks so much like Reuben as to make no difference. Meyer would have a wife, Esther would relax, the Burstein line would continue, Second Avenue would rejoice, Lillian, his darling girl, would be a wife and a mother, his daughter-in-law, and they would have to stop their nonsense and behave like decent people. Although he would like to see her pregnant and naked. He would like to put his hands over the pale, shiny arc of her belly, trace the blue veins in her big breasts. He would like that, once, before she marries his son.

"But it could be Meyer's," he says.

Reuben's understanding of homosexuality is gracious and it is generous, but it does not allow a healthy man to lie next to a naked Lillian and not respond. Afterward, Reuben imagines, a homosexual would go back to sex with men, the way you have veal once in a while when something special is on the menu, even though you're a steak man.

It's Lillian's turn to shrug.

"Marry Meyer," Reuben says. "Esther will make you a wedding. We can do it soon."

He looks at her waistline and her hips. They could announce the engagement next Sunday, set the date, and two months from now, a very nice wedding. And if people think that Meyer got caught with his hand in the cookie jar, so much the better.

"I would rather marry you," Lillian says.

He doesn't hide his dismay—and his pleasure, which is as real, is too deep down to show.

"So, I don't have to marry," Lillian says, and adds, like one of Yaakov's Bundist girls, "Free love."

"Free love? I don't think you can afford that, doll. You're going to raise a little *mamzer* instead of giving the baby a name, instead of giving Meyer a family and giving me and Esther grandchildren?"

Reuben sips his coffee. He calms himself.

"Go see Meyer. Make him happy. Make everyone happy."

And Meyer does what Reuben knows he will. He blinks a couple of times and he smiles, hugely. He drops to one knee on their flowered carpet and says, "Lillian, please marry me." And Lillian presses his handsome head against her stomach and says nothing.

A week later, her flow comes and for days on end the two men treat her as if she has stolen something from them. For days on end, Lillian sees Sophie around every corner, her blue hair ribbons floating in the sewers, her doll on the back of a peddler's cart. Even in the apartment, the town of Turov seeps in. Lillian slips her feet out of her pumps to stretch her legs and there is her mother, lying on the green floral carpet, her long, pale breasts covered with cuts, one deep gash at the base of her throat, revealing bone and white tendons. Her shoulders heave twice and she vomits blood as if it is all being pumped out of her and there is one last second when it seems that she sees Lillian and then the shade is drawn inside her.

That night in Turov, Lillian had closed the eyes of the dead and had run to the chicken coop, blood dripping from the hem of her nightgown across the floor and the yard; she left red, speckled footprints from the broken wineglasses.

The chickens had settled themselves on their laying boxes, the smartest ones coming toward Lillian for a midnight snack, their beady eyes gleaming in the moonlight. Blood pooled around Lillian's feet and the sight and smell of it was nothing new, even to the chickens, and they dipped their beaks into the blood and cocked their heads. It was a small coop and Sophie was not behind the laying boxes, or under them, or under the coop itself, or by the fence behind it. There was a strand of blue yarn caught on the rough wood of the door and Lillian sees that blue yarn everywhere, like she sees the blue ribbons.

She'd thrown her nightgown on the ground to wash off at the pump. There were half-naked men and women everywhere, old men in overcoats and prayer shawls, women with tablecloths and bedsheets around them, and the neighbors across the road came out of their house in their nightclothes, their grown daughter in the father's arms, red and slack like a skinned rabbit. Lillian picked glass out of her feet, rinsing them off until the cold water ran clear. Back inside, she had spread her wedding quilt over Osip and a plain brown one over her mother. She'd stood with her feet on her father's shoulders to pull the ax out of his neck and she covered him with the tablecloth. She dressed. She took the ax with her.

Turov had been like Kishinev after the massacre, like Bessarabia, like Nanking, like Constantinople, humans destroying one another like hurricanes through houses: babies torn to pieces or fed to dogs, streets piled with corpses and people on their way to being corpses, toddlers clinging to the hands of their dead mothers, and police officers looking away, poking a stick through promising debris. Lillian took it in as best she could, her hand over her eyes as if against bright light, looking for Sophie.

She went ten miles up and down the river, to Turov and away from it, up to her waist in the water, Osip's boots in her hand as she walked through green-and-brown river weeds, pulling them apart, looking for Sophie. She walked up every path to every farm, and spoke politely to men who looked like the cousins and uncles of the men who had slaughtered her family. In one little village, a collection of six houses, there were Jews who hadn't even thought of leaving home: a tired old man, waiting for death with his rooster and his scythe and a sharp-faced girl with a shy Christian husband; she had changed her name to Masha overnight and practiced making the cross, looping it like a bow, the entire time Lillian talked to her.

They were like the Jews in Ekaterinoslav who'd woken up on a Monday believing, if they thought of it at all, that the years of milking cows side by side with their gentile neighbors would protect them and had instead found themselves on a Tuesday night laying their dead children out in rows on the synagogue floor, shoulder to shoulder, head to feet, there were so many of them, and the synagogue itself only as big as a small barn.

Lillian searched for days. Christian women pulled their little girls close when she walked by, even when she was across the road; they must have read her rage as clearly as if they'd seen her father's hatchet in her hands. When she got back to Turov, the bodies in the house had not been moved. The chicken coop was empty of chickens, the eggs stolen, and no Sophie. Lillian walked the half-mile farther to her aunt Mariam's home. She lay down on her aunt Mariam's narrow bed and hoped that God might allow her to die in her sleep.

Aunt Mariam had her own story, as people do. She'd slept in a cowshed five miles away for three nights, and when things had set-

tled down, she walked home along the Pripiat River, singing only
Russian folk songs, in case anyone was listening. She'd stood in her
sister's bloodied house and wept and then she'd swept the floor and
watched over the corpses, until she began to see signs of life, she said
to Lillian, and she'd heard voices that she suspected did not come
from the bodies before her, but the voices made her feel less alone,
and finally she came back to her own home, no bigger than and no
different from a goat shed—she says so herself. Mariam washed herself by the pump, she put on a clean dress, her gray one, she said, as
if she had a dozen in her armoire, and she brushed the dirt off her
felt slippers and she watched Lillian sleep until the longing for company and conversation overtook her.

Sweetheart, sweetheart, sweetheart, she said, wake yourself up.
She said, You are my only family now, and Lillian let herself be
hugged. She let her aunt make tea, a few leaves floating in hot, gritty
water poured into a chipped cup.

Lillian wished herself grateful and thankful for her aunt's kindness. It could have been worse, as her aunt kept saying, and with every
sip of that awful oily tea, Lillian thought, God, You have put out a
light in the world, my Sophie. You opened the door for the murder-
ers of my mother and my father and my husband, and You chose, as
we believe You can, to let us be set upon by our own neighbors, drunk
and angry over life's latest difficulty, and as if that is not enough, my
parents, who You might have given a little comfort in their hard lives,
and my husband, who You know could not have hurt a fly, much less
defend himself, and above all, my daughter, You Illness, You Malig-
nancy, as if that is not enough, Aunt Mariam, crazy and of no use to
anyone, ever, You let live. And not a scratch on her. *Dayenu*, Lillian
thought and put the cup down so hard, it split along the old cracks
and Aunt Mariam spit three times against the evil eye and then
braced herself against the wall and said, I must say what I must say.

Lillian, she said, we have not always been close. But you poor thing. I have to tell you. I saw your Sophie, floating down the river. I saw her little blue hair ribbons in the weeds—I would know them anywhere. She said, as if to herself, I ran along the riverbank, I cried for help, but who was left to help? I couldn't fish her out myself— I'm not a young woman. Mariam cried and cried all three days, and Lillian couldn't bring herself to ask if all this was to somehow comfort her, to put an end to her uncertainty, or to hasten her departure, and how would she know? She grieved, Mariam said, for her sister and for her dear little great-niece and since God, in His infinite wisdom, had allowed these things to happen, if this particular chain of tragic events should lead to her becoming the owner of a two-room home, with hearth and windows, who was she to question His ways?

Yellow fliers appeared in Turov. On the fourth day, Aunt Mariam pressed one into Lillian's hand: COME TO AMERICA, THE NEW WORLD. 45 RUBLES A TICKET. Beneath the words there was a drawing of workers, you could see they were workers because they were short and bowlegged, with caps on their heads, and instead of a chicken under the arm, or a bolt of cloth, each little man had a bulging sack of money with the American dollar sign on it, and they were running, running with their bags of money to a pillared building across the street marked BANK. The puffs of smoke from the factory, the street lamps, and the workers' shiny black shoes all had a round, friendly quality.

"Turov is cursed for you now," Aunt Mariam said, waving her hand at the empty yard and the dark house, as if she was too polite to say more. "Go to America—you have a cousin there, Frieda. My other sister's daughter. My niece. I happen to have her letter."

LILLIAN DIDN'T SAY, But I don't know Frieda. She didn't say, Will she be kind to me? She didn't say, You have always wanted our house. There was no reason to stay, and no one to stay for. Lillian

If I Had Chains,
I Would Pull You to Me

IT HAS RAINED FOR HOURS, AND EVEN LILLIAN'S POCKETS ARE wet. She has carried her packages under her coat, and her wet hand slips off the wet key. It is Sunday night and all she wants is to rinse off in the tub and dry her hair in front of the fire. She can take her time; Meyer is rehearsing tonight and Reuben is going over his books. She can clean her face, properly. Meyer likes her to blacken her eyelashes and rouge her cheeks and lips. Lillian thinks it looks whorish, but that must be what Meyer wants; he wants people to see sex when they see her, to see bright-pink cheeks and a fitted blue satin suit, and not to see Meyer-and-Lillian, a combination that does not in any way say passion-and-romance. Fear-and-despair, it might say. Shame-and-discomfort (drubbing, abashment, unease, and also uneasiness).

Tonight she can wash out her stockings and sit in her velvet robe with a glass of wine and see what terrible things have befallen the people who write to the Bintel Brief. If Reuben were coming, she'd

have to pull herself together; he doesn't buy her nice things to decorate the dresser drawers. Some nights he likes her to be in her robe
already, as if she can't wait. Other nights, to show her, or to show
himself, that this is all strictly business, that her wants have nothing
to do with anything, Reuben will say just a few minutes after he
walks in, "I don't have much time today," and even as he looks away
and jerks his tie loose, Lillian nods her head and walks directly to the
bed, without a word. They both know it's a lie, that he says it whenever the distressingly beautiful and useless truth is upon them. But
the nights he walks in with a kiss and kneels down to start a fire and
they play house, with a hot dinner and wine on the table and him behind the newspaper calling out remarks in Yiddish while she washes
the dishes—these are their favorite nights. She tells him the sewing
room gossip, which is not uninteresting (whose bosom is not what it
seems, which gentleman has taken to wearing a corset), and he tells
her ("This is *entre nous*, you understand," he says) how much he owes
his investors and which old friends he will have to drive out of business in self-defense.

Whenever Reuben comes over, more is required of her, and she
doesn't mind. Smoothing almond cream on every part, soaking her
hands in warm olive oil for ten minutes and then in milk to get rid
of the smell, repinning her hair so that it looks artful and enticing,
not like she's been running her hands through it all day. If Reuben
were coming tonight, which would otherwise be very good, she
would get no time to read.

She bumps open the door with her hip, holding Meyer's American cookies, Reuben's herring, her own hairpins and curling papers.
Her cousin Raisele stands in front of her, head cocked, arms ex-
tended sweetly, as if she has come to America just to help Lillian
with her wet packages. Lillian holds on to the boxed cookies and the
herring, she thinks to put her key in her purse, and she does not faint
as Raisele thought she might. Raisele herself thinks that fainting is a

brilliant way to handle awkward situations, and she has practiced buckling her knees and letting her head drop loosely from her neck so many times that she can perform a faint wherever there's a little floor space.

Lillian takes a step forward and stops six inches away from her cousin, who is not dead, not in Russia, not anything Lillian can grasp, except that the girl is standing in the middle of Lillian's apartment looking frightened. Raisele is sorry now she put on Lillian's dressing gown and oiled her hair. The orphan in the storm, the poor little cousin from the old country, is not a person wrapped in velvet and scented with lavender.

Raisele already likes America. She liked the music she heard coming out of the bars; she liked the sharp looks from men in American hats and suits; she liked the shiny, sheer stockings on the quick legs of the American girls and the bright signs she couldn't read. She liked the quick escape from Ellis Island, the friendly doctor. She liked her quick meal with Cousin Frieda, who was happy to see Raisele alive, happier still that the girl didn't need a place to stay. ("You didn't get my letter?" Raisele said. "No matter.")

And Raisele likes Lillian's apartment, which had a lock like paper. She liked Lillian's bath oil, which she used on her body and in her hair, to make it smell sweet and lie flat after her bath in Lillian's nice tub. How Lillian has come to this is a mystery to Raisele, but it speaks very well for America. Lillian's green velvet robe is a little tight through the chest but also nice. Raisele noticed that the whole apartment was decorated in different greens, like a garden, and the carpet makes the flowers, and she liked this, too.

She heard the key turn in the lock and she moved to the center of the room. She put her arms out and dropped them. She clasped her hands. She held her hands behind her back. She held out her arms. She watched the door.

. . .

ALL SINS BEGIN IN FEAR, and Raisele is sick with it; she may have miscalculated, her splendid adventure might end before it even begins, she might wind up with only a fraction of what she has come for. Raisele drops to her knees, pulling Lillian's free hand to her.

"Sophie is alive," Raisele says. "She's alive."

And then she faints.

LILLIAN PUTS RAISELE to bed and empties the tub. It doesn't matter whether Meyer or Reuben comes tonight, or when, or which one, or if they come at the same time, toss a coin, and have her by turns on the kitchen floor.

Lillian climbs into bed next to Raisele, who has thrown the dressing gown on the floor and sleeps naked, curled on her side, her arms crossed over her chest. She is warm as an oven. Lillian takes a deep breath to calm herself, and she smells her mother beside her, perspiration and green onion and the singed, nutty scent of buckwheat groats tossed from one side of the skillet to the other in a perfect, nonchalant brown arc. The bed is suddenly filled with Lillian's dead, and Raisele rolls over into the middle of them, and puts her hands on Lillian's shoulders. She says in her light, lisping Yiddish, "Shall I tell you?" and she does, without waiting.

Mostly, the families fled west, except the Pinskys. The Pinskys cut behind the Krimbergs' yard, heading to the road east (Raisele does not say, looking for whatever might have been left behind, looking to strip their neighbors' houses of whatever last things someone might have been unable to carry). They found a small muddied heap near Lillian's house, by the steps of the chicken coop. The heap was Sophie, blood and filth at the hem of her nightgown, her feet speckled with gravel, and Mrs. Pinsky, who had buried three babies, said to Mr. Pinsky that the Leybs were all dead, they must take the child with them to Siberia, and she would not hear no.

Kachikov, the constable, told me all this, Raisele says. And what could I do but write to you at Frieda's place and come to America to tell you myself, in person.

"I didn't get the letter," Lillian says and kisses Raisele on the forehead. She pulls the blanket up to Raisele's neck and tucks it in around her. Raisele opens her mouth, and Lillian puts her hand over it. There is a roaring in Lillian's ears, and she wouldn't be able to hear Raisele even if she could let her speak.

Lillian puts on her old cotton wrapper and stands by the window. She will have to give that green velvet dressing gown to Raisele or burn it; she can no more wear it again than sleep in a coffin. Her skin is prickling, the hair on the back of her neck rising and falling, as if ghosts are leaving and entering the room. How can this be worse than sleeping on top of her parents' graves, saying Kaddish so many times the words ran together like nonsense, worse than sitting for days by the Pripiat River, watching for a little sock or Sophie's blue petticoat, sitting in the mud in only a nightgown and blanket, until the weather changed and Mariam came with the flier for America? Those first black, wet days, winter rain fell on the stones inside her, and when she left Turov, everything froze.

Sophie's name, the sound of it in Raisele's mouth, her name said by someone who had seen her, seen her laughing and chasing the chickens, seen her in her flannel nightgown and thick socks, braids one up, one down, seen her running in the yard, ducking Lev Pinsky's dry red paw. Sophie's name is a match to dry wood. Ice is sluicing down Lillian now, running off her in sheets. Trees of fire are falling across the frozen field, brilliant orange, blue-tipped and inextinguishable; fire leaps from the crown of one tree to another, until the treetops send waves of fire back and forth between them, tossing flames like kites. Lillian's veins are bleeding fire, her hands and feet rippling with it. Hawks and sparrows drop down from the blackened sky. Lillian's face hurts. She stands in front of the window, her wrapper open, and presses her face and body against the cold glass. She has clawed four dark red scratches on her cheeks, and she will have them for weeks and the fire will not go out.

Alive. Not dead.

Esther Burstein opens the door to her home in Brooklyn. The wood floors shine under thick rugs, the silk curtains billow gently, the lace and linen runners on the sideboard and dining room table are brilliantly white and as crisp as toast. Lillian feels like the filth of the world, like shit on the bottom of Esther's famously small shoes, and Esther is looking at Lillian like that's just what she's thinking, too.

What Esther says is, My dear, what a long trip. What she says is, Coffee, tea, some pound cake, Belle just made some of her delicious cookies. And she rings for Belle, a very, very homely colored woman. Esther likes beautiful things, and it is almost painful to look at poor Belle, her wandering eye, her bowed legs, and whatever the disease is that has splotched her arms half white and half brown. Belle puts down the tray and leaves, smiling at them both.

Esther says, Belle is a wonderful help in the house, and Lillian nods. If she were married to Reuben, she would have only plain girls with diseases in her house, too. Lillian has not taken off her navy cotton gloves (she knows now about wearing gloves when it's not cold). She is afraid that if she reaches for the cup or the cake, blood and mud and shit will run off her, onto all of Esther's beautiful things.

"I have looked for Mr. Burstein," Lillian says. "I have things to discuss. I want to discuss with him."

She can hear her *w*'s sinking into *v*'s and Reuben is not here to carry on about it, and Esther, of course, doesn't care. Lillian can sink back into the mud of Turov and Esther will not be sorry.

Esther sips her tea from her Spode cup. The cups, which are milk-thin and gilded and slide the tea into your throat as from a porcelain spoon, are a great comfort to her.

"Tell Meyer about it, dear, and he'll let Reuben know. And Reuben will get in touch."

"I am looking for him three days."

Esther knows that. Esther knows that whatever Lillian has done, it has displeased Reuben tremendously. He is in a miserable, argumentative mood and Esther has held her tongue for a week. She has had Belle fix his favorite foods, and when he complained that she was trying to make him fat, she didn't say, It's my fault you eat the way you do? She had Belle make baked chicken and asparagus and carrots and no potatoes for the next night, and when he sulked like a boy over the absence of potatoes, she brought in a potato-and-onion casserole with bits of green scallion and a river of yellow butter around the edge and he ate most of it.

"You and I know that Reuben knows everything. If you are looking for him and he is nowhere to be found, it may be Reuben does not want to be talking to you right now."

Lillian looks at her gloved hands. If she were Esther, she wouldn't help her husband's whore even this much. She would throw her into the street or tell her, Sure, chase him down—everyone knows he's finished with you.

"Thank you," Lillian says. "Just let him know, please."

Esther presses tea and cake and cookies on her, but Lillian will at least manage to leave this house without eating or drinking. At the door, without even thinking, Esther tilts Lillian's blue velvet hat to a more becoming angle.

"Meyer's *shaineh maidele*. Go find Meyer. I think you should discuss with him."

Her fingers are quick, and her smile is small and knowing, and although it is hard, it is not malicious. Three thousand miles later, when Lillian is standing in Seattle's Skid Row holding the hand of a colored prostitute who looks at her with Esther Burstein's wise, mean smile, it is clear to Lillian that she could have gotten the fare to Odessa easily. That Esther would have found seventy-five secret dollars and given it to Lillian, that Esther would have packed her bag and driven her to the pier. It never occurred to Lillian, because she is proud and hardheaded and deserving of exactly what she's getting, to ask someone who wanted her to go, for help in doing just that.

AT FOUR O'CLOCK, Lillian is in the Blue Bonnet, sitting with two copies of *A Tale of Two Cities* (one in Yiddish, one in English), acting like a woman waiting. Reuben comes in, looking like God about to smite the Egyptians.

"So, you go to my house, you disturb my wife. Is that necessary?"

"I wanted to see you."

Reuben doesn't say anything. What Lillian wants to tell him is worse—he can see it on her face—worse than when she thought she was pregnant, and whatever it is, he doesn't want to hear it. Reuben says all the time, like Maréchal Pétain, Tell me the truth, especially if it's unpleasant, but he doesn't mean what Lillian is about to say. He means, Tell me the director quit or the ingenue got fat or Esther has invited her sister for two weeks or the box office is weak. He doesn't mean this.

"I have to go home. To Russia. I have to go to Siberia."

"Siberia? Who goes to Siberia if they can help it?"

"My neighbors from Turov do. They took my daughter, they save her, they go to Siberia."

"Who says?"

"My cousin Raisele says."

Reuben has heard about Raisele already. Cute, hard little twist, eyes like a thief. She's looking, Reuben has no doubt, to get Lillian out of the way, to give Meyer what he needs in exchange for a warm bed, new clothes, and a new life, and if she figures out about him and Lillian, she'll let him know that whatever Lillian does for him she can do it, too, and Reuben is guessing that she will not be happy with Charles Dickens, a decent wage, and tea at the Royale. She will be as uninterested in love as Reuben liked to think he was.

"She makes up this cock-and-bull story and off you go to Siberia? Or maybe it's true and what is your plan, Lillian? A warm coat and you get off the boat in Odessa and then what? You just ask the friendly policeman, every nice Russian man from Minsk to Pinsk, 'Have you seen my daughter?' "

To make it clear that he cannot let her go, that he would rather Sophie was dead than that the child should be a reason for Lillian to leave him, he says it in Yiddish, too, in a mincing, threadbare suppliant's Yiddish.

"Oh where oh where is my darling daughter? You'll be dead before you get to Kiev," he says.

"Will you help me?" Lillian says. Who else will help her? Surely Reuben could take her to Russia, she could be in furs, they could make love on the ship. They would have a bed, not like her last crossing; they would have their meals at a little table for two, with a rosebud in a white vase, beside a round little window that looked out on the ocean.

"I'm not going to help you die." He is all dignity now, armored in who he is and what he has done and who the world knows him to be, armored in his family and his theater. If Esther were here, she might say to Lillian, Wait a few days, smooth his feathers, and, seeing that Lillian couldn't wait, Esther might say, as she has certainly said to herself, a hundred times, Well, beg then, if you want it so bad and you are not above bending the knee for something he should want to give you. Beg him.

Lillian begs. Reuben forces himself to stop listening. She will find the child and live the rest of her life in some wretched village, or more likely, she will die alone in a snowdrift. Helping her gets him nothing. But he could. He could offer, they could take a cruise ship together, white fur rugs, white satin sheets, and pink lamps.

Lillian sees what Reuben sees. Everything that Reuben thinks about Raisele may be true. Everything that Raisele tells Lillian may be true. Lillian says nothing, and Reuben can't answer nothing, and Lillian kisses the back of Reuben's hand as if he is the young lady and she is the soldier off to the front. It is a gesture of such elegant regret, such restrained and inconsolable loss, that for a moment Reuben thinks he made a terrible mistake not putting Lillian on the stage. And then there is nothing but the shadow where she stood. The lines around his mouth and eyes darken and draw down like faded chiseling on the white, set stone of his face. He leaves for Pittsburgh the next day, a few weeks ahead of schedule, with Gloria, with Gloria's dachshund, with the intention of sparing himself the sight of Lillian floundering. When he returns, Lillian is gone and Yaakov is not talking to him.

Reuben walks carelessly through the Goldfadn costume room when he gets back. He compliments Miss Morris. He picks up a blue button beside Lillian's sewing machine as if he is tidying up, and he flirts with the plump, pretty girl who always sat behind Lillian. It has not occurred to Lillian or Reuben what her leaving will do to him, that he will lose most of his vision within a year and when he cannot bear to make his way with a cane and a helper, he will retreat to the house in Brooklyn, eat without appetite through the winter, and die in the spring, lying beside Esther in their big four-poster bed. They will put his coffin on a rose-trimmed wagon with white plumes at each corner, and twenty men, all in black, red-faced and weeping, will pull the wagon through the Lower East Side, and people will stand on line for hours to pay their respects, and the eleven Yiddish theaters will stay dark that night. Meyer will grieve, genuinely and suitably, and then he will go to Hollywood, as Reuben suggested before he went blind, and Meyer will change his name and make a handsome living playing good-natured Italian gangsters and good-natured Italian priests.

LILLIAN FINDS MEYER at the apartment. It might go better with him than with the old man. They have an understanding, they do try to help each other, even if Lillian is not the wife Meyer wants, and is pretty sure she isn't even the proper sort of mistress. (Lillian is right. Ten years later, Meyer will be seen in certain nightclubs with his dark-haired, severely attractive wife, and in others with a very slim, very blond young man. His wife will be as patient as Esther Burstein, and the young man will be as easygoing as Gloria ever was, and there will be many times when Meyer, at fifty, will look in the mirror while shaving and wonder when he became Reuben Burstein.)

When Lillian walks through the door, Meyer is reading the paper. She comes up from behind, slipping her hands around his neck, as mistresses do, and he is glad to see her.

"Your cousin went out," he says. She brings him a cup of tea and she looks up at him from underneath her lashes as if she and he are happily in love; he appreciates the gesture; he appreciates her. Lillian puts a few of his favorite cookies on a plate and Meyer pats her hand. He likes her. Maybe not quite as much as in those few minutes when he imagined they might have a child and marry and Lillian would rescue him from himself, but he wishes her well. Despite her temper and her stubbornness, she's been a good friend to him, the kind of person who keeps your feet on the ground when you're tempted to dream about a villa in Italy with some handsome count, the kind of person who pokes you in the ribs at the right time so you can make the right answer to the rich, homely woman who might make the villa possible.

Lillian tells Meyer about Sophie, about Siberia, about the very expensive steamship ticket. He sees that he was wrong. Lillian is a lunatic disguised as a sensible young woman; she is worse than Yaakov—she wants to die twice. Meyer will not give her the money. She asks him over and over, not hearing him say no, not stopping when he says, In a pig's eye, he has nothing better to do with seventy-five dollars, that Raisele is giving her a line—anyone can see that; that even if she gets a ticket on the Red Star, she'll never get herself across Russia; it's a crazy idea—he won't dignify it by calling it a plan; it's a death wish—that's obvious.

Lillian stretches herself across his strong back, crying, and even as she strokes the side of his face, she hates herself for doing it. She hates herself for being stupid as well; she should have spent more time stroking Reuben when she told him about Sophie; God knows Reuben responds to her touch. With Meyer, she could be draping cold noodles on him for all he cared for her hands and her body. Lillian kneels on the floor in front of him.

"Help me. You don't want me—you know you don't. You'll find another woman. It is no loss for you, my leaving."

Meyer knows she's not saying that he's so highly sexed, any woman will do. He knows what she's saying.

"Think about it," she says. "I am going to find her no matter if you help me or not. I like you, Meyer. You were always my friend. Be my friend."

It's clear to Lillian, even as she says this, that Meyer is not her friend, that he had wanted to be but everything public between them was for show and everything private between them was the mating of fish and frog, or else, on a few cold nights, the shamed, exhausted company of invalids. Actual friendship was out of the question. Later it will seem to Lillian that only Yaakov Shimmelman was truly her friend and everything he recommended or encouraged or suggested pointed her toward death.

Meyer looks around the little apartment, with the gaudy pillows and the silver bowl filled with oranges. It wasn't a bad idea, but he's over it—he can see its limitations (which include blackmail and babies and a sense of failure every time he looks at Lillian's naked body). He has other plans now, and Lillian the seamstress is not part of them. In his next arrangement, he wants to be Lunt and Fontanne, whom he has seen on Broadway in *The Guardsman* and admires as absolute icons of stagecraft and personal charm. Also, Meyer has heard from a man whose very good friend knows Alfred Lunt extremely well that Lunt and Fontanne are both as gay as Dick's hatband.

Lillian changes out of her work clothes in front of Meyer. She takes everything off. She steps carefully into her pink silk underpants. She pulls on her stockings with a snap and steps into her buckled pumps. She pulls on her skirt and then fastens her brassiere. She buttons her shirt. Every pin she tucks into her hair is a soft insult, just to say what kind of man he is not. Meyer watches her the way you watch a train pulling in and out of the station when you know that yours is coming later, he watches her fiddle one last time with her garter, and his flat, sorry disinterest is her answer.

"It may take a few paychecks to get myself a ticket," she says.

"I'm not throwing you out. You can stay. Your little cousin, who ought to have 'Gold digger' tattooed right there on her forehead, she can stay, too, if you like."

"You don't want Raisele?"

"What, you're selling her? You're pimping for your cousin?"

Lillian shrugs and finishes pinning up her hair. She sprays Evening Blossom on her neck and shoulders.

"I don't want her," he says. "She scares the bejesus out of me. Take her with you when you go, please."

And Meyer leaves, stepping over Lillian's crumpled gray worsted skirt and her black smock from the costume room.

Lillian watches Meyer walk down Second Avenue. The women's heads turn, the men touch their caps, he gathers them all like white roses. Lillian hangs her skirt up and sits in the rattan chair. She has three dollars and her clothes, rhinestone earrings from Meyer, and a small library in Yiddish and English. Sophie turns four tomorrow.

LILLIAN WALKS TO SHIMMELMAN'S FINE TAILORING. Yaakov is on his knees in front of a pretty woman standing on a box. He has pins in his mouth, sprayed out like little silver spikes, and he doesn't look in Lillian's direction.

"Good afternoon, miss. I'll be with you right away. Right away," he says loudly, like an actor with a slow audience.

Lillian sits down. The woman is in a blue silk dress and stands perfectly still. The hem of the skirt flutters a little, and Yaakov tugs on it gently. He doesn't touch the silk stockings on the legs beneath the hem. He shuffles around the woman on his knees, puts his fingertip on her hip, to turn her. She speaks to him in perfect radio English.

"You're a genius, Mr. Shimmelman," she says, ducking into the changing room and talking to Yaakov while she undresses. She is nearly naked, dangling her navy-blue dress over the slatted door, laughing in a friendly and knowing way and making Yaakov laugh, too. He can't help himself—he turns red, pretending it's a cough, but it's a laugh, a man-to-woman laugh, and Lillian wouldn't mind that much if she weren't on fire. The woman walks past Lillian, the high green satin collar of her coat ruffling her shingled hair, rising up to her pretty pink cheeks. She picks up a pair of green suede gloves from the counter. "What would we do without him?" the woman says as she goes out.

"Yes," Lillian says to Yaakov in English, to show that she's calm, "what would we do without him?"

Yaakov looks at her. She is not calm—she is sitting like a burning log. She presses her back against the wall, and Yaakov stands over her.

He would rather she hadn't come to his shop. She doesn't belong here any more than he belongs in her Second Avenue love nest sipping tea while Bursteins march in and out. Their entire life, their romance of sorts, their short but happy marriage of the soul, is conducted in the Royale. Yaakov has loved his wife and boys, then Reuben, then Lillian, as it turns out, and for the rest, frankly, all those other people—they come by for a visit or they forget all about you; it doesn't matter. In the little life of Lillian and Yaakov, she admires his English, his provocations, and his politics, and he admires her fine eyes and pretty ankles and her tenacity and her worldview, which is on the dark side, like his own, like any sensible person's. They meet and talk every day in the Royale, they eat Reuben's little cakes and give Reuben the business, which is their privilege, and in this love story there is no reason, no occasion, for Lillian to have seen Yaakov on his knees, and there is no occasion for him to see Lillian like this, so sick with something, barely holding herself together with hot thread and a burnt needle, as his wife used to say.

Yaakov touches Lillian's shoulder. She is sweating right through her cotton jacket.

"Tea," he says.

Lillian shakes her head. She has lost every sentence except one. She says, "Sophie is not dead and I must go and get her." She says it twice.

A short fat man opens the door and hands Yaakov three pairs of pants.

"Let 'em out," the man says. "Business is good."

Yaakov nods. He can't think of any of the hundred smart remarks he usually makes to the businessman.

"All three," Yaakov says.

"All three," the man says. He laughs. He punches Yaakov in the arm, to show how good business is, and he leaves.

Yaakov looks over at Lillian to reassure her, to save her from herself (From who else, Lillian would say), and he sees that sitting there, head cocked and hands clasped in her lap, she has fallen into the light, bruised sleep of the traveler. Yaakov watches over her. He hems the skirt with one eye on Lillian, in case she should fall over. She sleeps upright and unmoving for half an hour.

"You've wandered away from the Burstein empire?" Yaakov says.

They are on their third cup of tea.

"I want to go home."

"Of course you do."

"Reuben won't give me the money. Meyer neither. Reuben says I am going to my death."

"Could be. You already live without your little girl—why not go on living without her? That's the question."

Lillian leans over on the bench and puts her head down between her legs for a few seconds, and Yaakov waits. This is just conversation; if she cannot survive just conversation, she'll never get where she wants to go.

"Imagine, it's a year now, she's got a new *mamele,* a new *papeleh,* nice people. What's their name?"

"Pinsky."

"Nice people?"

"She was nice," Lillian says. She can hardly remember them right now. Fat, sad Rivka. Clever, bullying Lev. "He was a *bulvon.* He pulled Sophie's hair."

"Could be worse. She lives with the Pinskys, she has moose for friends. She rides in a droshky, she wears a cozy fur hat. Why not?"

He says all of this in a sweet, coaxing tone, as if they can both imagine Sophie's happy life, and when Lillian lifts her head and slaps him hard across the cheek, he sits still, not displeased.

"Because she belongs to you? Is that why?"

Lillian is horrified.

"No. Because I think they are not nice. Or maybe they are dead and there is no one to care for her. Because she is a little, little girl. Not that she is mine. That I am hers."

Yaakov nods. He does not say that it may not matter to a little girl in Siberia that the mother she cannot see and may not remember so well loves her so. That it may be that Lillian will die in any one of the ways Yaakov can think of (and he has his album of memories from home, as everyone does: the rocky river, the treacherous slope, the unexpectedly bad night in his own village, with gentile boys setting torches to the homes of people they'd known all their lives) and that her daughter will not feel the cold squeeze of the heart that is Lillian's due, the sense that something essential has fallen away forever, and as Lillian lies dying, thinking of Sophie, Sophie will be thinking how nice it is to have new shoes, how glad she is that she wore her sweater on such a cold day.

"I can make the money," Lillian says, and Lillian and Yaakov share the same image for a moment; Lillian in a short red skirt and monkey-fur jacket, standing on Fourteenth Street looking for business.

"Don't be ridiculous," Yaakov says.

"What's ridiculous? *Az me muz, ken men.*"

He has a better idea, Yaakov says. It's a plan that takes into account how little money they have and the current attitude toward Jews on oceangoing vessels and Lillian's complete inability to pass as a shipboard manicurist or a shipboard hairdresser or a traveling shiksa. It so happens, he says, that it is nothing to get across America, big as it is. It so happens that it is another three thousand overland miles from Odessa to Siberia, much more than the fifty or sixty miles Yaakov calculates lie in the Bering Strait, a little strip of water between Alaska and Siberia. He has read the Rand McNally atlas and the other maps and charts many times, just for pleasure, and the blurred ivory pamphlet of the Yukon Telegraph Trail, and the elegant turquoise map showing the tiny dots of the islands of the Bering Strait are among his favorites. The fact is that however far it is from one place to the other, and however difficult it will be, they both know she must go.

Lillian puts her arms around his thin, shifting shoulders. She holds him and he holds her, and thinks, Little, little girl.

THEY SIT FOR A LONG TIME and then they walk up Franklin Street, to think more clearly. Yaakov swings Lillian's hand and says, as theater people do, in the jaws of sorrow or boredom or unbearable anxiety, What do you say, dinner and a show? They carry two pastrami sandwiches and two beers into the depths of the Goldfadn. Old tins of Henry C. Miner Blue Label Face Powders in Pink, Champagne, Brunette, and Cream, and the Theatrical Blending Powders in Sunburn, Indian, Othello, Mulatto, Japanese, Canary Yellow (unopened), Natural, Juvenile, and Pale Flesh. Gaudy, almost empty tins of Rexall's Theatrical Cold Cream, "Prepared especially for the Profession and General Toilet purposes." Old costumes from old plays: soldiers and vagrants, bereft mothers, devout fathers, a pope, an innkeeper, Hamlet as a young rabbi, Lear as a queen with difficult daughters. There is a skimpy white dress and a cardboard caduceus from Gorman and West's doctor-nurse routine, which would still make Yaakov laugh if Reuben brought it back for a Saturday night. There is Archie Rice's huge bow tie for his society satires, and Archie's cracked patent-leather dancing shoes.

Yaakov holds up a costume to show Lillian. It is a ragpicker's tattered jacket and patched pants, with drooping, filthy kneesocks sewn into the trousers. Yaakov pulls on the lining of the jacket, and the ensemble turns inside out, black gabardine frock coat, shiny black trousers that were fashionable twenty years ago, a yellow-and-red paisley cravat, and gleaming yellow socks signifying high living and, with the green wreaths embroidered on the ankles, hilarious, goyish decadence as well. Yaakov holds Archie's bow tie to his neck and says, "Hey, waiter, you got frog legs?" He tosses the bow tie aside. "No, sir, that's just my rheumatism." And Yaakov slaps his thighs, *ba-da-boom.* "We had fun."

Lillian looks at him.

"Before I met you," he says, "before I met anyone you know . . ."

He pulls out a trunk for Lillian, spreads an old curtain over it, and blows away the first layer of dust.

"You sit. I'll give you a show, like they used to do, then you applaud wildly, then we have a conversation, a real tête-à-tête, about getting you home." Yaakov spreads his arms wide and drops to one knee. "The choo-choo train away from you it takes me, nobody knows how sad it makes me, so kiss me, Tootsie, and then, do it over a-gain."

He does a quick, graceful Charleston. Lillian claps politely. It cannot be that he has brought her here in this bad time, before things get worse, to give her a little song and dance, but every time Yaakov dances, she sees who he was and falls a little in love.

"You pack your things, I talk to a few people, and tomorrow night, or the next night, off you go, like Eliza on the ice floes." Is he telling her that she, Lillian, will pack her three dresses, her two skirts, her thesaurus, and a jar of cold cream and hop on some New York City–Siberia express?

"It can be done," he says, nodding. "I'm telling you."

Maybe. Maybe it can. There's no reason to be uplifted by his faith in her, there's nothing he's seen—her willingness to spread her legs for not one but two Bursteins, her fancy, tangled English, her skills as a seamstress, where she comes in only a little ahead of the poor girl with the harelip—nothing to make any living person think that she can get to Siberia and find her daughter. But here, in the basement of the Goldfadn, among the dead, it doesn't seem to be a question. She can feel them underneath her, pushing at her, pressing at the backs of her knees, lifting her up and out of the grave. Yaakov, closest to the top, straightens her skirt and brushes a last crumbled leaf from her cheek, so she can join the living, not just to do what they do, which even the dead can manage, but to feel what they feel and keep on, which even the living find hard.

"*Az me muz, ken men,*" Yaakov says.

"That's what they say," Lillian says in English, and she settles herself on the trunk for the show.

Yaakov drags out a rolled-up muslin scroll, as tall as a man, mounted on two wooden poles topped with black-and-gold eagles. He pins one end behind a trunk and unrolls the other, showing her a painted scene, brilliant blue streaks in front of brown-and-orange hills, small faded clumps of trees appearing in the foreground. Chips of orange, blue, and brown paint fall to the floor steadily as Yaakov unfurls the scroll.

"My first job," he says. "This Is Your America, education and entertainment, ladies and gentlemen, a nickel a night, only three cents for children. Fifty years ago. I was a little pisher. My oldest brother brought me here—he could have been lead man but he never got the English. Me, I picked it up like nothing."

Yaakov pauses and walks out a few more feet, revealing more trees, more river.

"Monumental Grandeur of the Mississippi Valley. Here we have Chamberlain's Giant Domes." He sounds like someone else; it is his *New York Times*-reading voice, with a sharp, silvery edge. He sounds knowing and companionable and almost sorry that it is so easy to fool people.

"Lillian, see the Indians?" Yaakov inscribes a few big circles in the air and tugs at the scroll to uncover two Indians standing on the riverbank under a rainbow bending over bluffs that rise like gray castles behind the river. The Indians look small with their enormous feathered helmets tumbling to their shoulders, and it seems unlikely to Lillian that she will meet people dressed like that in America.

Yaakov pushes the scroll into a corner and lifts out another one, unrolling it a few feet at a time. "You see, one scene leads to the next. The Domes, the Grassy Plains, now the Indians Hunting Buffalo, now the Village of the Dead, very popular because of 'the curious manner by which the Indians dispose of their dead.' Which is not as curious as the Jews: you stop breathing for two seconds, watch out, you're in the ground; and not as curious as the Catholics: they keep you in the parlor for weeks so everyone can get a good look and have a beer."

Yaakov unrolls another scroll and peers at the scene.

"I always liked this one. Sit a minute. 'The richest soil in the world from which America can raise all the tropical fruits in the world, oranges, figs, olives'—never mind is the olive really a fruit— 'and all that you can imagine. Behind the levee' "—Yaakov points to two blue halves of a lake separated by a patch of white, bare muslin where all the paint has come off—" 'we see the extensive sugar fields, the noble mansions, the beautiful gardens, the modest Negro quarters from which you can hear their lovely traditional spirituals.' We used to have two little colored boys hide behind and sing."

Yaakov smiles at Lillian.

"I would throw cotton bolls out to the crowd. That was one of my jobs, cotton-tosser, and also thunder, horses' hooves, smoke when needed, gunshots, and so on and so on, through the Mississippi Valley, around the Indian Burial Mounds, into the Great Stalagmitic Chamber, beautiful big spikes of crystal pointing up and down, *g* for *ground*, to help you remember, *c* for *ceiling*—that's the stalactite. We make our way to the famous Encamping Grounds of Lewis and Clark, all America knows them, and on to Indians scalping the settlers and also killing the buffalo with their bows and arrows, very talented—they didn't need guns. The Negroes burning down plantations, the plantation owners hanging the Negroes from the willow trees. The settlers shooting Indians while riding horseback; they don't use bows and arrows—why should they?"

Yaakov drops the mural and wipes the sweat off his face. Lillian looks at him in the gray light and wishes she could see who he was fifty years ago, a little boy with a big show, trembling with excitement, unaware of a future. Yaakov meets her eye for a moment. He shakes his head.

"So that's America," he says. "Easy-peasy. Let's get ice cream."

Lillian walks over to the scrolls. "They'll be ruined if they lie here. All the paint will fall off them."

She has tried to take care of things in this country. She puts her belts in one drawer and wraps her stockings in a shawl so they don't catch on the belts or on the rough wood inside the dresser. She has tried to take care of Meyer's nice things because they matter to him, and she has tried to take care of herself for Reuben, and she has been and done for both of them to the limits of her patience and her nature, and surely if Yaakov cares so much about these pictures, even though nothing matters except getting to Sophie, she can pretend to care about this, too. "Let's put these away," Lillian says.

"For what?" he says, as if they are nothing to him, scraps of cloth and drops of paint that could not matter less in the modern world. And they are nothing to him now. They've served the last useful purpose they'll ever have. Yaakov burned everything his wife wore and everything his boys loved, and he would burn these scrolls if it would not bring down most of the Lower East Side. He avoids souvenirs and keepsakes. He's determined not to be like those women carrying tin candelabra and locks of brown hair, still looking for the husbands who ran off to Arizona; not like the man wandering Essex Street at midnight, holding a poxy doll and a colored daguerreotype of a sweet-faced little girl. He would put his foot right through the scrolls but Lillian takes his hand and they go up the stairs and over to the Blue Bonnet, where they will not meet anyone they know.

In the morning, Yaakov studies a dozen atlases in the Mid-Manhattan Library, careful as a bank robber. He looks again at the teal-and-brown insert of the Bering Strait, at the tiny islands strung as close as pearls, only a hard day's walk from one to another, and he steals the two best atlases and the ten-page booklet about the Collins Overland Telegraph Trail of the Far North, illustrated with inviting pen-and-ink drawings of thirty log cabins, like lakeside cottages, each just another day's walk from the other. In his shop, he slices out the five most beautiful maps of the Pacific Northwest, Canada, and Alaska, and he will sew them inside Lillian's overcoat under the lining, making a buttoned silk pocket for each one.

RAISELE BEATS HER FIST against the door. "I have food," she says. "I have champagne."

It is no surprise to Lillian that Raisele has brought a loaf of challah, a slab of liver pâté with a ribbon of white fat around it and olives cut like flowers decorating the ends, half a roast chicken, still warm, and a packet of four marzipan fruits, two tiny pink apples, two miniature bananas, packed in green straw. It would surprise Lillian if Raisele had paid for any of it, and it would surprise Lillian if the little basket of marzipan had not originally held six pieces of fruit.

Raisele puts it all on the table and takes a marzipan banana. "I love this. I love these little candies. I love this country." She holds the basket up to Lillian, who shakes her head. "Don't say I didn't ask." Raisele balances the marzipan on the pointed tip of her tongue and then chews it. She tears the foil off the champagne and pops the cork. "It wasn't easy to get this," she says. "I had to go all the way to Boylan's Pharmacy." Boylan's Pharmacy is not run by Mr. Boylan—it is run by Meyer Lifschitz—and it is not a pharmacy, it is the primary distributor of wine and spirits for the Lower East Side. Lillian assumes that Raisele is sleeping with Mr. Lifschitz or promising to sleep with Mr. Lifschitz, or else that Raisele has arranged for Mr. Lifschitz to encounter his murderous competition while in Raisele's embrace. Whether Mr. Lifschitz turns out to be home with his wife playing canasta or lying in a pool of his own blood on a narrow cot, this picnic is someone's partial payment for something.

Raisele and Lillian lie back on the green divan, staring at the ceiling the way you do when you have had three glasses of champagne that is really gin with a spray of seltzer. Raisele puts her head on Lillian's shoulder and kisses her sweetly on the cheek. She pats Lillian's hand. If Raisele were a man, Lillian would be afraid to be alone with her.

Raisele raises her glass toward the window, toward the river. A little gin spills onto her hand and she licks it off.

"Bon voyage," she says. "Good luck."

Lillian looks at her. "It's not an adventure, Raisele."

Raisele doesn't want to fight about it. It is an adventure, and it's another chance for Lillian, who doesn't even deserve one. Lillian has no knack for this city. She had not one but two chances to make something of herself, and she turned her back on marriage and on babies, on a very nice arrangement with the old man and on a full-time charade with the Matinee Idol that had all kinds of potential. Lillian should get another chance in a smaller city. Raisele wants Lillian to try again. She wants Lillian to go.

Lillian sips at the bubbling gin. "People drink this? Tell me again what Kachikov told you."

And Raisele tells her. She says, I told you. The Pinskys are cutting behind the Krimbergs' when they find little Sophie. Raisele says again how dirty Sophie was, with the scraped knees and the gravel stuck in the tender places of her hands and little feet. Raisele says again that Mrs. Pinsky could not bear to leave Sophie behind, a Jewish girl and an orphan, because of the four babies Mrs. Pinsky had buried. Lillian says, Four? I thought it was three, although she only remembers the one time, when she must have been twelve and Mrs. Pinsky came into their yard naked, blood running down her legs. Mrs. Pinsky and her mother lay down on the bed, and right before sundown her mother put Mrs. Pinsky in one of her old dresses and gave her half a chicken to bring home for dinner.

Raisele says, "Maybe it was three."

Lillian says, "Rivka Pinsky took Sophie? Kachikov didn't tell me. I saw him, he saw me. I must have crossed through the village and that goddamned province a hundred times looking for her."

Raisele pours herself a little more gin.

"Well, in the end, he told me. We were friendly."

"Oh, yes. And Mariam, her story about the little blue ribbons?"

Raisele shrugs. "Who knows? Can we blame poor Mariam? She made a mistake. She thought I was dead, burnt to a crisp in the barn, but she was wrong about that, too. There's no telling how someone will react to these things. She was unhinged—she made a mistake."

"She thought she saw my dead daughter floating past her in the river, but she was mistaken?"

"Yes, mistaken." Raisele looks away. "Plus, she's crazy. You never noticed? I'm saying, by the time she realizes, by the time she sees it clear in her mind's eye, as clear as she ever will, you're here. And the Pinskys have come and gone."

"Someone must have seen the Pinskys take Sophie—"

"At midnight, while goyim murdered people in their beds? Who was looking? Anyway, I wasn't there," Raisele says.

"Where were you?"

"Safe," Raisele says and clinks her glass against Lillian's.

Lillian doesn't know what answer she wants from Raisele. There is no catching her out. Going after Sophie seems foolish, and worse than that, it seems to be the act of a crazy woman, and it seems to be what Lillian must do. She must believe Raisele. She must leave this apartment and her lovers and her habits. She must leave the Royale and Canetti the greengrocer and the radio in the costume room and the clean embroidered sheets that Meyer insists on. She must go someplace godforsaken only to discover that her child is dead, or to never find her at all, and still she has to go.

Raisele sees Lillian's hesitation. She says, "Remember how she wore her socks, one of each, and that doll, she loved that dolly—what was her name?"

"Tseidele," Lillian says and she lies back squeezing her eyes shut, to keep the image of Sophie, like the end of a dream. Raisele, who is usually the last to sleep and the last to rise, pulls one of Meyer's soft green blankets over her cousin, glad that nothing holds her hostage in this wide, abundant world.

LILLIAN PACKS AND RAISELE PACES. Raisele's found twelve dollars in Meyer's underwear drawer and also two pairs of wool socks and also a large cotton handkerchief, which could be useful. She would take more things for Lillian if he had them. She goes through the whole dresser, Meyer's shirts and Lillian's clothes, and she picks up and puts back and then pockets a pair of Meyer's silver cuff links.

"Maybe trousers," Raisele says.

"If I had."

Raisele shakes her head in mild disbelief at the weakness of other people and pulls open the closet door. They look at three pairs of men's trousers, black worsted, Harris tweed, and green gabardine. Raisele takes the tweed trousers, which look as if they are not only for the outdoors but made from the outdoors, and drops the wood hanger on the floor. She tosses the pants on the bed.

"Now you have."

Lillian folds the pants. This is the help she gets. She gets a woman who would steal the pennies off a dead man's eyes (and Lillian can hear Raisele: The man is dead, so who needs the pennies more, me or him?) and a crazy man who so loves death he is sending Lillian on ahead in hopes of a big reunion in the afterlife, a heavenly Café Royale, where the cakes are free, the tea is strong, and all is not only forgiven, it is undone. She folds a sweater and Meyer's wool overcoat, rolls a wide leather belt on top of two camisoles, and tucks her winter knickers and Meyer's socks and handkerchief into the bottom of her satchel. She'd rather bring stockings—it would make her feel better to imagine a trip involving silk stockings and her pretty navy-blue pumps with the diamanté buckles, but she knows better. She holds the stockings and the shoes out to Raisele, who takes them instantly.

"These are . . . nifty," Raisele says as the stockings and the shoes vanish into her own small bag.

"Yes," Lillian says. "Ducky, nifty, swell."

"Yes. They are swell."

Lillian's bag is almost full and there is still a dress hanging in her closet, and a drawer of blouses and jerseys. Lillian sees Raisele looking intently at the dress, and she smiles. Raisele is a wolf, the way other people are lambs, or saints, or sparrows.

"All yours. Whatever fits. *Zay gezunt.*"

Raisele has already made plans. She has found two plain girls from Odessa, and they both have jobs, and they have a big couch and no other boarders and no prospects, as such. They are lonely now with just each other and evenings at home, and Raisele has talked them up, alone and together. She has told them every interesting thing she knows about the Bursteins, she has brought them chocolate-dipped fruit from Stricoff's Candy Shoppe, and she has allowed them to take her to the Thursday-night Odessa Mutual Aid Association Theatre and Ballet with Grand Buffet Following. Raisele is more fun than anyone, the sisters say—she should move in already, they could not love her more.

Raisele plans to walk Lillian to the corner, kiss her three times like the theater people do, and come back to the apartment for a final inventory. She believes that you can do things that may appear bad and still be a good person. She believes that if you do not actively wish people harm, you have done no harm. She will leave Meyer his furniture (except the maroon silk cushion, which she has admired since the first night) and his clothes (except a blue cashmere muffler), and she will take the green chiffon peignoir set since Lillian doesn't want it, and she will take all of the food in the icebox that she can carry. Raisele looks through the icebox one more time and holds up a salami for Lillian.

"No. Take what you want. Meyer says out by tomorrow, absolutely."

Raisele, who has been hoping that Meyer would come to see what a perfect companion she could be, more pliant than Lillian, more agreeable (which wouldn't be so hard, Raisele thinks; Lillian seems to have decided that in this country, of all places, men want to know how you feel), is disappointed but doesn't say so. Raisele never tells anyone how she feels, and even when she becomes the Vilna Art Theatre's next ingenue, even when she replaces Ida Liptzin as *the* Juliet and creates such a sensation with her new naturalistic style that Broadway actresses sneak in to see her, even when the man from Samuel Goldwyn presses his card on her after dinner at El Morocco and suggests that if her screen test is what he thinks it will be, she'll be changing her name very soon, Raisele Perlmutter is never inclined to tell anyone how she feels. Her screen test, like her movies, shows an alabaster face with pale eyes and pale lips playing against the image of the vamp, sleek rather than beaded or flounced. She is genuinely ironic, genuinely indifferent, genuinely modern.

THE BAR IS NEAR BLACK, and Lillian jingles her pennies and the set of stainless-steel safety pins Yaakov has attached to the inside of her overcoat (You never know, he said). She's glad that no one can see her sweating through her loose serge dress and cotton stockings. She can see Yaakov's face only because she's standing right beside him. The other men look like shadows, and there are no women at all. Men sit in twos and threes at small round tables and stand pressed against the long, dark counter. It is a serious bar, she can see. It's a place men come to drink, and it smells the way such places smell, of wet wool and sweat and urine and smoke, and the floor has been splashed with beer so often the grain gives up hops and malt every time you walk across it.

"You've been here before?" Lillian asks. It's hard to imagine Yaakov sipping tea at one of the tables.

"Oh, yes," he says. "Before."

"With Reuben?" she asks, and she would like this to be the last time she says his name. She won't be able to see where she's going if his face is in front of her all the time.

"Our Reuben?" Yaakov lowers his voice. "In this shithole?"

A man with thin red hair and white sideburns taps Yaakov on the shoulder.

"Shimmelman," he says, and the two men face each other. They shake hands quickly, and the red-haired man looks at Lillian. Lillian feels that she's smiling politely, but the man is frowning and squinting, so it may be that her smile is not right or that she's not smiling at all.

"All the way to Chicago, Mr. O'Brien," Yaakov says. "And a meal."

"Sure," the man says. "Didn't I say so? And is this your daughter?" he asks, one eyelid lowering slightly.

"Yes," Yaakov says as if it will protect Lillian, and she brushes her hair back and links her arm with his.

O'Brien shakes his head as if he's never heard such a bald-faced lie, as if Yaakov is making use of the sacred bonds of family for his own wicked sheeny purposes. He puts his hands in his pockets in the manner of a man watching a horse race on which he has sensibly placed only a small bet. Yaakov takes out his wallet, and the red-haired porter looks away, toward the door, ignoring the movement of Yaakov's hand entirely.

"One dollar yesterday, and this makes five," Yaakov says, and puts the bills in the porter's hand.

"Let's have a drink," O'Brien says.

The two men drink beer, and Yaakov pays, as he must. When he gets up to accompany them to the train station, the porter pushes him back down.

"I tell you what, mister," he says. "It would be a little strange, the three of us on the platform. You leave the young one with me. Say your farewells here and now."

Lillian and Yaakov look at each other, and O'Brien checks his watch. Yaakov picks up his empty glass. He could smash it to pieces and write Lillian's name on his chest. He puts the glass down. It's not necessary; her name is there already.

Yaakov holds Lillian to him so hard the four buttons of his overcoat press through her sweater and her blouse and her camisole into her skin, and she clasps her hands around the back of his thin neck as if he is her father.

"*Zay gezunt hey,*" Lillian says. Go with God, and she means, Go with my love. She means, Come with me. She means, Do not leave me. She means, I cannot do this without you. She means, Do not let me go.

Helping Lillian is the last fine thing Yaakov will do. After she leaves, he stops singing in the Royale, stops teasing Reuben, stops mocking Meyer. Reuben's fatigue is his own, Meyer's lies are his own, the world's crimes and errors in judgment are his as well. He spreads towels at the edge of the bathtub, in case there is splashing. He pulls his heavy armchair up against the front door. He climbs into the hot bath, everything arranged on the mat beside him, and there is no Reuben this time to fish him out.

Orphan Road

L ILLIAN AND MR. O'BRIEN TAKE THE SUBWAY UPTOWN, CHANG-
ing trains silently until they come to Pennsylvania Station. She
looks up at the giant stone eagles guarding the entranceway, at the
columns as big around as ancient trees. Amphistylar, or am-
phiprostyle, she thinks, because she has been giving the thesaurus a
rest and has begun the dictionary at the beginning. She doesn't
think, How like Bernini's Roman colonnade they are. She likes the
warm honey color of the stone floors and the very high ceiling, and
she sees that the big windows are already dark with soot and that
thin beams of light crisscross the room. If Yaakov were with her, he
would be telling her that the floor is genuine travertine marble from
Italy and the ceiling is one hundred and fifty feet high. He would
gesture to embrace the whole hall and mention the baths of Cara-
calla and the Basilica of Constantine and that she might care to
know that the Waiting Room was modeled on a tepidarium, which
means nothing more than "warm room." Yaakov Shimmelman is a

great admirer of Stanford White and Charles McKim, and he has seen the public displays of their drawings and walked past their buildings, just to admire, and it has been his particular pleasure to alter the pants of Mr. White's chauffeur on three different occasions.

Lillian follows the porter past the lunchroom at the station's north end. She sees the ticket and telegraph offices and men's black overcoats. She sees flappers, fringe and silk shoes in the green of this summer's fashion, poisonously bright, and older women in bisque and pale gray with hats to match, and then the porter gives her a sharp poke to step lively down to Track 107, the Pennsy, he says, Broadway Central. She sees the starry blue ceiling, she sees the icy marble steps, she sees the Pullman porters who seem so much cleaner and finer and kinder than her own, she sees a man selling Italian ices and a barbershop open twenty-four hours, and then they are on the crowded platform with the legitimate passengers, immigrants with six kids and no bags that match, and businessmen and drummers with their big sample cases, and a few women in pairs, looking daring or cross.

The porter swings up into the coach car, and Lillian scrambles after him. He puts out his hand for her bag, but she holds it fast. She sees green baize-and-rattan cushions and glossy wooden doors, and she can just make out two men opening their newspapers behind etched glass when the porter turns down the corridor and pulls open a louvered door. He pushes Lillian and her bag into a closet, and she hears the key turn in the lock.

"Twenty-two hours," he says. "Not a sound."

There is a blurred, narrow bar of light at the top of the door before he closes it, and then there is no light at all. There is thick black mesh between the slats, and the mesh itself is painted over. Lillian is used to the yellow street lamps and the red-green-red of traffic lights shining all night through the parlor window; she's used to lying in Meyer's bed watching the stars come and go from the city sky and tracing the tips of the buildings, which never disappear entirely into the night. This is the dark before the world was born.

Lillian closes her eyes and opens them and there is no difference. She can feel the brass clasp on her bag, and she fingers it, turning the bag this way and that in case it might catch some stray light and shine for her. She sits down and something hard and narrow, the rim of a bucket, presses into her spine. Lillian straightens her back away from the bucket and bumps her head on a wooden shelf. She reaches her arm behind her, around the bucket. There is a wall, then the bucket, then Lillian, then her bag. The wooden shelf is just touching Lillian's head when she sits up straight. The best position will be her head on her bag, her feet against the bucket. Whatever is sloshing gently in the bucket will spill out at some point, and it would be better to have it spill on her shoes than on her face. It would be better to die. In the dark, Lillian makes a pillow of her coat and inches her legs from one wall to the other. There is no adjusting her eyes; the closet gives up nothing. She rocks to sleep with the train, to Albany.

She's dead. She's blind. Already she can feel the sticky pull of the blood on the floor. She sees her grandmother's teapot broken in four pieces, she smells the spilled tea. She cuts her knee on a shard of china. She knocks over a bucket, and whatever is in it soaks her nightgown. Her own blind fingers touch fingers, and she should recognize the hand instantly, but she doesn't. She steps over the hand and into the backyard. There is a beautiful sunrise, and Lillian sees that Sophie's bed has been set in front of the Lebanskys' chicken coop and is neatly made. Osip's wedding band spins around on the dirt like a golden top, and Lillian runs to catch it. She sees the tail end of Sophie's brown braid and her blue hair ribbon go around the corner of the chicken coop. She sees Mariam's dyed-black curls and her soiled scarf pass by, and she hurries to catch them.

The doorknob turns a little. Someone shakes the door. Lillian wakes just in time to keep herself from screaming.

No luck, darling, a man says. A woman laughs. Lillian can tell that she's excited, she would go with the man into the closet if the porter hadn't locked it to keep Lillian from falling out at some sharp turn. The man says, We'll have to wait until Albany. I can't wait, the woman says, and Lillian thinks saying that to a man is a terrible mistake.

The train stops, and Lillian can hear the world moving past her, two inches away. She smells people leaving, sweat and bombazine, rubber, cheese, someone has brought his garlic salami with him, rye bread and lavender and beer, baby shit. There is the crying baby, there is the muttering mother, Shush, shush, it'll be all right, there is the conductor, Albany, Al-ban-ee, there is the rustle of skirts and a thick rubber heel kicked against her door. Goddammit, the man says. Now people are boarding, Lillian can feel the air surging the other way, new air, a little fresher. Footsteps, men's voices flat and sharp, men who talk when they must, men who leave talking to women. Where have the lovers gone? Lillian wonders.

The train moves. In the dark, things shift. The things Lillian has been sure of so far—the door, the wall of the bucket that protects her from what is in the bucket, the edge of the shelf, the bristles of the cleaning brushes, which press into her left leg, an umbrella's metal tip lying harmless against her right foot while the handle makes a small rattan curve under her—seem to move. She cannot remember the shape or plane or curve of anything from one moment to the next; it is all moving with her. She shifts her hip away from the cleaning brushes and the bristles lean toward her like a cat.

Lillian falls asleep and the dream happens fast: red straw, broken teapot, severed hand, Sophie's empty bed. Lillian screams, not five minutes after she's closed her eyes.

The porter pulls open the door and she falls out, just as she'd feared she would, as blind in the hall light as she was in the closet. The porter swallows a bite of his sandwich.

He says, "You can't yell like that, and you can't fall about, neither."

He wraps Lillian's two hands around another sandwich and shoves her back in the closet, prodding her with his boot. He whispers through the mesh, "Schenectady or Rome, you can use the facilities." The sandwich has fallen to the floor and Lillian finds it by her shoe and eats it before she can think about what it is or where it has been.

She hears the lovers' voices again. Why didn't you get off in Albany, he says. Why didn't you, the woman says. She sounds cheerful. She says, We get off at Albany and we stop at the hotel and you go home to your wife and I go home to my husband. I just figured why do that again? They're going to raise hell, the man says. Oh, I know. She laughs and Lillian is happy to hear it—it is the sound of bells on a warhorse, and she wonders what terrible things happened to this woman to make her so brave. Lillian would like to tap on the door and say that while she admires the woman from inside the broom closet, she does not admire the man, and she's pretty sure he'll leave in Rome or that other place and if the woman manages to keep him in her bed until Chicago, he will glide away early one morning and take the train back to Albany with a present for his wife. Let's get a drink, the man says.

They walk away and it is darker than before. Lillian can see nothing of the country she is passing through. She smells traces of the man's bay rum and the woman's attar of roses. Apple orchards, green, red, yellow, brown, and dark plowed fields and muddy grazing cattle, and hoboes ducking through railroad yards and shoeless children in flour sacks waving to the train as it comes 'round the bend, and clusters of shacks and red silos and large bodies of water whose names Lillian doesn't know—this great slice of America is less to Lillian than what was left of Yaakov's Stalagmitic Chamber and exquisite Indians, and it is behind her within hours.

"Just wait," the porter says. "Wait."

There are endless footsteps down the hall past her door, the narrow wave of fresher air over caramel, wet wool, singed hair, smelling salts, hair tonic, Pears soap, tobacco. Lillian catches the lovers' scents again, but they don't speak, and then she smells the train station, ash and oil, hot wick and wax as if a hundred candles have just been put out, toasted bread, tar, damp, tired people hurrying along.

The porter opens the door. Lillian is on her hands and knees, the floor floating beneath her like a dirty sea, his shoes as dark and glossy as wet stones.

"Off with you," he says.

Lillian had thought that she would stay on the train and they would go on together, as they had. He is the only person she knows.

"This is La Salle. You'll be wanting Union Station. Across the river," he says, but the girl stays on all fours, stubborn as a dumb animal and he wants to kick her. He pulls her up and presses her against the wall and pushes her satchel into her arms.

"Be a good girl," he says.

She looks at him and although he himself has rarely raised a hand to his wife, and not in the last ten years, he looks at the girl's face and thinks, This is why we hit you. She sees it, she sees the thought, she sees the hand lifted and the shadow falling before the hand, and she closes her eyes and thrusts her face toward him because this is nothing to sit and wait for, and Dan O'Brien sighs and pulls her out onto the platform and drags her up the stairs from Track 123.

"For fucksake," he says. "Go to Union Station. You'll be wanting Andy McGann, Great Northern. McGann's the man. They call him Red."

Lillian cannot muster a word or a single step. She can no more walk than fly.

"That way," the porter says, and he gives her a push that is all that's left of his wish to hit her so hard her eyes would roll back in her head and she would trouble him no more.

Lillian stands. She picks up her satchel. Finally, she says to the

first well-dressed man she sees, Union Station, please, and he shakes
his head. It's not that he doesn't know, Lillian thinks, it's her. It's
that there is nothing in it for him to tell a dirty foreigner where the
train station is. She tries another man, not so well dressed, and he
looks at her sadly, as if he knows how it has been for her and how it
will be for her, and she casts her eyes down as if she is the most unfortunate person in the world, and then she smiles hopefully. She is
thinking that she will have to act the woeful, winsome girl a million
times over just to get to the goddamned train station when he says,
East Van Buren Street, three blocks to Lower Wacker, right turn,
two blocks along the river, left on Adams, take the bridge—it's there
on your right, after the river. Lillian has no idea what he has said or
how she would repeat it. The man walks off and Lillian stands on
the corner. A man and a woman step into the street right beside her,
the man puts up his hand, and a taxicab pulls up and away.

Lillian has ridden in taxicabs with Reuben and with Meyer. She
puts her hand up, too, palm out, with the Bursteins' grand sweep,
and she lifts her chin like they do, and the cab stops in front of the
dirty girl in heavy, scuffed shoes. Lillian has thirty cents ready in her
right hand. The rest of her money is in a slit in the lining of her left
boot, in one of the hidden silk pockets Yaakov has made for her, and
underneath the bottom of her satchel. Thirty cents seems right; it's
what Reuben paid for them to come home when they went uptown,
it's what Meyer paid when they went to Ye Olde Chop House.
Thirty cents could be the going rate for metropolitan taxicab rides,
and if it's more than that, Lillian will not hesitate (falter, stutter,
fluctuate, and also shilly-shally, blow hot and cold, or straddle the
fence). She will throw down her three dimes and run like hell. She
hears, Thirty cents, miss, and tosses the money over the seat. Lillian
is up and out and looking for a man named Andy McGann, known
as Red.

The symbol of the Great Northern Railway is a white goat
against a red mountain, and Lillian sees the goat a dozen times before

she finds the train. A nice American family is in front of her on the platform, the father and mother shiny as a magazine cover and the two children in little travel suits, the girl with a curly-haired doll, the boy with a big picture book. The little girl holds Lillian's gaze for a second and looks away, distressed to be looked at like that, and Lillian looks away, too. Farther down the platform, two elegant women are carrying two fancy little dogs. Porters pull two matched sets of violet suede luggage past Lillian, and she thinks that it's not enough she has to stand in Union Station, sweating underneath her lover's overcoat, in a dirty dress, her hair lank with grease and piled on her head, she has to be ignored by women who smell like flower beds, with luggage nicer than her clothes, carrying dogs who look better than Lillian. She can't wait for this kind of vanity to pass; she imagines that at some point she won't care what she looks like or what other people look like, she won't notice who notices her; she'll see life as a big wheel rolling smoothly from the past to the present to the future, from her life as a woman to the next life as a water bug or a tulip, all lives equally desirable or undesirable and the wheel stops for nothing, which is how Yaakov explained Buddhism to her.

"Ticket, miss?" a porter says, and the way he says "miss" would be a lesson to Meyer Burstein, it is so rich in contempt and nuanced surmise and the quick conclusion that the only way this woman will leave Chicago is flat on her back with her panties down.

"I am looking for Mr. McGann."

Another porter passes by and says, Red, and Lillian says, Yes, it is Mr. Red McGann whom she seeks, and the two porters laugh but the plump one with the fatherly face calls out in a voice like a claxon, Red, Red McGann, Track 27, and another porter picks up the call and here he comes, Red McGann, a bit taller than Lillian, muscle running to fat, skin white as paper except for two spots of pink on his high cheekbones. He has round, boyish blue eyes, and his hair is streaked with rust and slicked-back high, hard and smooth as the prow of a ship.

Red McGann takes Lillian by the elbow like an uncle and walks her toward the next-to-last car. He asks her how she came to him, and Lillian tells him she has been sent by Mr. O'Brien and she adds that Mr. O'Brien allowed her to sit in the broom closet and treated her with great kindness and gave her a cup of coffee and two sandwiches and Mr. O'Brien has said that Mr. McGann will do the same for five dollars.

Red McGann smiles. It is not the worst smile she will ever see, but it has the kind of tenderness you find on the faces of boys who love their dogs and kick them.

"O'Brien's a fine man," he says. He takes Lillian's satchel, gives her a hand up into the railroad car, and pulls her into the women's lavatory. He stands with his back to the lavatory door and puts the satchel behind his legs and says, "Let me take your coat for you" and he hangs it on a hook on the wall. He locks the door. He unbuttons the fly on his blue wool trousers and lays his muffler on the floor. He puts his square white hands on Lillian's shoulders and pushes her to her knees on top of the muffler.

"Can you really spare the five dollars, love?" he says.

Lillian looks up at him, looks up the length of him, from the blue wool and glimpse of flannel shorts beneath, up the considerable expanse of his blue tunic, to the creases of age on his neck, to the underside of his chin, where she can see that he has missed a few gray whiskers in shaving. She cannot really spare the five dollars—she can use every one of them come Seattle. She puts her mind on Seattle. She breathes through her mouth so as not to have to take in the scent of Red McGann, so as not to remember any more of this than the cracked black-and-white tile under the navy-blue muffler and his black shoes on either side of her. She pushes her hair back and licks her lips, and Red McGann sighs. You're a pet, you are, he says.

She cannot raise him. He is as soft in her mouth as oatmeal. Lillian handles him as if he were a lover, as if he were Reuben after a long day. She reaches inside his shorts and cups his balls, she takes hold of the shaft with two fingers and then with her whole hand, and all the time she is thinking, Seattle, Seattle, Seattle. She tugs steadily and he rocks with her, and puts his hand behind her head so she won't hit it against the porcelain sink.

She fits her lips around him tightly and minds her teeth. She makes her mouth as soft and inviting as she can and holds her lips firm against him. Red McGann says, Oh, good girl, good girl, and he thrusts toward her and hardens slightly. Lillian opens one eye to see if this will get them where they must go, and he softens again. She leans away and wipes her mouth on the back of her hand. She puts her other hand around him again and sighs. I cannot make a fire with wet wood, Mr. McGann, Lillian thinks, and as if he has heard her, he puts his hand over hers and holds it still. Lillian keeps her eyes down; it's not likely that he wants to look at her.

He pats her head. He pushes back the hair that has come loose from her twist.

"There it is," he says. "If I had to sign for my life, I'd be a dead man. No lead in the pencil."

It sounds as if he's smiling, which surprises her, but she cannot smile back. He pulls her up and dusts off her knees. He shakes out his muffler and puts it back around his neck.

"No harm done, love," he says.

"No harm done," Lillian says, and thinks that it's more true than not.

Red McGann is not a bad man and he wants Lillian to know that, and he wants her to say it, too. He wants that now more than he wanted the other. He wants her to see that he was willing to save her five dollars and that another man would have asked her to rosin the bow and taken the money as well, and he has heard that some of the fellows charge extra for the water and the sandwich, which he does not. He wants Lillian to agree that there are some things you want so much you don't care about their provenance. It doesn't matter if they're stolen or paid for or forced out by pity or fear. It only matters that you get that drink, or that release, or that money, or that baby, and when you are standing on the side of need, in the thick of not having what you must, the trouble that may come later, even the trouble you can guarantee, is of no account. And if Red McGann said that to Lillian, she wouldn't argue with him.

He hands Lillian her coat.

"I'm shattered," he says. "That's the truth of it."

Shattered, Lillian thinks. Aren't we all. And at that she does smile and Red McGann is uplifted.

"Ah, really, no harm done," he says again, and he shows Lillian the broom closet. "I'll see you out in St. Paul—you can do your business then."

Lillian adjusts herself in the pitch black inside. Again there is the painted mesh screen between the slats, the bucket, the brush. There are the same three shelves above her, the same damp wood floor, a box of soap flakes, but no umbrella. Lillian stands in the closet for a few seconds and cracks her neck. She hears a man singing to his little girl, Trot, trot to Boston, Trot, trot, to Lynn. Watch out, Sarabeth, or you'll fall in. Lillian uses the lavatory before dawn in St. Paul and gets her dry ham sandwich in Fargo, North Dakota, and has her bad dream in Minot, North Dakota, and again in Spokane, and even in the dream she can feel herself standing to one side saying, Yes, yes, teapot, ax, severed hand, I know, for God's sake, I know. She begins to scream, she wakens, she quiets herself. Lillian falls out of the broom closet at Seattle's King Street Station, and Red McGann picks her up by the elbow.

"You must keep sharp," he says. "The world is a terrible place."

September 3, 1925

Ain't It Fierce to Be So Beautiful, Beautiful?

SEATTLE'S KING STREET STATION IS FAMOUS FOR TWO THINGS, and no one tells Lillian about either one.

King Street Station is a big, handsome barn of a place, and civic-minded people in Seattle compare its dark-red brick tower to the campanile found in the Piazza San Marco in Venice, Italy. Lillian walks out of the train station and she never even sees the tower.

She looks from face to face, from sign to sign. THE SEATTLE HOTEL; THE TYPEWRITER CAPITAL OF AMERICA; THE WANG DOODLE ORCHESTRA TONIGHT ONLY; THE CAVE CAFÉ AND GRILL: SOMETHING DOING ALL THE TIME. On either side of the main entrance are ten-foot-high posters, NO SPITTING bannered across the body of Hygeia, the Goddess of Health, who holds a tidy single-family house in one hand and doves nesting in a sapling in the other, the hem of her green robe falling over DIRT, DISEASE, CRIME, and a half-dozen spittoons. Travelers pour out around Lillian and find their way to cabs and hansoms or waiting families or bellboys for the better or bigger travelers' hotels.

Lillian doesn't need a place to stay; according to her notes from Yaakov, she needs only to find the Alaska Steamship Company, Pier 70, which will take her to Prince Rupert, British Columbia. From Prince Rupert, Canada, he writes, a riverboat will take you up the Skeena River to Hazelton, and then from Hazelton to what people call the Telegraph Trail, and you follow that to Whitehorse and catch another steamship to Dawson City, and from there, apparently, according to Yaakov, small boats depart for Siberia. Yaakov has written it all out for her, Yiddish on one side, English on the other, and facts about Canada and the Yukon. She has seven dollars and twenty cents.

Out the rear door, Lillian follows the people who look most like herself: dressed badly but for all eventualities, cleaned up but not clean, and moving like small, scared fish in a very big pond.

The rear door, next to the faded sign for the Universal Negro Improvement Association, is not the best way to leave King Street Station. It leads directly to Yesler Way, the original Skid Row (run-down neighborhood, the dumps, desolation row, see also the slums), which began as Skid Road in 1852, when Henry Yesler, a big man in lumber, built up a narrow, rutted east-west strip through town to slide his logs downhill from the forest to the mill.

Lillian doesn't know the name of the street that runs past King Street Station. No one told her not to go out the rear door. No one told her that the local police don't patrol the area because the only people in that part of Yesler Way are out-of-towners who've gone through the wrong door and natives who are there to prey upon them. Seattle doesn't have enough police officers for all the brothels and opium dens and pawnshops and speakeasies and two-bit thieves and grifters. Lillian walks out the wrong door and doesn't see anyone but some colored boys shooting marbles and a red-haired woman lying still on the ground in just a skirt and boots, her white breasts bruised yellow and blue. Lillian looks around for the police or an upright citizen, but there is no one in uniform, and the men coming down the alleyway do not look like upright citizens.

SOMEONE IS KICKING Lillian in the ribs lightly. She opens her eyes and what she sees makes no sense to her. It is the dark, smooth leg of a young colored girl, her foot in a white Mary Jane and a white cotton anklet with white lace crocheted on the folded edge, and a shiny round toe is prodding Lillian's side. The little girl, in a white pinny and blue high-necked dress, looks down at Lillian and says, "Lady, Miss Lady, don't you wanna get up?"

Gumdrop knows right away what she's looking at. Natives do. Natives come early and stay late on their home ground; they understand what's going on before it's even begun, taking in the significance of events before the shapes have risen and configured themselves. Lillian's father saw the narrow yellowing edge of the birch leaf in late August and knew that his son-in-law would have to borrow money in October. Reuben saw Lillian's stained, pinpricked fingers and knew that she could offer something. Cousin Frieda saw the hats and flashing bracelets of the American women and knew that she would lose a husband and make a living in the New World's shallow, swift-moving fancies. Gumdrop knows that this woman, lying in an alley off Yesler Way, is her own age, not dead, not American, and very possibly of use.

Gumdrop kicks Lillian again, harder. She bends down to whisper in her ear, her diction as precise as a Sunday-school teacher's. In a serious and utterly adult voice, she says, "Get up now. In about two minutes, they'll have the clothes off your back." Lillian opens her eyes fully and Gumdrop says, "Now."

LILLIAN WAKES UP in Gumdrop's bed. When she turns her head, it hurts to swallow and there are sharp pains everywhere. She tries not to move, just to watch the small woman who must have brought her here (there was a cab ride, there was someone carrying her up a flight of stairs, the back of her head knocking against the bannister) without the woman noticing. The woman leans over Lillian to smooth her pillow, her breasts brush Lillian's cheek, and Lillian understands that although there may be more to the story, she's lucky to be alive and this woman is the luck. There's nothing of the little girl in the alleyway now; the woman stands back from the bed, eyes narrowed, right hip canted, and when she throws one slim arm out toward the bay window, telling Lillian to sit up and greet the day, she is every actress Lillian has ever known, shining with self and gesture. Yellow silk blouse and flounced orange skirt, legs bright in silk stockings, tiny orange pumps with diamanté buckles. Lillian wants to say, I have shoes just like that, but she doesn't. She had shoes just like that, is all. The woman and Lillian look at each other, and Lillian pulls the sheets a little tighter.

"Nothing I haven't seen before," the woman says. She puts out her hand. "Call me Gumdrop."

"Call me Lillian," Lillian says, and wishes she had some other sporty name that she could choose to use or not.

Gumdrop opens the doors of her two armoires to find something to lend Lillian, and it's clear to Lillian that until now she's known only amateurs; Gumdrop is a professional, a professional with a specialty, and her specialty is The Little Girl. There are crisp white-and-navy pinafores, more shiny, round-toed shoes like the kind Gumdrop kicked her with, a black pair, a red pair, and a pink pair with pink-and-white ribbons instead of straps. There is a white ribbon-trimmed sailor suit with a saucy red-and-white beret, and a lavender wool coat with a cluster of silk violets on the lapel and a pair of lavender kid gloves sticking out of the velvet-trimmed pockets. It is the wardrobe of a much-loved, much-petted, and very spoiled ten-year-old girl.

Gumdrop is the colored Mary Pickford, and Lillian says so, and Gumdrop smiles for the first time. Gumdrop knows what she has and Mary Pickford is not a patch on Gumdrop in the nude. Her little bitty waist curves in sharply—an average-size man can put his hands around it and have his fingertips meet—and her bottom's bigger than you'd expect, which works out fine since she has to spend a lot of time showing her posterior view, one way and another, and her breasts are just like the Queen of France's or whoever it was who had famously nice little breasts, each one fitting perfectly into a champagne coupe. And she keeps all of herself soft and satiny brown with cocoa butter, except her nipples, which she rouges up twice a day because men like that, and her snatch is just a shade or two lighter than the rest of her where she shaves it smooth because men like that. Gumdrop is careful with her hands and washes them every night with one part lemon juice and one part white vinegar to two parts white brandy, preventing chapping and roughness, and if you asked her, Gumdrop would tell you that she believes, like Petrarch and like Madame Lola Montez, whose recipe it is, that the beautiful hand makes captive the heart.

Gumdrop asks Lillian everything about her life up until Lillian was left for dead and minus her belongings, and she is as thorough, as quick to go back to the missed stitch and the shaded detail, as any cop. Gumdrop's life of the last several years has led her to a greater understanding of how to get useful answers to unpleasant questions. She asks every question two ways, and when Lillian hesitates, which isn't often, Gumdrop smiles and pats her hand. The only thing Lillian won't tell her is why. She tells the woman who saved her life (unless it turns out that it was Gumdrop who robbed and beat Lillian and then repented, but that seems unlikely, as Gumdrop does not look like she repents much) about her quiet life in Turov and the massacre of her husband and parents. She tells her that she was the mistress of a famous father and son in New York City (and Gumdrop nods with appreciation), that she is a fair but reluctant seam-stress (and Gumdrop nods again; she herself would rather blow the late Warren G. Harding on a hot day than sew a button), and that she has decided that America is not for her and she is going home.

Lillian has lost all her money, she has lost valuable time and is still losing it; she is failing Sophie even as she's answering Gum-drop's questions, and she cannot bear to say Sophie's name or tell her story to this bright, hard woman who makes her living pretending to be a happy child.

Gumdrop pours two shots of whiskey. Mud in your eye, she says, and the women watch each other over the rims of their glasses. Gumdrop doesn't mind Lillian's lying. People who tell you the truth right away are people who aren't afraid of you, and that's either good news, because they're too stupid to be afraid, or very bad news, be-cause they know that the only person who needs to be afraid is you.

When Gumdrop cleaned Lillian in the tub, washing away the chalky dirt of Skid Row, patting around the bruises on the back of her head and neck, she'd noticed the thin silver stretch marks on Lil-lian's pale belly and the pink faded forking along the sides of Lillian's breasts, and when there was no pregnancy or baby forthcoming in Lillian's story, Gumdrop thought that whether or not Lillian was a liar (and Gumdrop knew she was), she wasn't exactly the right kind of whore. What Gumdrop's looking for is a couple of sensible whores, one of whom might have a specialty. Sensible whores are girls who understand men and make use of that; girls who can listen to men eight hours a day and cater to their darkest needs without wanting to kill them; girls who don't use too much opium or alcohol; girls who can follow instructions and make intelligent exceptions; girls who don't fall in love with their customers or with other girls. Love and drugs are bad for business; they lead to high turnover and a failure to move the product, and lately Gumdrop finds that she is interested in business. She has happened upon ambition, or it has overtaken her, and she finds that when you have a goal in life, almost everything that comes your way, even pain and disappointment, can be turned to useful account. Gumdrop reads the daily newspapers, colored and white; whenever the time seems right, she asks mild, pointed questions of her customers who own real estate, and later on, after her bath, she writes down their answers.

Snooky Salt is Gumdrop's pimp, and he is not the worst pimp a girl could have. He appreciates Gumdrop's specialty, doesn't send over customers who want a big fat woman with breasts they can bury their whole faces in, or older gentlemen who say they want a sweet little babygirl like Gumdrop but really want to be sweet little baby-girls themselves, for which Gumdrop has no patience and no accessories. A bad pimp would send the wildcatters up when they came to town, pockets filled with gold, looking for a woman as crazy as themselves, a woman they'd leave strung up on the bedpost with rope burns everywhere. Snooky doesn't do that. He's Gumdrop's own cousin Walter, and when she came to Seattle six years ago, he fronted her the money for the necessaries and set her up in nice rooms over the Black and Tan Club. The blood bond between them lets them relax with each other more than with other people in their line of work, and they like that, and Snooky is very nice, if a little big, in bed. Which is why Gumdrop hasn't told him she wants to fire him. She hasn't told him that she knows he's cheating her. And she hasn't told him that although she used to dream of being Seattle's first and foremost colored madam, she wants more than that; she wants to head a union of whores. She wants to be A. Philip Randolph, and really, if you pressed her and she was inclined to tell you, she wants to be V. I. Lenin.

Lillian and Gumdrop sip their whiskey and look out the window. "Thank you," Lillian says again. Gumdrop nods her head. They both know that Lillian owes Gumdrop something for not leaving her to lie in the dirt, but it's not clear to either of them what

Gumdrop can or should do with Lillian, who's a little too skinny for general tastes, and a proven liar, and a woman who believes that servicing two men in one day is not unlike being a whore. What Gumdrop has here, which is not what she wanted or expected or prepared for, is a houseguest.

Lillian doesn't feel like a houseguest. She watches Gumdrop tapping her smart little orange shoes against the linoleum and sees what Gumdrop sees: a lumpy-headed white woman with very few skills, no money, and not much promise. It hurts to be in a warm and pretty place, even if it's not everyone's taste, and to feel that you're the odd thing in it. Just being in someone's home hurts, even when that someone is a prostitute; Lillian had envisioned the occasional Canal Street boardinghouse or a rough log cabin (or even wigwams or igloos, like the ones she'd seen in Yaakov's scrolls, where whatever she would have to experience, envy—of brilliantly enameled plates and cups and saucers glimmering in a maple china cabinet and a bright, modern icebox, and a blue velvet divan and matching armchair—would not be part of it). Lillian watches Gumdrop smooth out the red-ruffled duvet and the matching red-and-white pillows.

Lillian can't tell Gumdrop that she's already thought about robbing her so she can get back on the road to Sophie and Siberia; she can't say that she already noted the Venetian stiletto stuck deep in the left edge of the mattress, its smooth handle protruding just a little. Instead, she tells Gumdrop how much she admires the china cabinet, which is true, and Gumdrop knows the truth when she hears it, and she smiles for a second time. She says that there is a bird's-eye-maple étagère going for peanuts right across the street but she fears it might be too big for the corner near the window. Lillian says she thinks an étagère would be very nice there, she thinks it would fill out the room. Esther Burstein, who comes up from time to time when Lillian is in Gumdrop's presence, had a tall, garlanded maple étagère that would be just the thing for Gumdrop's southeast corner.

The two women move from furniture to draperies, happy to ease out just a little from their daily armor and their present circumstances and gloss over the things that can't be said. (Gumdrop understands necessity and its companions, and she's already hidden all of her cash and her gold compact, and the stiletto is only one of three weapons she keeps handy.) They slide into the warm water of household matters like women of leisure; they make a tour of the parlor like English ladies, Gumdrop a glamorous toucan, Lillian half naked and barefoot. Gumdrop, who had planned to drop useless, dangerous Lillian at Fifteenth and Pike with her best wishes, changes her mind and says, as if Lillian has been reluctant and must be urged, You look famished—let's get some supper.

Supper at the Golden West Hotel ("The Best Colored Hotel West of Chicago," which is the kind of modest self-praise Seattle's colored people are known for) is chicken and sausage gravy and baking-powder biscuits and mashed potatoes and a kind of fried squash fritter Lillian has never seen before. Gumdrop takes very small bites and chews carefully, her narrow jaw moving steadily until there is nothing left on her plate and nothing on anyone else's plate, either. She is a marvel of efficiency and determined desire. Lillian eats slowly so she doesn't make herself sick with all this real food, and Snooky Salt sits between them, passing the biscuits left and right, pouring elderberry wine, a happy family man.

Gumdrop has told Lillian, on the way to the Golden West, that Snooky Salt is a snake. Not just because he's a pimp, Gumdrop said. Some pimps are not snakes. They're naughty enough, she said, but by and large, they're big men and not snakes. Big men, Gumdrop said, tend not to be vicious. They know you know they mean business. You look at a big, well-built man and he smiles at you. He sits back in his chair, legs apart. He offers you a cup of coffee and a piece of cake. You can sit in his big lap and talk things over, and he talks gentle to you, because he can. Snooky, said Gumdrop, comes from a long line of small, muscly men, all mean as snakes. They take offense quicker than you can say Jack Robinson, they have no regard for the niceties of a situation, and you have to tell them a hundred times a day how they're handsomer and smarter and braver than any of those big men they come up against. A big man can fool you with his gentleness and that warm, deep laugh so many of them have, Gumdrop said. I trust my Snooky, she said. He's pure snake. And Lillian watches him now for signs of snake, but he is as dignified as Reuben, as dapper as Meyer.

Snooky hands Lillian another biscuit. She is an excellent addition, he feels, and people are looking at the three of them; Snooky likes the new girl's nice posture and her big dark eyes and he can see her possibilities. Because of her color and skinniness and a certain set to her jaw, she's not going to be everyone's cup of tea. She might, however, turn out to be his. He puts bits of white meat and hills of mashed potatoes on Lillian's plate. Try this, honey, he says. I like a woman with a little meat on her bones. Lillian lets him. She's too tired to worry about how all this looks. She's wearing a green dress borrowed from the whore down the hall, she's letting herself be fed, in public, by a colored man in a black-and-white houndstooth suit and a lilac derby with boots to match, and she knows just how bad it looks. But there's no help for it. Or, she thinks as Snooky pokes a hole in the mound of mashed potatoes and pours gravy into it, there is help and she should not be fooled by the boots.

AT NIGHT, THE TWO WOMEN SHARE Gumdrop's big bed, and as they fall asleep Gumdrop says, Did they get all your money? Lillian nods yes in the dark, and Gumdrop finds Lillian's arm and pinches it, not lightly, to wake her up. Just how much did they get, Gumdrop asks, and Lillian says, Nine dollars and twenty cents, and Gumdrop laughs and says, Really, and she pauses and says, Even so, I can do you better than that. She pats Lillian's bottom and rolls to the far side of the bed.

It turns out that Gumdrop's needs are not unlike those of Meyer Burstein, or other leading lights. She needs a dresser, she needs a solid meal midafternoon, when things are slow, and a light dinner at about midnight. She needs regular trips to the Rexall's and she needs help with her busy schedule (there are a dozen large white men marching or skulking through the Black and Tan Club every day, looking for Gumdrop). She needs exactly what Meyer needed most: sincere, apparently judicious, and frankly limitless flattery. Gumdrop can smell how keen Lillian is to go, but she knows the money's a great lure, and the charm of having a white servant is irresistible to Gumdrop, although she doesn't say "servant". If Lillian will do for Gumdrop, for just a few weeks, she'll have enough money to move on. Four dollars a day, Gumdrop says, for three weeks, and Lillian says, Five, for ten days, and Gumdrop says, Four and a quarter for two weeks, and Lillian puts out her hand. Gumdrop shakes it and thinks, not unkindly, Jews.

For thirteen days and nights, when Snooky and Gumdrop are not called away on business, the three of them will dine downstairs at the Black and Tan, and when Gumdrop has a late-night date, Lillian will sit kitty-corner from the table where Snooky does business and spend a couple of hours reading the newspaper and nodding to Snooky's two other whores when they pass through (Ladivina, high-yellow and sulky and bored as a disappointed debutante, popular with customers who want to make her smile, or cry out; and Big Taffy, a fierce, chunky Welsh girl with no specialty at all except stamina). Snooky likes to see Lillian there, adding tone, and when he catches her eye, he gives her a big wink and a smile and sends over a bowl of peanuts and a root beer until he's finished with his business. Lillian works for a prostitute and is being courted by a pimp, and it is not the worst thing that has ever happened.

THE SECOND NIGHT OF HER NEW LIFE, Lillian wakes up screaming, and Gumdrop holds her firmly against her silk kimono and bare chest. Gumdrop says, as her mother used to say, "You're all right. Open your eyes and see the real world."

Lillian rests with her face against Gumdrop's warm shoulder.

Gumdrop says, "Go on. I know about dreams."

"I'm dead and I'm blind. It's bright red everywhere, like the inside of your eyelids. I can feel the sun on my face but I can't see. Everything has disappeared, the houses, the people, the chickens—this is in the town I come from, this is in Turov—and there's nothing; it's just white as a sheet. I rub my eyes and something is crumbling in my hands. It's dried blood. Blood was sticking my eyelids together. I try to rub the blood away, but it's sticky, it's on my hands, too, my hands and arms are red and wet. And the floor is red and poor Osip—we were married four years—is on the floor and is covered in blood, his clothes are black with it, and there are all these things on the floor between us. My grandmother's teapot is broken in pieces and there is a bucket."

Lillian knows what lies next to the bucket—she sees the hand, she knows whose hand it is—but she cannot say to Gumdrop, who is cradling her, My mother's severed hand is next to the bucket.

She says, "My mother is on the floor, dead. I'm naked in the room, everything is red, and I kneel down to my father, he's lying dead in front of the door in his nightshirt, and his ax is still in his hands. And my Sophie's bed—I have a daughter, her name is Sophie—is empty and I am screaming for her. That's the dream." Lillian remembers the rest of it, the sunlight, pale-gold morning light, catching Osip's wedding band and shining on the windows, but it doesn't seem worth saying.

"Sophie's a nice name," Gumdrop says. She props herself up in the big bed and puts her arm along the back of Lillian's bruised neck, and Lillian lays her head down on the little shoulder, which seems broad and full in the darkness. In the dark, Gumdrop feels like a big woman.

"My real name's Clothilde," she says. "I come from a small town near here—we were the only colored people around. My mother was a healer, my father did a little farming. Chickens"—and Lillian nods in the dark, picturing Turov, with all of Turov's residents, only brown-skinned—"a couple of goats. We got by, you know what I'm saying? We had a dog, which most colored people don't, because of the . . . past."

Gumdrop isn't sure what Lillian knows about dogs and colored people in America; Lillian doesn't know anything, not even enough to say, Jews don't like dogs, either.

"I loved that dog—she was a big black Lab. Delta, my father named her. Oh," Gumdrop says, remembering something, and she stops talking.

All day yesterday, Gumdrop had talked nonstop to Lillian, giving her the uncensored guide to Colored Seattle and the World of Gumdrop. She showed her around the neighborhood, where to go and where not to (yes to the Ubangi Room, owned by another cousin, no, absolutely no, to the Shake and Shimmy, owned by a white man with unusual habits). She told Lillian how to make a cocktail out of almost any three liquids, she told her why colored ladies needed hair relaxant and why lye was still better than anything more modern and less harsh, she looked at other women's shoes as they passed by on the street and she told Lillian their life stories (married to a rich old man—look at those shiny leather soles—she doesn't have to walk even two blocks; that one got herself a special lady friend picking out her shoes, telling her there's more to life than sex with the mister, there's pink suede pumps). She gave Lillian the skinny on the world as she knew it, in her bright, fluting voice, as if cocktails and beauty products and shoes were the things closest to her glittery little heart.

"I think the most important thing in the world is being brave," Gumdrop says now, in the dark. "I'd rather be brave than beautiful. Wouldn't you? Hell, I'd settle for *acting* brave."

She talks quickly, as if she has been talking for hours and needs to wrap things up before Lillian gets bored or goes to sleep. Lillian puts her hand on Gumdrop's chest and strokes it a few times, to say that she can slow down, that Lillian will lie there until dawn, just listening to Gumdrop breathe, if it will help. Gumdrop picks up Lillian's hand like it is a leaf or a ladybug and sets it back on the bed.

"My mother was brave," Gumdrop says. "My father died—he got the flu in 1916, like half the country. My littlest sister, too. It was a bad time. I was fourteen, my brother was eleven, my little sisters were eight and six. It was the six-year-old that died. Mabel. We kept the farm going, me and my brother, and my mother was busy with the healing, all those people down with the flu. Bad time. Two white men came when my mother was visiting the sick, and I told my brother go hide, and they took the goats and they interfered with me. The baby was born in the spring of 'seventeen. Beautiful baby girl. Oh," Gumdrop says, and she falls silent again.

The sun is coming up over Seattle, silvery light in the east making a new world, for just a few minutes, and the two women turn their faces toward the window to see it happen, so bright and pink with possibility, and then the world outside Gumdrop's window resolves into its familiar shape and they lie back down, Gumdrop curved toward the wall, Lillian behind her, waiting.

"Oh, you know how it is," Gumdrop says, and she sounds for all the world like Reuben Burstein, tired of someone's sentimental nonsense. "My mother helped me raise the baby, and then I got tired of life on the little farm and taking care of my baby and three others and selling eggs at the market and running the vegetable stand and nothing much ahead of me. Bright lights, here I come," Gumdrop says. "And I figure I'll send for them when I'm settled, when I have a nice place and I can take care of my mother and my daughter, both, and it only takes me two years to get on my feet and I send a letter and I don't hear a thing and I send another letter and five dollars; you can imagine what the mail's like out there in the countryside"—and Lillian nods, although she has never received a letter in her life—"and the minister sends back a note and after a couple of months, it does find me. My brother has shipped out and my sister is in a convent school and my mother and my baby girl are dead. D-E-A-D. Two years out, and some disease you couldn't even get by trying if you were in a civilized place, and it has taken them both."

Lillian puts her arms around Gumdrop's waist and opens her mouth to speak.

"We have to get some sleep," Gumdrop says.

GUMDROP IS SILENT AT BREAKFAST and busy until three in the afternoon, when she bathes and thinks about the two things she has to say to Lillian. One is that, as Gumdrop expected, Snooky wants a three-way, and the other is that Gumdrop would like to take the opportunity of this three-way (of this purported three-way, is how she plans to put it to Lillian, a three-way that will absolutely never be consummated unless Lillian is so inclined) to take back the money Snooky has stolen from her.

Snooky had floated the idea of a three-way last evening, while Gumdrop was lying with her head on his stomach and Lillian was reading downstairs. Snooky wanted to make it an invitation and not a demand because he liked Lillian and he didn't want any misunder-

standings and he didn't want the kinds of events that misunder-
standings can lead to.

"So don't misunderstand," Snooky'd said.

"I'm not misunderstanding a thing," Gumdrop said. She sat up
on top of him. "You want me to ask my Lillian, who is not a professional, if she would care to engage in a ménage à trois before she
ships out."

Snooky pulled Gumdrop to him and licked the little hollow
above her collarbone.

"I like her," he said. "And you like her."

"I like her fine," Gumdrop said, as if she didn't.

"Oh, you like her," Snooky said. "You could get comfortable with
her in the sack, G."

Gumdrop shrugged. Snooky Salt, like Otto von Bismarck,
thought of himself as the iron fist in the velvet glove, and he offered
the velvet side to Gumdrop one more time.

"I could give her a fin as a good-bye and good luck," he said.
"Help her get on her way to East Buskavitch, wherever she's
headed."

Well, Gumdrop thought, his mind is made up. Good-bye and
good luck, Lillian.

Gumdrop has given Snooky's proposition a lot of thought. She
has tried not to suspect him of stealing from her, which is hard for a
sensible woman who can do arithmetic, but she has tried because
she knows that there are serious consequences to suspecting things.
When Snooky first suggested that he collect for her, Gumdrop said,
No way in hell, and Snooky shrugged sadly. Soon after, she had to
remind a new customer to put the money on her nightstand and the
man cut her on the chest with a riding crop. Snooky heard about it
and horsewhipped the man on Jackson Street, to everyone's satisfac-
tion, and Snooky came to Gumdrop, big-eyed and sorrowful, the
whipped man's two blood-speckled dollars in his hand, and said that

he could not bear to let her be so mistreated and please would she let him collect. He would take the extra time, he said, to meet every customer on his way out of Gumdrop's door and collect the fee, keeping his share and giving Gumdrop her full half (minus what she owed him for the original capital expenses) at the end of every day. And he has. But Gumdrop has heard a little of this and that, she has managed a conversation with Ladivina, who is sullen but not stupid, and she suspects that Snooky raised her price some time ago without raising her cut.

Gumdrop sees her stolen money every morning and every night: spires of silver dimes, an extra ten cents taken from every dollar she has squeezed out from between her legs for the last two years. She sees pale-green dollar bills in a metal strongbox, at least thirty of them hers if she has figured correctly (and she has done the calculations dozens of times—she does them the way other people count sheep, figuring for daily income, days missed due to illness and holidays, weeks worked, months worked, and it is at least thirty dollars that's owed to her for at least the last two years), and the box must be in the back of Snooky's closet, between his lilac boots and his cherry-red ones. There must be at least a hundred dollars in the strongbox (Snooky Salt is not a banking man), and it doesn't seem impossible that with Lillian's help Gumdrop can sex him up, drug him, and take back her money without too much commotion. She can give Lillian what she owes her, plus another five for helping with the reparations, and the two women can be on their merry way, Lillian for Outer Mongolia and Gumdrop for St. Paul, where unions and colored education are all the rage.

On her next-to-last evening in Seattle, Lillian jots down a few reminders for Gumdrop.

"Fasttrack is coming tomorrow," Lillian says, and she writes "Mr. FT 3:00" in the slim black ledger she's bought for Gumdrop. They both love the set of ledgers, the black laquered covers, the red ribbon bookmarks sewn in, the blue lines crossed with pink ones. It has the look of business done by glamorous and practical women. "Which is my last day."

Gumdrop sighs. Fasttrack Peterson prides himself on all the things he can do with his tongue, not one of which is appealing or even restful, and he spends ten minutes of every session telling Gumdrop about all the pleasure he's going to give her, and then a lot of writhing and wriggling and carrying-on is required of Gumdrop. The only pleasure Fasttrack gives her is when he hands her a tip and shuts the door behind him. Fasttrack is the least of Gumdrop's problems for tomorrow.

She says, "Forget him, Lillian. Snooky has my money."

"What can you do?" Lillian says, and she means, What will you do? She means, What can anyone do in the face of a cousin stealing from you? She wants to do better by Gumdrop, and she adds, "Screw your courage to the sticking-place and we'll not fail."

Gumdrop nods, as if she's been waiting for exactly this advice. She says that if Lillian will just pretend to go through with the three-way Snooky's been asking for (and Lillian is no more surprised than Gumdrop; she hasn't known a lot of men, but she's known enough), Gumdrop will sort it out with Snooky at a favorable moment, and should it be awkward, Gumdrop will have Lillian to help out and they'll do something clever to get around him. She hands Lillian her overcoat, the long tear up the sleeve mended neatly and the hidden pockets still filled with maps but none of Lillian's money from New York, which is no surprise to either of them. She lays Yitzak Nirenberg's empty satchel in front of Lillian, who knows enough not to look for the three dollars she'd tucked under the satchel's bottom, and to say nothing more than thank you. Gumdrop says, My stars, you got nothing, and she gives Lillian a second set of underwear, more or less Lillian's size, which means it belongs to Ladivina down the hall, and she folds up two shirts and two undershirts that have been left behind by regular customers. The smart thing is to pack, just in case, and Lillian does, folding her tweed pants and her leather belt, all she owns barely filling half the bag, and Gumdrop says, Let's roll out the barrel, and they both wash up and pin their hair nicely and put on what Gumdrop calls party clothes, Gumdrop in pink silk and Lillian in Ladivina's green, dresses that come off easily and can be kicked aside without hesitation.

There is a host of things Gumdrop has not told Lillian about the evening to come. It isn't her experience that amateurs are helpful or that preparing them makes any difference. She once had to do a three-way on Jackson Street with a visiting second cousin who was willing but inexperienced, and it was a long, bad night. She couldn't get the girl to understand that their purpose was performance: arousing the customer, licking and nuzzling each other in showy ways that passed the time without too much bother (three short gasps, ten seconds apart, Gumdrop crying out softly, Oh God, my God, as if she were shamed and thrilled to feel such piercing sweetness, while mentally she reviewed *Half-Century* magazine's recent article on Baptist missionaries in China). Gumdrop operated on the general business principle of doing the minimum to collect the maximum, but her cousin had bucked over and under Gumdrop like muff-diving was her religion, jackknifing when she came, almost clipping Gumdrop in the eye, and then turning her attention to the customer so fully that they had to peroxide the scratches on his back, which pleased the man until he remembered he had to go home to his wife without an adequate explanation, and then there was no tip at all. Since then, Gumdrop avoids amateurs, and although Lillian has been better than useful these two weeks—keeping track of dollars in and dollars out, repairing lingerie and pressing her suits—there's no reason to think that for whatever might be coming she has what it takes.

. . .

"HE NEEDS TO BE DEAD DRUNK," Gumdrop says on the way to
Snooky's suite, pinching Lillian's hip, to make her listen. Snooky
waits on the bed like a sultan, his arms behind his head, and says,
What'll it be, girls? This here is Sadie Hawkins Day, which means
nothing to Lillian, but Gumdrop smiles like an imp. She steps out of
her dress and Lillian does the same, and Snooky notices Lillian's
plain patchy underwear right away. It's plainer than plain next to
Snooky's silk boxers, which are red-striped like a barber's pole and
they are shameful next to Gumdrop's finery, but Snooky says immediately that he doesn't mind. He says kindly as they get ready for bed
that he suspects she's saving her money for more important things
than fancy drawers, and when Gumdrop is out of the room making
her personal arrangements, Snooky hands Lillian seventy-five cents.
A little extra, he says, for your savings account. Lillian knows he's as
bad as Gumdrop says; he's worse. He's a pimp and a thief, stealing
from a hardworking woman, stealing from family, but he is a hard
man to dislike.

Gumdrop comes back and takes Lillian by the hand and says to
her, quietly, Turn over on your stomach. Lillian does, thinking, Oh
God, let this not be the biggest mistake of my life, although that's
not so easy to catalog anymore, and when Gumdrop spanks her
once, sharply, Lillian cries out in an unfeigned and completely satisfying way and Snooky laughs in anticipation. Gumdrop's little
brown hand on Lillian's round pink ass is a wonderful thing to contemplate, and he is filled with love for his cousin and with affection
for Lillian, whom he can already picture in three different and
equally terrific positions.

Lillian sits up and opens her mouth to object to the spanking, to
even the idea of spanking, and Gumdrop pinches her hard beneath
the sheet and winks hugely at her cousin. Shy, Gumdrop says, as if
she has tried and tried with this girl but will get nowhere without
Snooky's persuasive presence. And Snooky prefers it that way, prefers

that Lillian come to it on her own. He's not the kind of man who has to brutalize his girls for sex; they call him Brown Sugar, they call him Sugar Bear and Sweet Man, and he likes that, he likes that he never pays for it and he never hits for it.

Let's all relax a little bit, Gumdrop says, like she's had a sudden and bright idea. Lillian, she says, why don't you bring over that bottle of brandy and we'll have ourselves a little party. She pours half-capfuls for herself and Lillian and mugs of brandy for Snooky, and they play a few drinking games, and Lillian contributes one from Turov where you have to bang the spoon from the tabletop up into an empty cup. She's very good at it, and Snooky is not, and they all have a good laugh about that and drink more brandy. Lillian drops the straps of her cami off her shoulders, and Gumdrop catches her eye and nods. Snooky has a weak head, which most people don't know because he's usually careful, but Gumdrop knows all about this failing, from when they were ten-year-olds drinking behind the chicken coop and Cousin Walter, as Snooky was then, passed out cold.

Gumdrop waves her hand for Lillian to come closer. Snooky is flat on his back, smiling, nearly asleep. Gumdrop kneels beside Snooky. She runs her small fingers up and down his smooth, broad chest. She pulls lightly on his nipples the way he likes, and he moans a little and his penis twitches. Gumdrop looks at it and frowns. She doesn't want Snooky rousing himself at an inopportune moment. She rubs his chest in gentle circles and sings one of her mother's favorite songs from 1908, when she and Snooky were just babies, playing on the kitchen floor while their mamas sang and baked. She sings very softly and Snooky sighs in his sleep, and Gumdrop smiles down at him.

She soaks a handkerchief in brandy and puts it in his mouth, and he sucks on the cloth until the brandy's gone. She soaks it again and again until he stops sucking and his head falls to the side, his mouth open, his tongue pink and wet. A little brandy drips down his jaw to his collarbone. His chest gleams in the lamplight, and there is a pool of brandy in the shallow slit of his navel. His dick lies curled and thick on his leg, hidden in its purple sheath. It's impressive to Lillian, even in repose, but Gumdrop doesn't give him another glance. She kicks off her coral silk knickers and tosses her coral silk cami toward the bed. She stands in the middle of the room in just her brown skin and a pair of Moroccan silk slippers covered with pink and orange sequins, toes pointing up. She is ready for action and unimpeded by clothing.

Gumdrop is as comfortable out of her clothes as in them, and she thinks that Lillian must find it easier to see her ready to steal and naked than ready for work in a starched white pinny and gingham bows. In Snooky's overdecorated suite (the Moroccan theme's more pronounced every day as the rest of the shipment comes in and Snooky adds a brass hookah and two carnelian rugs and ballooning curtains of orange-and-pink silk), even as Snooky lies on the bed snoring and drunk and they get ready to rob him, Gumdrop looks beautifully like a small Greek statue in a Turkish harem (seraglio, palace, women's quarters), and Lillian says so.

Gumdrop can see that Lillian is tired; performing and nerves have taken it out of her, but the evening's not over. Not by a long shot, Gumdrop thinks, and time is of the essence. Lillian lies down next to Snooky, and Gumdrop lays her hand on Snooky's thigh and nods to where he has his business stiletto, the one with the stained brown leather handle sticking out from the edge of the mattress just enough that if you were having a good time in bed and were interrupted by urgent business, you could be on your feet and ready before the girl had put her legs together. Asleep, Snooky looks like a strong, clever boy.

"You stay here," Gumdrop says to Lillian. "If he stirs, give him more brandy. If he puts his hand on you—"

"I let him," Lillian says, thinking, I may not be a professional but I'm not an idiot, and she settles herself beside Snooky with the brandy and her legs right next to his fingertips.

Gumdrop searches for the strongbox, and because she wants it so much, she looks in the wrong places, fumbling with knobs and hinges that would ordinarily be no trouble. She runs her hands through all the shelves of the linen closet, blue blankets, mended white sheets, patched pillowcases, one set of yellow satin sheets so thick and slippery it was like making love on mayonnaise and not something Gumdrop wanted to do again, and then, there it is, gray metal corner sticking out on the uppermost shelf. Gumdrop can't reach it with a footstool. She walks back to the bedroom and sees Lillian sitting up expectantly, ignoring Snooky's hand making its blind, sleepy way between her legs. Lillian gives her the thumbs-up, and Gumdrop drags a chair over to the linen closet. She should let Lillian do this, she thinks, just as the strongbox falls through her hands and crashes to the floor. The lid flies open and coins scatter, and Snooky, who has seemed dead to the world, bolts up in bed, erect and alert and on his way to the closet before Lillian can do more than grab at his ankle.

"Clothilde!" Lillian cries out as he brushes her to the floor with the hard edge of his palm, and Snooky, who never expected to hear that name from a white mouth, stops to look at the woman crouching beneath him, her hands scrabbling up his leg. In that moment, as Snooky is startled by the presence of the girl Gumdrop was, a ten-year-old smoking corn silk and stacking tomatoes blemished side under, Gumdrop jumps over the tangle of Lillian and Snooky and runs back to the bed to pull out his stiletto, kept in the same place, exactly, that she keeps hers. Snooky comes toward her like a maddened bear, his eyes shiny and red, his mouth open, ready to make her sorry she thought to fuck with him and his hard-earned money and more than sorry she was ever born, but Lillian is holding on to his left foot, so he is severely hampered until he twists his handsome torso and kicks her hard in the stomach with his right. Lillian lets go. Snooky punches Gumdrop in the face and sends her flying onto the bed, but she doesn't drop the stiletto. Snooky reaches for Gumdrop's wrists to force her hand open, thinking that he'll fuck her and beat her senseless, and if she's out of commission for a week she'll remember this lesson, and he'll have to do Lillian, too, because it's somehow worse that a white girl to whom he has taken a fancy for no reason is trying to steal from him. He understands Gumdrop's thinking, at least, and he says so. He says, You should have asked me for the money, baby, and he grabs her wrists and pulls her arms nearly out of their delicate sockets, and her fingers tremble around the handle of the knife.

Lillian falls on him, pulling at his shoulders and screaming in Yiddish and English, *Gazlen,* murderer, get off her. She scoops her arms under Snooky as if he is a drowning swimmer and she must pull him back to shore, but she trips, the sheets are wet with sex and sweat and brandy, and as Gumdrop puts her hands up to protect herself from these two big people crushing her, Lillian's full weight falls on Snooky's back and drives the stiletto into his heart.

Gumdrop rolls off the bed as Snooky falls forward onto it. She and Lillian lie on the floor, six inches away from Snooky's outstretched hand. He gasps and turns himself over, and the hilt of the knife catches the setting sun. His eyes open and he blinks several times like a man being woken by a bright light. He pulls himself up until he is almost sitting, muscles rigid with effort, and then falls back, and the stiletto slips, as it is designed to do, farther into Snooky's chest cavity.

Lillian can't look at the metal edge of the handle, protruding only an inch or two above Snooky's smooth brown skin, or at the thin red streaks beginning to appear around it, and she can hardly look at Gumdrop, covered in goose bumps and drops of blood and breathing hard, but she can't let the knife slide deeper into the man's chest and do nothing. She takes a pillowcase off one of Snooky's pillows and tears it in half. She wraps the linen around her hand and grabs the square edge of steel and pulls the stiletto out. Blood flows like a wild river, like wine from a dropped bottle, and Lillian is wiping splashes of it off her face and jamming the torn pillowcase into the hole in Snooky's chest. Gumdrop lies on top of him, holding the linen tight with her body. Lillian wipes his face with a cold cloth. Gumdrop whispers, Walter, Walter. Snooky breathes painfully, blood seeping from the stiletto wound and then pouring from his mouth.

If Gumdrop and Lillian hadn't been so afraid of the short and empty life, of their histories, rife with errors of omission and commission, if they hadn't both been afraid they would never do what they told themselves they could and should, Snooky wouldn't be dying, and he knows it, too. He looks up at them and he says, You got the wrong man, girls, and the two of them pat his hands helplessly. They know he's right, he cannot be the right man, but there's no telling who the right man is.

Lillian pulls Gumdrop off the bed. They stand in the pile of brandy-soaked sheets, their feet dug into the cool twists of Snooky's red silk duvet and they can't move, they can't look, they can't have done what they've done. Long after the details of his death are hazy, long after it seems to Lillian that Snooky tripped and fell on Gumdrop, long after they've forgotten each other's stories and the names of each other's daughters, they'll remember blotting the blood from his nose and mouth with their hands, plugging the hole in his chest with lace-trimmed cotton.

Gumdrop closes his eyes with her thumbs, as her mother used to do, and she says to Lillian furiously, You may as well stay in your underthings. We have to dump his body. We have to clean this apartment so it looks like we were never here. And then we have to skip town. When she finishes speaking, Lillian puts her arms around her, and Gumdrop stands there, unwilling to be held by anyone except her dead cousin, with whom she shared the same slanting copper eyes, the same elegant hands and feet, the same fascination with appetite and its uses, and then she goes into Snooky's new marble-trimmed bathroom, and vomits.

Lillian finds her shoes and Gumdrop's, and she finds their dresses and their marcasite barrettes. She picks up the crystal decanter that was knocked to the hearth rug and puts it back with the others on the sideboard. She sets the little French end table right and stacks the unbroken gilt-trimmed ashtrays on top of the mantel. Stop it, Gumdrop says, and Lillian pays her no mind. She mutters Kaddish and folds and shelves the clean towels that fell to the closet floor, and she wipes blood and brandy off the nightstand and off the red-and-gold Moroccan bedside lamp.

They do everything they have to do. They wrap Snooky in the duvet and haul him down the stairs, trying not to drop his heels or his head. When they get to the swinging door between the lobby and the stairwell, Gumdrop goes through to the front desk, high heels clicking on the parquet, and leans back and fans herself like she's taking a break between customers. There is no one at the desk, and Gumdrop waves for Lillian to edge out into the lobby, and the two of them drag Snooky down the side stairs to the alley and arrange the trash cans in front of him. Lillian touches Snooky's warm face, his small, hooked nose, his dapper mustache, his neatly curled ears, until Gumdrop slaps her hand away. Watch over him, she says, and runs back upstairs for Snooky's lilac derby and his lilac boots, because he loved them so, and she puts the hat by his head and places the boots by his feet, as if he is only sleeping. Like the Egyptians did, Gumdrop says, and Lillian, who knows nothing at all about the ancient Egyptians and their burial practices, nods and tucks the ends of the duvet under him.

Gumdrop and Lillian have both seen dead men before, and Snooky looks like all of them, his features shrinking slightly, settling with sorrow. They stand over him for a second, shivering in the cool, rank air, and run back upstairs to finish dressing, to divide up the money and get out of Seattle before anyone can wonder where Snooky Salt and the little whore Gumdrop and the white girl have gone to.

Gumdrop says, "Which do you want, the cane or the pocket watch?" Neither of them wants the bloody stiletto, kicked under the bed when they moved Snooky's body.

Lillian doesn't answer. She doesn't want to take anything. She is not going to leave Seattle like a grave robber, and she says so. Gumdrop shrugs agreeably. Lillian is still carrying Yitzak Nirenberg's satchel, she would still be wearing the Kurlanskys' dead daughter's coat if it hadn't fallen to pieces, and it's kind of Gumdrop not to say, Who are you kidding? Lillian picks up the pocket watch and puts it down. It's as big as an egg. Gumdrop thumbs it open and shows her that beneath the heavy cross-hatched lid with TOUJOURS GAIES engraved on the front, there's a second lid with a scene of three women in sheer gowns, tossing a ball. It is the fanciest thing Lillian has ever seen, and she could use a watch—she's never had one, and it feels like real gold. If she should come on hard times, as she expects, she could sell it instantly.

Do you think, if I had to, I could get five dollars for this? Lillian asks, and Gumdrop says, I sure do, maybe seven, and Lillian takes the watch and the eight-inch gold watch chain and drops them both in her middle hidden pocket. Gumdrop sighs. She has wanted to be fair, and you could say she has been—she has given her friend dibs on the things left behind, but she didn't show Lillian that within the malacca cane there is a very fine sword. A hundred times in the next few months Lillian will wish she had a walking stick and a sword— she'll wish it so hard there will be days when her only prayer is for those two things—and it must be better that Gumdrop doesn't have to know this and that Lillian doesn't have to know how easily she could have had them both. Gumdrop gives Lillian thirty-five dollars, because there is far more than thirty—there's a hundred and forty dollars in the strongbox—and Gumdrop takes what's left and they both think she should. Gumdrop has been the navigator and the engineer of the terrible event, and Gumdrop had to see the knife go into her cousin's chest, and Gumdrop had to walk past her cousin and her lover and his hat and his best boots, and both she and Lillian think that a hundred and five dollars must be at least what that costs.

Lillian and Gumdrop are two blocks away from the Golden West when Lillian says, If you just show me the way to the Alaska Steamship Company, I'll beat it out of here. Giddy with relief and nerve-dead, Gumdrop sings out the first verse of "Bonnie Banks o' Loch Lomond" and as they get well away from Snooky's corpse, a little singing does not seem out of order. Gumdrop skips by Lillian's side. "Ye'll take the high road and I'll take the low road, and I'll be in Scotland afore ye. . . ." Gumdrop loves all things Scottish; she had a Scottish grandfather—she found his photograph tucked in the family Bible, an old, angry white man with pale eyes and Gumdrop's own pointy chin. Snooky liked to tell folks they were descended from a Chippewa Indian chief, but if Gumdrop had a nickel for every colored man who claimed to be the son of an Indian chief, she could have stopped turning tricks before she started.

Climbing into the cab with Lillian, holding Lillian's satchel for her so that the hack will think he's seeing a white woman and her colored maid (an eccentric white woman in man's clothing and a very nicely turned-out colored maid, but people see what they expect to see), Gumdrop thinks that she may have misunderstood her own desires. She can't have killed someone she loves for a hundred and five dollars and by accident; there is no way to make peace with

that. She must have killed Snooky, like Moses smote Pharaoh (and
didn't Moses love Pharaoh; didn't she read the two boys played together on the palace floor?), to set herself free. She must have killed
Snooky to be reborn. Whoever's going to start that union of
whores—and it is an idea whose time has come—they will have to
do it without her. She'll go to St. Paul tonight and she'll get a job
teaching school—there's no reason she can't; her English and her
diction and her handwriting are first-rate and have the tiniest trace
of Aberdeen (and when the administrators ask for her college tran-
script, she will say, keeping her hands still and looking them straight
in the eye, that she was convent-educated right through her two-
year degree, and given a medal for Elocution and another for Rhet-
oric by the Sisters of Mercy in Spokane, Washington, whose fine
school unfortunately burned to the ground in the terrible fire, almost as bad in its way as Chicago and Seattle—they might have
heard about it—and all of her school records ashes now, as they can
imagine, but she came through it certified to teach English in that
great state, and she will hold the principal's gaze and he will see that
this is a fine young lady and that there is no wedding band and that
right beneath her thick, lowered lashes is a hint of something that
should have been eradicated by the good sisters).

And now that Gumdrop is thinking clearly, she realizes that
what she's looking for is a fine Jewish man with a progressive frame
of mind, like her regular Wednesday-night customer, Sam Blumen-
thal. After she's taught in a colored school for a few years and made
friends with open-minded white people, she'll marry the kindest
man in that social circle and her children will be light-skinned colored people or dark-skinned Jews, and they can choose which college they prefer and which life, and what they will not know is
subsistence farming or tricking on Jackson Street or murder.

Gumdrop helps Lillian out of the cab, and they split the fare,
and Gumdrop kisses Lillian good-bye. If they had kissed this after-

noon instead of tonight (and it is only ten o'clock; seducing and robbing and killing Snooky took three hours from beginning to end), it
would have been the kiss of women who had begun to be friends and
had to part in a hurry, still in that first excited bloom, after intima-
cies have been exchanged and before dependency and disappointment have sprouted. But it is their only kiss, and although they are
not enemies, they're not friends any longer; they are co-conspirators
and ashamed. Lillian has the advantage of her color, Gumdrop has
the advantage of almost everything else, and when she kisses Lillian
she slides her tongue into Lillian's mouth and it is like a tiny pink
slap, one of Gumdrop's familiar warning pinches. Lillian backs away,
and Gumdrop laughs and turns her toward the steamship waiting to
take her a thousand miles up the Pacific coast to the town of Prince
Rupert, in Canada.

Six weeks later, Clothilde Browne, lately of Spokane, does surface in St. Paul, in a navy-blue suit and navy-blue suede pumps with
ankle straps, and she does what she set out to do. She teaches at the
best colored school, she meets a fine Jewish man, she converts under
the eye of a wary rabbi (there is nothing new anyone can tell her
about the wide-ranging, vengeful, and capricious hand of Yahweh),
and she marries Morris Teighblum in the rabbi's study. They have
three children in five years, Sylvia, Samuel, and Louise, and
Clothilde gets her figure back every time. The children are very
proud of her, and a little frightened by her temper, and when they
need to be comforted (when they throw themselves a pity party,
their mother would say) they go to their father. Clothilde Browne
Teighblum gives money to the NAACP, anonymously; she wears a
smart hat, a fitted suit, and matching gloves to thirty years of
Hadassah luncheons at which she is unsnubbable because, like an
English gentleman, she does not allow herself to take any notice of
the intended insult.

When she sees young colored men in the park on summer afternoons and thinks of Snooky Salt, of his narrow, twisting hips and his hooded eyes, when she thinks of his body in the alley, comforted only by his lilac derby and lilac boots, it does make her smile a little, because she was such a bold girl, and it makes her sick because she can still see the amber light flicker and go out in Snooky's eyes. She can still see his surprise and his fearful pain, even now that she's an old lady, and she can still feel the place in her heart where she stabbed him.

What Folks Are Made Of

WITH HER SATCHEL, HER PINS, AND HER NEW GOLD WATCH, on the Alaska Steamship Company's worst steamship, Lillian has fallen among Christians. The captain meant to do her a good turn and put her in with the only other women, and now she's lying in one of three rope hammocks in a small room that stinks of fish, listening to Mary and Martha Hornsmith pray. They pray like old Jews; they mumble, they sway, they discuss a little among themselves, they interject (Martha puts in regularly about their father's illness and their brother's war injury). They pray for Lillian all the time and they tell her so.

"Your eternal soul is what we're praying for," Mary says, and Martha nods.

Martha says, "It is the lost sheep that Jesus wishes us to save," and Mary nods.

It's not because Lillian is a Jew that they're praying. They're not the kind of missionaries who think that everyone else is a heathen.

They pray for Lillian because when she climbed into her hammock on the first night and put out the lamp, Mary Hornsmith asked her forty-seven personal questions Lillian couldn't answer (Yes, I had a child—I think she may be dead but I am going to Siberia, just in case; yes, I was married and he is dead, too; yes, I come from a small town that was burned to the ground by Christians—thank you for asking) and finally said that she was a prostitute from Seattle, on the lam from her pimp. She said her name was Gumdrop Brown and she led them to understand that she was tired of her life of sin, which had been spectacularly awful. They were thrilled and distressed to hear about the goings-on at the Black and Tan Club, and they were tireless in their prayers for her good fortune. They were clearly kind, decent women who'd become missionaries because they'd had the bad luck of a drunken father, a dead mother, an injured and useless brother, and a farm sold out from under them. Otherwise, they would have been wives and mothers in Goldville, Oregon, and Lillian would not have yielded to the impulse to mock them and hide from their round-faced curiosity in Gumdrop's wicked raiments.

In the morning, Mary puts her own hand-knit brown scarf around Lillian's neck when the waves splash up at them. In the evening, the traders, prospectors, and merchants file in to dinner. They all lift their hats or their heads or tug at some part of their hair when they see the three women, and the Hornsmiths are particularly pleased that Gumdrop shows so little interest. Martha brews them each a cup of chamomile tea in mugs she has taken from the dining hall. They would not want to stay on when the men are smoking and playing cards and drinking hard liquor, Martha says, and Mary and Lillian follow her back to their cabin like ducklings.

LILLIAN TAKES HER TURN with a sponge bath in the cabin, making what she can of the sliver of carbolic and the tepid water. Martha

Hornsmith is not a woman to stay in the room while a prostitute, even a reformed prostitute, removes her outer clothing, but Mary is, and she sits on the piano stool they all share and watches Lillian wash, as if it is the most interesting thing in the world. When she sees the round scar on Lillian's shoulder she says, My goodness, that one must have hurt you something awful, and Lillian wants to tell her something fanciful, a fabulous story of villainy crushed and virtue rewarded, a narrow escape from something too awful to articulate but not too awful to indicate, but Mary's face is all kindness. Lillian says, Oh, yes, this one, a soup spoon—my mother burned me with it when I was a little girl. Mary does not say, Oh, my goodness, again. She pulls up her plain gray blouse and rolls up her cotton camisole to reveal her soft white middle and a pink-and-red crescent of scraped, striated skin. Boiling water, she says. Terrible what life makes folks do, isn't it?

They are nearly to Prince Rupert and down to the last of Martha's chamomile tea when Lillian confesses. I am not Gumdrop Brown, she says. I am Lillian Leyb. Mary takes Lillian's hand in hers and says, The Lord does not care what you call yourself, my dear. Martha, a little shrewder, puts down her embroidery hoop and says, Lillian is a much nicer name. You can't go among decent people calling yourself Gumdrop. Leyb? she says.

BY THE TIME THEY LAND, they know that Lillian was never a prostitute, never had a pimp, never danced in her scanties at the Black and Tan. They knew all along she was a foreigner (Miss Brown, my foot, Martha whispered the first night. You could cut that accent with a knife. And Mary said, She might have changed it to Brown when she got here), and they can see she's in pain, and in a hurry, because they have been both.

Martha tucks a cambric handkerchief into Lillian's sleeve, newly embroidered with navy silk initials, L.L., and Mary presses a small cherrywood cross on a tarnished chain into Lillian's hand and says, The Lamb of God, dear—hold on. Lillian puts the cross in her pocket, next to Yaakov's safety pins and Snooky's watch, and jingles the three Graces, the very useful stainless-steel safety pins, and the Lamb of God all the way into Prince Rupert, which is not the Gateway to Gold that it once was.

ARTHUR GILPIN IS A GOOD MAN and Prince Rupert's only constable, and his wife has been dead for nine months. He has lain by himself and cried into his dead wife's nightgown almost every one of those two hundred and seventy nights, except when he was too drunk to climb to his bed. It makes him sad to go with the town whores, or with the Haida girls who come by canoe, thirty at a time, passing through the river towns for a few nights, selling goat-hair blankets and themselves, silk flowers from Eaton's pinned to the tops of their heads, walking into Prince Rupert in moose-hide boots and city dresses, which suit them not at all.

The Haida girls are more wary than the local whores, but less bitter, and they don't playact like the locals. (Oh, Mr. Gilpin, Marie simpered when he went right after Helen died, does this tickle your fancy? And he wanted to slap her for what she thought of him and of herself, and for what she must think of his Helen.) If the Haida girls like what you are doing, they gasp or smile or pull at your hair; if they don't, they lie still and stare at the ceiling and when you are done they close their eyes, and even without language, you know they are giving thanks.

When the Haida girls come, they use the empty, doorless rooms of what's left of the Winslow Hotel, throwing their thick, light blankets on the floor for the evening, kicking the mouse droppings and dead birds into the corners. The more entrepreneurial girls set out a whiskey bottle and strips of salmon and you can pay as you go. With a Haida girl, under the ripe, oily blanket, with a shot of whiskey in you, her hair covering your chest like spilled ink, you could fool yourself for a few hours, and that's why Arthur Gilpin has stopped going to them. He thinks that if he has to bite his tongue so as not to propose to a stout, pockmarked girl whose name he doesn't know, after an hour of plowing her like a field while she lay beneath him, placid and firm, smiling vaguely the whole time, it is time to stop going altogether.

Tonight he's made his rounds through town twice, and twice people have told him there's a girl dossing down at the Winslow, so he is obliged to look in there. He sees that Ben Newland's pigs have come and gone and that the girl is there, sleeping behind the bar. She smells like pig shit and fatigue, and she's not half the size he thought she'd be. He wakes her, as he would a drunk neighbor, taps the tip of her boot with his own, and she flips onto her back and sighs, without waking. He puts his hand on the girl's shoulder, to rouse her from the bad dream she's having, and she opens her tired eyes, unseeing.

She says, Oh, Sophie, and she puts her arms around him and cries like her heart is breaking. Arthur Gilpin holds on to her, out of nothing but the kindest intentions and his constabulary obligations, and thinks that another man might take advantage of her. He cannot help but imagine how and he burns with shame and lets her drop back to the floor, and then, she does see him. He can see that she sees him, that her embracing him was a mistake; it just shows how tired the girl is. He pulls her to her feet and she struggles for balance, worn out and dirty-faced from her walk into town. When he grabs her by the waist, she falls limp in his arms. They must look like a slapstick routine, he thinks, like something from the Keystone Kops. He uses his no-nonsense tone, the one for young boys getting into trouble, just a little louder in case she is foreign.

He says, "What are you doing?" And the girl squints at him as if this is a trick question.

"I am en route to Dawson City," Lillian says, and she speaks as loudly and forcefully as he does.

"Really?" Arthur says. "Who's taking you?"

It may be she has a lover, or a husband, but she doesn't look like a woman with a husband, and the lover has probably run off and left her here in Prince Rupert, which is a dumping ground for traders' wives and prospectors' sweethearts and all sorts of baggage that has to be shed before a man can make his way north.

Lillian leans back against the bar.

"I am taking myself," she says, looking outside at the night sky as if she's about to pick up her satchel and go, which she is, if she can just get past this tall, suety man with the dreadful bushy sideburns and eyes as sad as any she has ever seen.

He spreads his arms out, as if to embrace her, and he pulls her wrists together in front of her.

"You can't get that far this time of year," he says, her wrists like soft, splintering wood in his hands. "We've already had snow."

Lillian sets her jaw, and he thinks she's going to make a break for it, fake to the right and go left. He lifts a hand off her wrist and onto his nightstick, hoping he won't have to use it, and just as she's expecting him to say, You're under arrest, for whatever they can arrest you for in Prince Rupert (and Lillian has been out in the world long enough to know that she has some defense against criminals, and none at all against the law), Arthur Gilpin says, "Let me make you dinner and offer you my home for the night."

Lillian picks up her satchel and she thinks of Yaakov. Every dinner invitation he got, he'd say, Thank you, yes, and then he would say, to every host, I warn you—I can resist everything except temptation.

Helen Gilpin was a sensible woman and a sensible prairie cook, and she loved her husband. She served him a big meal at noon and supper at six, and although it was not the best thing for him, she had a piece of fresh pie or a slice of lemon cake for him every night right before bedtime. She liked to watch him eat and she liked to reach over and brush the crumbs off his undershirt, over the shelf of his belly, when he ate the lemon cake in bed, like a boy having a treat. Arthur Gilpin thinks every day of Helen's venison stew and her chicken fricassee and her light hand with pies and the lemon cake, and he doesn't try to make any of them.

He sits across from the girl at his kitchen table, and they eat what he's been eating for the last nine months: greasy meat pies from Mrs. Hennepin, who does for him once a week, boiled potatoes, and dried apples soaked in brandy.

"My wife was a fine cook," he says.

Lillian nods. She can hear the whole terrible story aching to come, and she knows that she cannot say, Oh, please, officer, I am full up. I have no room for another story of love and loss. Lillian asks for seconds, and eats all of it, swallowing a little over the meat pies, the pastry burned and raw and oozing beads of lard, the gray meat filled with gristle and small chips of bone. She says, Sit, please, and gets up to wash the plates and the two bent forks and the two chipped mugs, which is all she can offer. He is so moved by her young back, by her fear, by her misfortune, by her hands swimming efficiently through the soapy water, like Helen's, that he says, You can stay here while you get your bearings, and Lillian thanks him twice and makes her refusal clear without even turning around. He eats the last of the apples and pours himself a little more brandy, and thinks he was a fool to have offered, and lucky to be turned down.

Helen Surges Gilpin's trousseau included a narrow wrought-iron trundle bed made by her uncle in Calgary, and Lillian lies in it wearing one of Helen's sprigged flannel nightgowns. Her dirty clothes and shoes are on the floor. Lillian listens to Arthur wash his face and brush his teeth and check the front door one more time. She listens to him undress (boots, the slight swish of the suspenders off his shoulders, his chamois shirt, his bow tie, his constable's jacket, the sigh of a big man taking off clothes that have come to pinch a little over the last years), and she listens to him settle into his double bed, on his side, as he cannot sleep on Helen's side, which is where he has secretly arranged three of her embroidered pillows, and sleeps facing them, one arm around the middle pillow, the other curled under his head, his hand resting on his brow as if for protection.

He thinks of Helen and hopes to dream of her. His dreams are the best part of his day. Her breasts and belly press against his back, her yellow hair comes out of her braid and tickles his cheek. He thinks of all the nights she lay on her back and opened herself to him, and he crosses his arms around the middle pillow and pulls it to him. The night he remembers best, when Helen was only beginning to be sick and they didn't know how bad it would be, her fever broke and she pulled off her nightclothes in the wet bed, saying they were too awful to sleep in and he got up to bring her a fresh nightgown and she stopped him. She pulled him back down and put her cool hand, just her fingertips, on the middle of his chest and stroked the length of him, and he hopes he will dream of that night.

Lillian lies in Helen Gilpin's uncle's bed, thinking about Joseph Stalin. They were getting rid of the old-style Jews even before she left Turov, and the Leybs were old-style. The Pinskys were modern. They were clever people; Lev Pinsky made noises like a Bolshevik when there were Bolsheviks around. He talked about the proletariat and the New Economic Policy whenever he saw gentiles. He used to sit in the yard with her father at the end of the day, and the men would have a little schnapps, and her father would say, *L'shanah haba'ah b'Yerushalayim,* Next year in Jerusalem, and Lev Pinsky would say, What's your hurry? They'd have a little more schnapps if supper wasn't quite ready, and Pinsky would move a chess piece after a while and her mother would shake her head and Osip would breathe deeply, which is how he showed his disapproval of things outside the Torah. Lillian brushed and braided Sophie's hair every night, and sometimes for fun she would give her four braids, not two, and Sophie would run to her grandfather, wiggling her four braids. Was Osip nothing to any of them, Lillian thought in Helen Gilpin's uncle's bed; was there no more of him than a sighing absence? And on one such evening Lillian's father took Sophie on his lap and said, This is the Jewish future, and Lev Pinsky said, I hear the Jewish future is Tikhonaia, in Siberia, and it'll be a Paradise, by Jews and for Jews and not in the goddamned desert, either. He tugged on Sophie's braids a little too hard, as he always did, and Sophie yelled and Lillian picked her up and brought her into the house. Lillian's mother said to Sophie, You'll live, Miss Sarah Bernhardt, and then, When he's in Tikhonaia, freezing his balls off with the Chinese, he won't be so quick to bother little girls. Lillian laughed and Sophie stuck out her lip and nodded, too, and her mother patted Sophie's cheek, and it was a great moment of solidarity for the three Leyb women, disliking Lev Pinsky and his careless ways.

Oh, Tikhonaia, Lillian thinks now, that's where they've gone, and she puts on her pants and coat over the warm, sweet-smelling nightgown (she has not worn a nightgown in months; she cannot bear to give this one up) and she carries her shoes and satchel downstairs and her hand is on the latch. She pushes the door open and snow blows into the front hall. Arthur Gilpin, in his undershirt and trousers, lays his hand on hers and takes the satchel.

"You can't go in this weather," he says.

"I have to," she says, and it is like that between them for a few moments, and then he handcuffs her to the bannister and sits on the step beside her.

"I cannot let you go out there," he says. "You'll be dead in a day." There's no arguing with that, or with the steel handcuffs or the dead wife, but Lillian says, "I could take care of you, sir," and he looks at her and says, "You can't take care of yourself," and there is no arguing with that, either, at the moment.

The constable sighs and says, "Promise me you'll stay in for the night and I'll take off the handcuffs," and Lillian sighs and thinks what kind of woman would she be, to lie to such a sweet man. She looks away, because she can't bring herself to lie to him (perhaps a stronger woman would), and she can't bring herself to tell the truth (Take this strip of metal off my hand and I'll disappear into the night and you can count yourself lucky I don't take that wool blanket with me). Arthur Gilpin shrugs. He unlocks Lillian and walks her up the stairs and handcuffs her to the iron bedpost.

"I'll be downstairs," he says, "sitting by the front door."

"I'm sure you will," Lillian says and there's no rancor on either side. They wish each other good night, and in the morning he unlocks her wrist again and sits outside the bedroom door while she dresses (she keeps the nightgown on; she will have it for a long time), and then he handcuffs her to the kitchen chair. "I don't like to," he says, "but you're too quick for me, and I'm afraid if I keep hold of your shoes or your coat, you'll go anyway, headstrong as you are."

Lillian nods; headstrong is a nice way to put it.

"You can't travel in this weather," Arthur Gilpin says, and he sets the table for two. He makes buttery scrambled eggs and fries up some bannock and a half-pound of bacon. He makes black coffee with plenty of kick and skims the cream off his last bottle of milk to make it rich and sweet for the two of them. Lillian eats with some awkwardness, but the constable helps her. He dabs her mouth a couple of times when the eggs get messy, and he says, Oh, pick up the bacon with your hand, why don't you—it's just you and me and the kitchen clock. And she does, and he does, too, to be companionable.

At close to nine, he says, I sent a boy for the trusties at Hazelton, the Hazelton Agrarian Work Center for Women—that's the proper name. Here's what you'll hear me tell them. You've stolen my watch but you're not a bad girl. That's what I must say. I'll say I suspect there was a bad influence and that's why I'm sending you to Hazelton—they have women in trouble but not really bad there. I don't feel that your character is so damaged you must serve a long sentence, I'll say. I mustn't say too much good, as being a constable's little sweetheart won't win you any friends in there. Ladies rule at Hazelton. But you'll winter at the work farm—your sentence will be up by spring. I'll bring you some things at Christmas, like I heard you've repented, and he smiles broadly, as if he is not a Christian at all, as if he thinks repentance happens as often as water turns to wine. Come spring, he says, you're off and away to Dawson, Bob's your uncle.

When the two Hazelton trusties come for Lillian at ten o'clock, he has washed the dishes. He unsnaps the handcuffs and she stands in the front hall, with her eyes downcast, like a chastened girl. Arthur Gilpin says what he said he would and Lillian says nothing and he is cool and regretful, as if they'd never shared a meal or held each other.

October 5, 1925

Hard Times, Hard Times

F AT PATTY IS HAZELTON'S ARTIST. SHE WORKS IN A LOW-
ceilinged atelier under straitened circumstances and produces
beautiful images. She has admirers. She has a patron. She keeps the
room warm enough to minimize gooseflesh and shivering, the
curses of her profession, along with sudden spasms, hepatitis, and
changes of heart. She digs the point of the needle into the curve of
Lillian's hip with one hand and fans herself with the other. Fat Patty
perspires heavily, and you can't work a fine line with sweat blurring
your vision. Lillian bites down on the rag Fat Patty has put in her
mouth.

"It's pretty clean," Fat Patty says, and Lillian doesn't argue, she
doesn't pull the rag out and point to the streaks of hardened dirt and
the dark, oily hem. It was good of Fat Patty to even bother lying to
Lillian, and to thank her and be less the foreigner, Lillian says, "I've
had worse than that in my mouth."

Fat Patty laughs and pulls her hand away before she blurs the ink. She laughs the rich, dirty laugh fat women have, as if there are things about men that they've seen and hidden in the folds of their bodies, things that men don't reveal to smaller women, and her side-kick, the walleyed girl everyone calls Mama's Little Helper, laughs, too, and elbows the dwarf who goes with them everywhere and whose name Lillian has never heard. The dwarf chuckles, and Lillian thinks, Shame on me, and then she thinks that it might be a good sign that she can still be ashamed. We are the only animals that feel shame, Yaakov said one night at the Royale. Or need to, Reuben shouted, both hands slamming the tabletop, and they laughed the way men do when they are particularly enjoying being men.

Fat Patty's cell is Hazelton's full-service department store, and all the women there have been her customers. The dwarf is head cashier, standing by the door, taking and hiding the payments that can be hidden (chocolate from a soft relative, a pound note, more needles, a lipstick in a gold case), and even making change occasionally, a little extra something for Fat Patty, in appreciation, and then there are all the other payments, the food Fat Patty likes, the attention she likes, the first seat at the first table at every meal, and Lillian assumes there are other things, the things that go on between the women at night, or even in the courtyard, under cover of sewing a quilt on the farthest bench. Lillian tries not to watch, but how can you not watch two people having sex in public, while thirty other women go about their business as if the one woman has not dropped her head back like she's been garroted as the other leans forward, her hand rippling under the cloth, and they are both flushed and rocking unsteadily, and then they slow and one wipes her face with an embroidered handkerchief—they are renowned famous, the pair, for their beautiful needlework, and no wonder—and then she wipes each finger of her lover's hand and they spread their skirts like hens settling, and no one is watching except Lillian and Mrs. Mortimer, the librarian, who watches everything.

The walleyed girl with the wild spray of moles across her face, as if someone has spit a mouthful of brown paint at her, is Fat Patty's sales manager; she shows customers a few designs, she mentions what's most popular and what's cheapest, and she gives everyone a little bit of time to decide. MOTHER is very popular and FATHER not at all. Names of your children, especially your dead children. A few women ask for the names of their idols: Cleopatra, Queen of Sheba, Theda Bara. PEARL HART appeared a couple of times, on a back, on a bicep, after her famous run on the banks of Canada, and MARY, MOTHER OF GOD, is popular, too. Fat Patty is not much on representational figures, but she has a nice flowing script and a few iconic designs. If you have done time at the Hazelton Agrarian Work Center for Women, you can leave with an elegantly written name in a furling banner or in the midst of a bunch of blue-and-red posies, round and neat as cartoons, but you will not get a hula girl, a jumping trout, or Joan of Arc, and the grifter from Toronto who showed everyone her lower back with Joanie on a Pony, multicolored against the French flag, peeved Fat Patty badly and was sorry for it.

Fat Patty is Mr. R. H. Macy himself, invisibly pulling strings to move the merchandise, spying on the competition. (Gypsy Lou has a small business in curses and tattoos but what the women value in Gypsy curses works against her with the tattoos; they think she's not clean and that her designs have hidden meaning.) Fat Patty even offers special rates in the summer, when no one wants to get a tattoo because of the sweating and the risk of infection. The walleyed girl tells Lillian this and when Fat Patty pauses for a moment, to burn more paper in the teacup and mix it with water to make ink, the girl says, "Think nice thoughts," which is what Mrs. Mortimer is famous for saying to the women she has successfully pursued. Lillian laughs and Fat Patty swats Lillian on the hip, the way you do a careless child. Looky here, she says, and it's no kindness for her to get Lillian's attention so fully, because all Lillian can do then is focus on the jab of the needle and the sting of the sooty ink and then Fat Patty's warm, beery breath and then another dab of the rag to clear away the blood. Lillian leaves Fat Patty's room with a strip of cleanish cloth soaked in witch hazel pressed to her hip under her drawers. Lillian needs more of Sophie with her, with the edges and corners of memory beginning to fade and alter suspiciously; but at the first curve of the *S*, she puts her hand on Fat Patty's and they agree to make it seven blue stars instead and the dwarf says, "You got the Pleiades, now. You know, Orion chased them, then the gods made them into stars," and Lillian grips the rag. To have had Sophie's name on a banner or in a spray of blue-and-red daisies would have been a mistake; it would have been presumptuous.

"Sister, it wouldn't help," Yaakov would have said and Reuben would have pounded the table and roared, "It wouldn't hurt," and they would have all laughed until they cried. Lillian thinks her tattoo of seven girl stars must be in that category; it can't help but it couldn't hurt. She lies down on her cot, she turns her sore hip to the ceiling, and listens to the lovers sixteen beds away.

BY THE END OF HER FIRST WEEK, Lillian feels that she has lived at the Hazelton Agrarian Center for Women most of her life. Lillian has a tin cup, two jumpers, an apron, three pairs of knickers, and a pair of felt slippers. She has a seat for mealtimes at the end of the farthest table. On her right is a deaf-mute, who has done nothing but be deaf and dumb and not too bright; on her left is a redheaded prostitute who robbed a customer of his watch and his automobile and then ran him over, breaking both his legs; across from them is the matricide, who killed her mother through neglect. She is at Hazelton and not in a proper prison because it was only neglect, and the woman says this at every meal; she says to Lillian and the other two, her captive audience, "It's true I neglected my mother. I had other family obligations and the unfortunate result was the neglect of my mother. It's true." Every day there is a tin cup of water for each of them at every meal and a mug of weak tea at supper. Everyone has a soup bowl and a spoon, and if someone does not turn in her bowl and her spoon at the end of the meal, everyone stands in the dining hall until morning, or until midday, or until all the spoons and bowls have been accounted for.

ON LILLIAN'S ELEVENTH DAY, a new girl walks into the dining hall in a faded blue jumper two sizes too big and an apron with a singed front pocket, her long braid swinging behind her. Some of the women speculate out loud about what she must have had to do that Matron hadn't cut it right off. Matron sits the girl down between Gypsy Lou and Epiphany Smith, the Jamaican. Everyone else is Norwegian or Swedish, Irish, English, Scots, or Newfie, and two Cape Breton girls who stole bits of jewelry from all the houses they cleaned. The new girl looks at her dinner partners and nods politely and eats the pea soup and the bannock and the roasted potatoes. Gypsy Lou pokes her in the side and says, "You're a Chink," and the Chinese girl nods politely. Lou says, "Fucking Chinks." The Chinese girl nods politely again and moves her spoon to her left hand and kneels on the bench and presses the spoon against the back of Gypsy Lou's neck and holds her face in the potatoes and stewed squash and lets up only when Lou stops thrashing.

The new girl eats Lou's squash and offers her potatoes and the rest of her soup to Epiphany Smith. When they form their lines after the meal, stopping at chapel for ten minutes of silent prayer and then walking in pairs without talking (but there are notes passed, hand to apron pocket, and there is a set of hand signals and feet scuffings for basic information), the matricide walks on one side of the new girl and Lillian walks on the other. The new girl looks at each of them and smiles. Her smile is like Gumdrop's, which was like Esther Burstein's, bright and narrow and no more about happiness than a scimitar.

"Chinky Chang," she says. "Grifter."

Lillian has gotten the hang of threshing peas and roasting them for coffee. She has come to expect fried peas at breakfast and pea soup and pea gruel and a bit of chipped beef on a slab of mashed peas for Sunday dinner. The threshing and roasting is filthy work, the green skins of the peas sticking to her palms and fingernails, the roasted brown dust in her hair and eyelashes and eyebrows like sand, and after two weeks Mrs. Mortimer approaches Lillian and says, Perhaps you would rather do embroidery. She says, blinking her big eyes, I understand that you have some skill. I can sew, Lillian says, and she lowers her eyes as she sees the other girls do with Mrs. Mortimer, but I would most like to work for you in the library. Mrs. Mortimer says, Patience is a virtue, and assigns Lillian to the laundry room, which is as awful in its wet way as the threshing room is in its dry one.

Lillian walks into cooling and cold wet linens, tubs of hot water, pools of soap on the floor, everyone's debris—strands of hair, a broken tooth, fingernail parings, sticking plasters, and worse—floating on the water's surface and then clinging to the cement floor. The new girl is beating sheets, water dripping from her black braid, and the two Cape Breton girls have stripped to the waist to wring the linens. They've rolled their blouses down like belts; their chests are red and wet, their bare, broad backs glazed with steam, and they nod to Lillian and curtsy to Mrs. Mortimer, who looks at their breasts and says, Lillian will help press. Chinky has unbuttoned her blouse to the waist, torn her sleeves at the wrist so they push up past her elbows, and tucked her skirt into her belt. Lillian thinks that she will do as they do, that she has not come this far to die a wet death in Hazelton, Canada. She has just undone her collar when the Cape

Breton girls hurry into the press room and close the door behind them. Lillian turns.

Gypsy Lou has a cup of lye in her hand, and as her arm swings back to toss it in Chinky's face, Lillian, whom Gypsy Lou has not noticed even once since her arrival (wrong table, wrong type), acts without thinking, which Chinky will tell her later is the worst thing a girl can do. She throws a wet sheet over Gypsy Lou, and Chinky punches the woman so hard she drops, and the cup of lye rolls away, to mix with the other poisons on the floor. Mrs. Mortimer passes by the laundry room door, carrying the freshly ironed lace runners she uses on her desk and her escritoire. She looks in at the three of them, Chinky and Lillian breathing hard over a body under a damp sheet, and she nudges open the heavy swinging door. She lifts up a corner of the sheet and sees Gypsy Lou's pale face, her fluttering eyelids, and she says only, "Ladies, tidy up." The Cape Breton girls wait until Mrs. Mortimer has gone, and then they come out, blouses buttoned, hair repinned, and filled with compliments. All over Hazelton, it is a great day for the foreigners. "You're stuck with me now," Chinky tells Lillian.

MRS. MORTIMER NODS TO LILLIAN most days after that, and one evening before vespers, which is a great social occasion, women slipping in beside their crushes, small goods exchanged from pew to pew, the librarian says to Lillian, "Your people are great readers, I understand. People of the Book." Lillian thinks of her illiterate mother and her father's stories of suffering through cheder, the youngest son of the poorest man in the village, and she says, "Oh, yes, we certainly are." Mrs. Mortimer hands her *Bulfinch's Mythology*.

Lillian reads to Chinky, skipping to the part she has nearly memorized. " 'If no other knowledge deserves to be called useful but that which helps to enlarge our possessions or to raise our station in society, then Mythology has no claim to the appellation. But if that which tends to make us happier and better can be called useful, then we claim that epithet for our subject.' " She reads as if Reuben is still beside her, ready to rattle the teacups if she makes a mistake. Sometimes when she's very tired, she loses her way with the *w*'s. She doesn't mind; the rough, uncertain sound of a girl just come to America from a small village in Russia, the accent she used to have, comforts her as she falls down into sleep.

" 'Literature is one of the best allies of virtue and promoters of happiness.' "

Chinky snorts. "Mortimer'll give you some happiness, I bet."

Mrs. Mortimer is Zeus and Hera at Hazelton. She is the lord of all, she is the pursuer of nymphs and virgins, and she is the jealous goddess, filled with dark suspicions and darker vengeance. She does, finally, invite Lillian to the library. Chinky says, Wear two pairs of drawers. It is a small room lined with books that no one wants (pamphlets of uplifting verse, privately published, Mrs. Beeton's housekeeping guide, Lutheran cookbooks, opera libretti, and the occasional first-person account of life among the Canadian Mounted Police, or the Eskimos, or beet farmers). Mrs. Mortimer has arranged a circle of seven chairs within it. Lillian has been invited to read. The other women have also had their turn as *lectrice,* as Mrs. Mortimer calls it, and the five of them have their own fairly accurate ideas of what will happen after Lillian reads a half hour of "The Lady of Shalott" or "Tristram and Isolde." They have all read their Bulfinch as well, or struggled through it, and even if one or two find themselves reading from *Elsie Dinsmore* or *Was He Worth It?* because of their limitations, the principle and position of *lectrice* is upheld. When Lillian and Mrs. Mortimer are alone, discussing King Arthur and the knights and romantic friendship and the south of France, where Mrs. Mortimer spent two happy summers in her youth, Lillian holds her breath.

In the event, nothing happens. Mrs. Mortimer pours two tiny glasses of sherry and asks what parts of Bulfinch Lillian most enjoys. Lillian says the myths, an obvious and true thing to say; poor Scylla and Cupid and stupid, adorable Psyche take her mind off Mrs. Mortimer's exquisite hands. She is a horsey, chapped-looking woman in gray worsted and thick laced black shoes, but her hands are long and pretty, with elegantly oval rosy nails and a fine tracing of blue veins on the back. They are the hands of a Victorian lady, and Mrs. Mortimer is not unaware of their effect; she favors heavy lace cuffs stiff with sizing, each row of Battenberg peaks glazed and sharp, and she wears a large ruby cabochon on her index finger.

"What I enjoy very much," Lillian says, "are maps."

Mrs. Mortimer sips her sherry and raises one thick, graying eyebrow. "We don't have maps, my dear."

Lillian sips her sherry, too. There's no reason for Mrs. Mortimer to lie, but someone in the Hazelton Agrarian Work Center for Women must have a map. Someone must, on occasion, need to get somewhere.

· "Surely," Lillian says, "there's an atlas or two, something to show us where we are in relation to Africa or India, or the girls' hometowns."

"Just so," Mrs. Mortimer says. "That is precisely why we don't have maps. This is a place of refuge and improvement. Maps encourage thoughts of the larger world. Of escape."

"For myself," Lillian says, "it's the art of cartography. I admire maps."

Mrs. Mortimer shrugs. Everybody here wants things they can't have, the shrug says. I admire you, for example, but I can see you would be a treacherous, twisting, hard-hearted girl in the end. You would choose to become a tree or a deer or an ugly little bird rather than accept my embrace, or you would accept and watch for your reward, and when I brought you a map of Canada, at great personal risk to myself and my probity, you would flick your hand over me without pausing or give me the tiniest rub of your leg and you would sigh over how much you had given away and your coldness would shame me. Mrs. Mortimer leaves a few drops of sherry in her glass and stands up. Lillian is acutely aware that she has been found wanting, that she will not get a map from this woman and that what Hera hated even more than infidelity was ingratitude.

Chinky says, For crying out loud, and coils her hair around her head like a Scandinavian housewife and begs a tiny sprig of silk violets from Fat Patty. She sings at vespers and forces out a few starry tears and Mrs. Mortimer is taken with her. She gives her Bulfinch, which Chinky hands over to Lillian. I don't care, Chinky says—just find me something about a young girl and an old woman, and if you can't, then two sisters, maybe. Or two flowers, two swans, what the hell—you get the picture, she says. And Chinese would be good, if they have that. Chinky picks up *Screen* magazine, laughing, and sucks on a mint candy from a box the redheaded hooker has passed around.

Chinky becomes a favorite. She does try to get a map for Lillian, whom she loves, but she doesn't try so hard as to jeopardize the honey in her tea, the bar of Ivory soap, the promise of early release, perhaps right after the March Event, when folks from Hazelton and beyond come to buy the famous embroideries and the scones and cakes and to listen to the Hazelton Women's Choir. Chinky asks a few times, until Mrs. Mortimer says, That would be for your Jewish friend, I presume, and Chinky shrugs and says, I can't even read a map, myself.

Lillian goes on. She makes the effort to do one thing after another. She begins to walk around the courtyard in even the coldest weather, sometimes with the deaf-mute, who walks daily, and sometimes with the Christian Scientists, who are great believers in fresh air. One of the walkers, pale and lean, with a shock of dark hair and a gap-toothed smile, says to Lillian as they mark off another mile,

"What are you walking for?" Lillian says, "I have to get to Russia, to my daughter." The woman says airily, "I am walking for my spirit." After a few weeks, Lillian knows that Emily Anne Warren means she is walking to calm her spirit so that when she gets out she doesn't accidentally on purpose poison another woman who ruffles her feathers, and Emily Anne knows that Lillian has a very hard road ahead of her. She brings Lillian two lead disks from the threshing room.

"If it were me," she says, "I'd wear them in my shoes to build up my legs, you see."

Lillian does see, and Emily Anne's brutal good cheer is relentless.

"You gotta build up those arms," she says. "You can't save your baby with those skinny things." She says, "No run-down lazy bitch is walking to Siberia."

At night, Lillian rubs her legs with liniment and reads her way through the library, although she is not part of the reading circle any longer.

"Jesus H. Christ," Chinky says. "I didn't even know the Micks had mythology. Morty's making us read *Cuchulainn*."

Chinky puts a slice of stolen tea cake on Lillian's cot. She shares everything with Lillian, the cakes from the library circle and the newest ladies' magazines, which are like cocaine, they're so popular—the women fight over their shiny, gorgeous pages, poring over every word and picture, even the small, blurry ads at the back for bust enhancement, wigs of human hair, and marital aids. Chinky has offered to do to Lillian what Mrs. Mortimer does to her.

"It passes the time," Chinky says.

Lillian says, "Have you ever been in love?" and Chinky laughs and shakes her head.

"Never have and hope to never be."

Chinky crosses her heart and kisses her pinky finger. She lies on her cot, arms folded like a corpse, and waits until lights-out. She walks quietly to Lillian's cot and says, "Shove over." She runs her fingers around the ribbed cotton of Lillian's underpants and then pats Lillian's stomach. She puts her small hand between Lillian's legs.

"Relax," she says. "It starts like this," and Lillian parts her legs a little, her thighs tightening, rushing water spreading under her legs, up through her chest and throat, until her ears buzz with it, and she sits up quickly.

"I can't," Lillian says.

"Sure you can, goose. We got three more months."

Lillian lies back down, and even as she hears her own voice, from a great distance, saying something indistinct (she is not saying Chinky's name, of course; she thinks Reuben's name but doesn't say it; she thinks her own name, too, but what she says is No, no, no), even as she feels Chinky's strong, sharp shoulders under her hands, even as she hears Chinky saying, Hey, quiet now, quiet, Lillian, use your head, she knows that as soon as she is on the other side of this pleasure, it will be like it never happened. Penis, hand, it could be a foot or a doorknob, Lillian thinks; it is nothing brought to nothing, and that's her fault, not Chinky's. Chinky, God bless her, touches her with determined skill and a speedy but real kindness, like a nurse on a battlefield. Water poured onto desert sands, Lillian thinks as her body relaxes. Five minutes after the last drop has emptied out, has dropped from the cold wet lip of the pitcher to the ground, the dark spot will be dry again and the sands will drift over, undeterred.

Lillian has lost track of time; she has lain silent next to Chinky for too long to be polite, even under these circumstances, and she reaches her hand out to touch Chinky and thank her, although that might not be the right way to put it. The mattress creaks a bit, and Chinky is back on her cot, wiping her hand on the underside of her pillow.

"Don't let the bedbugs bite," Chinky says.

. . .

CLOSE TO CHRISTMAS, a terrible time for women who have had to leave children in the care of people they hate or have hurt or hardly know, who have had to leave heartsick mothers ("I'm glad my poor mother had not had to endure a holiday without me," the matricide says primly) and lovers who may or may not have made other arrangements by New Year's. Arthur Gilpin comes with a fruitcake and a yellow cardigan with glass buttons. He has sat through a short Christmas performance of "O Come, All Ye Faithful" and "O Canada," and for the first time the Hazelton choir sings "Wicked Polly," tackling the lines "Her nails turned black, her voice did fail, she died and left this lower vale" with tremendous, even rollicking enthusiasm. Mrs. Goode, who assists Matron with cultural activities, had supposed the women would be shamed by Polly's punishment and fearful of sharing her fate, but they sing it like a fight song and Matron makes a note to move Mrs. Goode to laundry.

Matron allows Lillian and Arthur Gilpin to sit in the library, under Mrs. Mortimer's basilisk eye.

"Thank you for the sweater," Lillian says. "It does get cold here."

"That's what I hear," Arthur Gilpin says, and he avoids her eyes.

She doesn't look bad. She looked worse, is the fact of the matter, when she was lying in pig shit behind the Winslow bar, but not much worse. She has put on a little weight and a little muscle, so she doesn't look so worn, and although her skin has the pale-yellow smoothness of starch and early nightfall, she seems springy, surer in her step. She looks, he cannot help noticing, like every prisoner he's ever seen: weary and watchful, angry with the world and careful, most of the time, not to show it. He thought it would be different for a woman.

"I don't suppose you still need a housekeeper?" Lillian asks.

Arthur Gilpin looks at his hands. He smooths his wiry side-burns, trimmed neatly. His collar is clean and his boots are blacked.

"Or a wife," Lillian says, and she's sorry to have said it when he stands up to look at the books on the shelves.

"They don't keep you too up-to-date, do they?" he says.

"I think they hope that old-fashioned books will inspire old-fashioned morals."

Arthur Gilpin snorts and Lillian smiles. He sits down again and pushes the fruitcake a little closer to her.

"I'm getting married, as a matter of fact. In January. Fine woman. A widow."

"That's very good," Lillian says, and she summons up Esther Burstein. "I am so pleased for you. Congratulations."

It is ridiculous to speak as if they are old friends, or as if they had had a youthful infatuation, never forgotten. He sent her to jail, for her own good, as he kept saying, and now she is in jail and he is getting married to a fine woman in January and she should tell him that it is very kind of him to visit her.

"Did your wife, that is, your fiancée, accompany you to Hazelton?"

Arthur Gilpin looks ill at ease, and it is the smallest comfort to Lillian that he cares for her enough to conceal her existence from his future wife.

"Not this time. But she would very much like to meet you, and when you are . . . when you leave Hazelton, she, Mrs. Wexall, invites you to stay with us before you begin your journey."

Well, Lillian thinks, clever Mrs. Wexall. She picks up her cardigan and cake, she shakes Arthur Gilpin's hand, she wishes him a Merry Christmas as she had meant to do when he came in, and she holds Mrs. Mortimer's eye, which is not unsympathetic. Lillian goes to Fat Patty's, where everyone gathers to watch the redheaded hooker get MERRY CHRISTMAS tattooed above her twat.

O Beautiful City

MARCH COMES, AND JUST AS SHE PLANNED, CHINKY IS GONE before the snow melts.

"You can travel with us," Chinky says. "My family's okay." Chinky presses Lillian's hands in hers. "I can wait for you in Vancouver," she says. "What's two more weeks?"

But Chinky longs to get to Vancouver and beyond, to fleece the marks, and to see Mr. Chang like a horse yearns for the barn. Lillian sees it, plain as day. Lillian mashes down the straw in her pillow and says, I've got plans of my own, you know. Which is true, although the plans aren't much (get her satchel and maps and a hot meal and possibly some money from Arthur Gilpin; take a long bath; steal something from the new Mrs. Gilpin; walk to Siberia; find Sophie) and Chinky is too kind to ask how Lillian sees those plans working out.

Lillian says, "Two more weeks is a great deal. Your family waits for you." She says, "Your father needs you," and Chinky's face softens in agreement; there is no one in her family can do what she can.

"I'll think of you the whole time I'm traveling," Chinky says. She hands Lillian her best jumper, her pillow, and the rhinestone buckle she stole from Mrs. Mortimer. "You dream of me and I'll dream of you."

LILLIAN MISSES CHINKY all the time. She and Mrs. Mortimer look at each other like wife and mistress at a wake; they cannot bear each other's scent or voice, they can't even hold each other's gaze, but there is no one else worth being with. Lillian washes Chinky's jumper and dries it behind the compost heap. She hides the jumper and the buckle in her pillow, between the muslin and the corn husks, and when she puts her head down, the pillow's insides rustle around her, like the ocean roaring in a seashell.

Chinky must be on the steamer's deck by now, saying hello to Vancouver, feeling the salt spray on her face. She must be hurrying down the ramp, and there are her parents, and her mother is waving a white handkerchief so Chinky can come straight to her.

AS IT HAPPENS, Chinky is dry as a bone and she has been nowhere near the deck. She has been sitting in the dark for the last seven hours, next to a Mormon boy. When her sister got so sick she had to lie by the door to breathe fresh air, Chinky took her place on the bench, holding Xiu-mei's white Bible in her lap all night. It is a little before dawn now, when the sky goes black to gray and the dark water slaps the side of the ship without much force, and the boy sitting next to Chinky falls asleep and his head rests on Chinky's shoulder. She can study his long, wide nose, blunt like a shovel, and the freckles sprinkled across it, blazing orange and brown on his white cheeks. Even as his sleeping head rests on her shoulder, even as one tanned hand is splayed on her knee and a tiny hoop of her homespun catches on his rough nail, Chinky guesses that he has never touched anything more womanly than his father's milk cow. She pretends to be asleep so she doesn't have to pretend to be frightened. A decent Christian girl would be screaming her head off right now, alarmed by the boy's breath on the side of her neck. A decent Christian girl would have to leap up, right now, shaking all over with indignation. Chinky knows. She has leapt up and screamed and shaken hundreds of times; Chinky's number one job, her whole family's bread and butter, is acting like decent Christian people. Chinky plays The Girl, her sister is The Miss and sometimes The Invalid, her mother is The Blind Servant or else The Ladies' Aide (miscarriages that look natural and emergency baby-switching), and Mr. Chang is The Minister or The Medium or The Herbalist. Xiu-mei is especially good at being The Miss, in pert porkpie hat and gray skirt, clutching the white leather Bible in both hands, her eyes always lowered as if Jesus is appearing in the floorboards, but no one is as good at the show as Chinky's father.

Mr. Chang came of age in Nevada City, where you could walk from one end of Chinatown to the other all night, from herbalist to brothel to opium den, and never see a white man who wasn't a customer. Mr. Chang has a trunk of small silk bags: deer velvet for men, reishi mushroom for women who cannot have children, and saw palmetto for the women who don't want to. He has rubies ground into a fine red powder, and a big blue crystal that burns so hot he has to carry it in a fireproof box at the bottom of the trunk. Early on in a visit, Mr. Chang makes just one passing reference to these exotic things, and then he says, quickly, But that was in the old days. He tells the folks he is blessed to be a Christian, honored to travel this great country, from the lakes of Wisconsin to the mighty Pacific Ocean, carried westward by the word of God. It is only when it's getting dark, when they are almost on their way, that Mr. Chang lowers a lid in Chinky's direction and she lets slip that her father

knows other methods of healing when Christian prayer is insuffi-
cient. Papa, she says, remember the terrible influenza that carried off
our neighbors, but not us? Remember when poor Grandma couldn't
walk, the arthritis was so bad, until you . . . Her father stiffens and
jumps up, he threatens to hit Chinky. She runs out to the wagon,
braids flying, and her father stands in the parlor, small and slim and
offended by the mention of heathenish Chinese remedies when he
is so thoroughly a Christian. The lady of the house walks him out to
the wagon, apologizing for her interest, maybe a bun or a biscuit for
the little girl—it wasn't her fault—and the lady and Mr. Chang talk
for some time longer while Chinky eats whatever has been brought
out to comfort her. Or the mister walks Mr. Chang around to the
barn for a smoke and a little conversation.

Chinky's father used to tell her all the time, Do not pretend to
be—be. Mr. Chang is the best psychic anywhere, because he knows
how people are. He knows that women come for love, for their children, for woman problems and sometimes money trouble. Men
come for money and their manhood and trouble with a more pow-
erful man or a weak son, and sometimes, right when they're standing up to pay, the men will mention their suspicions about their
wives, and Mr. Chang has never known a man to be mistaken in this
but it doesn't always pay to say so. Often Mr. Chang tells people
what they want to hear and not what everyone for a hundred miles
knows to be the god-awful truth. No one comes to us because they
are happy, he says. Look at the hands, hardworking or soft. Look at
the shoes; rich people wear good shoes, he says, except if they're on
the lam. He knows how to fish for details, he knows how to flatter
folks. (Everyone thinks they're sensitive, Mr. Chang says. Everyone
believes they're a little smarter than their neighbors. Even the
farmers—you tell those men that no one knows how deeply they feel
things and their pupils dilate and you can see them thinking, How
come it takes a damned Chinaman to see there is more to them than

fifty years of rising before dawn to slave over the land?) Mr. Chang knows how to pause just so. Mr. Chang murmurs a few letters, a few numbers, and then he casts out a reasonable guess, and the sitter leans forward, rises up like a trout to say, No, not January, nothing happened in January, but June, it was June, and Mr. Chang says, Yes, I saw the J—I am so sorry I said January—and the sitter is so pleased that they are now focusing on June, which is when the trouble began, that the very word *January* disappears like clouds on a wedding day.

If Mr. Chang could have seen Chinky at Hazelton, she knows he would have been pleased. She is the girl he raised her to be: mild, slick, and false, a quicker dip than the ham-handed white girls. Every time Chinky sang the psalms at chapel, giving out with the tremolo her father taught her (You are a bird, he said. You are the sweet little bird of Jesus and you make them want to feed you), Matron teared up and Chinky should have gotten herself adopted on the spot, instead of having to rejoin the Chang Christian Road Show, which has moved on, Xiu-mei told her, to the greener pastures of Alaska. People up there are lonely, her sister said, reporting what their father said. Lonely men, worried women, and everybody still looking for gold.

She closes her eyes and settles into the bench so that the boy's lips slide from her collar to her skin. She wills herself asleep, floating on the little green river she imagined every night at Hazelton, silver fish flickering through it, pulling the current, pulling Chinky downstream and over the water-smooth rocks lining the shallow riverbed. She wills herself to breathe like the tiniest breeze through the greenest willow and she lets her hand, just the little finger of her left hand, trail in the water, brushing against the back of the boy's right hand. They touch each other, awake and asleep and awake, until the sky is thinly blue and the sun is doing its best to warm the people on the boat who begin to stir and loosen.

Cleveland—the boy's name is Cleveland Seward Munson—is not sleeping. He has not slept since the very ladylike Chinese girl pressed her gray gloves and white Bible over her mouth and ran for the open air and the other girl, the sister with the red lips and the thick braid, took her place. His body is on fire—he can feel the five golden angels of Joseph Smith dancing around his chest, squeezing his heart like a vise with their beautiful pearly hands, and his nether regions are so aroused and his pants are so tight that he pulls his jacket over his lap so as not to frighten this beautiful girl whose shoulder he is pretending to sleep on.

Cleveland's missionary aunt and uncle are waiting for him; they will go up into the wilds of Ketchikan, converting gold miners and fallen women and heathens like Chinky Chang and her family. Cleveland already knows, just from looking at the bow of the girl's mouth, which is like shiny red candy, and from her little hand, roughened at the edges by some very hard work, that she is not a heathen, not the way his aunt and uncle mean. Cleveland thinks maybe she was brought up on a farm, like he was, although he has never heard of Chinese farmers, nor of Chinese Christians, but there must be some. China is a big country—they must grow things there—and there are Mormon missionaries everywhere, and who's to say they haven't had some luck in China, which has so many heathens you could probably be the most inept missionary on earth, the kind Cleveland expects to be, the kind who leaves a crumpled pamphlet about the Latter-day Saints tucked into the doorsill because he cannot bring himself to look people in the eye and ask them to change their heathenish ways, and still you might get a few converts in China. A pretty gold cross lies in the valley between her breasts, where tiny seeds of sweat trickle down, and he could watch their slow slide into her bodice forever. He would not eat or sleep if it caused him to miss the rise and fall of her breasts and the silky trail of her perspiration.

Chinky and the rest of the Changs are not available for conver-

sion. They have been conspicuously Methodist for the last forty
years, and they have been flat-out grifters for the last two hundred.
Mr. Chang's oldest cousin was famous in Hong Kong for producing
virgins over and over; she had two houses on Flower Lane, virgins in
every room, Mr. Chang said. You tighten up the limbs severely, you
offer up the virgin's cry of surprise and pain, but there is no point to
it without blood, and that was the problem his cousin applied herself to. She rolled a few drops of chicken blood into a small pocket
of gelatin and made virgins. Brothels all over the world copied her,
Mr. Chang said. French queens copied her, Italian dukes. If she had
lived in a world in which you sent your papers to the United States
Patent Office instead of having to put arsenic into the tea of your
competitors, his cousin would have been a millionaire many times
over, Mr. Chang said. Mr. Chang revered his late cousin.

Chinky cannot expose this boy, sweet as milk, to the Changs; she
can already imagine her father sizing him up in the first five minutes. Is the boy better as a deaf-mute, taken in by the Christian and
compassionate Changs, given the power of speech right before the
eyes and ears of folks seeking exotic remedies when their cough
syrup and clear tonics have failed them, or could he serve as a young,
lovable Methodist minister who converted them all just recently,
and Mr. Chang will be the cheerful mute collecting alms for the
poor unfortunates of China, of whom Mr. Chang himself makes
such a sympathetic example?

When Cleveland begins to press his hand on Chinky's thigh,
Chinky lets her head fall forward and Cleveland can smell the back
of her neck, the sweat and the stolen rose water. He moves his
chapped lips against her not-very-clean skin, up to her small ears
with the fascinating gold hoops, no thicker than thread, and she lets
her hand fall to the inside of his knee, and their hearts are beating in
their throats, in their chests, between their legs, and they open their
eyes at last and kiss.

They kiss as if they were born to kiss each other, as if they have just been biding their time on this mudflat of Christians and heathens and grifters of all kinds. The *Derblay* is churning toward shore now—people are gathering their bags and boxes, their coats, their necessary goods. This is one of her father's favorite times, the gathering throng, the nervous, excited jostling of folks who are intent on getting where they're going. Do as they do, Mr. Chang says. Take what you want and go on the other way. Chinky has done the bump, the fall, the stall, and the pardon-me since she was three years old, and if she cannot move this big package and some cash without being spotted by her father, who will be trying to score while he waits for his daughters, she deserves to travel with the Changs forever, fleecing civilians and marrying a fat old man or having to play The Invalid for years after she's outgrown The Girl and The Miss.

The people on the dock are getting bigger. Cleveland can see hats now, can make out dogs, barrels, and boxes, distinguish beards from dirt. He cannot imagine what good it will do, but he says, "Ma'am, I am Cleveland Munson, your servant."

The girl says, "Chinky Chang," and takes his hand and presses it to her breast, the most extraordinary thing, and he would follow her right down to the very pit of hell, smiling all the way, and that is probably where they're headed, he thinks.

Chinky has to say something; she can't just take him through the crowd like a packhorse, without any prep. (She has a quick moment of sympathy for her father, who stays up late at night planning five moves ahead, planning spontaneous outbursts and accidental encounters so that things fall into place and the Changs make their swift, golden way through the world, unnoticed until it is too late.) While Cleveland is buttoning his vest and fumbling to put Chinky's satchel on the bench (it's not a proper name, and he is certainly never going to call her Chinky, he thinks, but he will; she will never let him call her anything else), Chinky has exchanged her porkpie hat for a pale blue snood that hides her hair, and has wrapped a ratty blue shawl around her shoulders, a far cry from the prim gray bombazine jackets she and her sister wear so that everyone will recognize their Christian modesty a mile away. Cleveland has just seen Chinky delicately slide a handbag off the wrist of a sleeping woman and then whip down the aisle to return with a big brown overcoat and a filthy brown cloth cap.

"You have folks waiting?" she says, and holds up the coat for him. He must have people waiting. Who would send this sweetheart out into the world by himself? His whole face, Chinky thinks, cries out, Fleece me. Cleveland puts on the coat and pulls up the collar, tilting the cap at a rakish angle, and he doesn't look like a sweetheart, he doesn't look like a Mormon missionary out to bring the angel Moroni to gentile people enjoying their day of rest; he looks like a young tough with big shoulders and no fear of trouble.

"Try to stay left when we get off, keep on staying left, and then go as far beyond the shipping office as you can go," Chinky says.

Look at people, her father used to say. The whole world goes to the right, every time. They pick the pill on the right side of the right palm, they pick the walnut shell farthest to the right. If you line up three cups, they pick the one on the right, and that's the one you fix with tea leaves in the shape of a cross or a triangle or a face.

Chinky tucks several items into the newly acquired handbag and Cleveland swings her satchel under one arm. "I'll just follow you," he says, and he does. His aunt and uncle are watching for a fresh-faced, sunburnt boy in overalls, and they have misremembered him as shorter and rounder. Mr. Chang is watching for his daughters, and he sees Xiu-mei, he sees only one gray jacket and one black porkpie hat. He is reluctant to cry out; he has his left hand on a heavy gold watch and with his right, he has loosened the hasp on a gold-and-garnet brooch. It's possible, he thinks, that nothing bad has happened, but he knows better. His youngest girl is gone. His wife will be crying for weeks, and there are routines they will never do again. He nods to Xiu-mei as she comes down the ramp. She lowers her eyes as if she is ashamed to have lost her sister, but Mr. Chang reads her like a marquee; she's not sorry—she's glad, she's already seeing herself with her sister's tortoiseshell combs in her hair. Mr. Chang stands with Xiu-mei for one moment, at the bottom of the ramp, pinching her inside the elbow until tears form and fall.

"I don't know," Xiu-mei says. "She gave me the slip."

CLEVELAND AND CHINKY go on to Fairbanks. The town is wide open for anything anyone can do, and Cleveland is a good welder and Chinky seems to have a way with sickness. When they come to open a hardware store, Munson's All-Purpose, Chinky stands at the back counter, in apron and moose-hide leggings (it doesn't hurt, she finds, to have folks thinking she's Inuit, and she puts on a little weight and braids her hair tight and up high and looks right at people as the native women do, flat and nervy, with a dark, dark humor that reminds her of her father's family). She knows right away how many fox skins to take for a pair of hammers, she knows how to deliver a baby, she knows, like her mother did, what to do to keep babies from coming. She whistles "Wicked Polly" and Christian hymns all day long. Cleveland handles the difficult customers and the cash register, and he is entertained every day by the scope of human foolishness. They live over Munson's All-Purpose the rest of their lives, even when their daughters move to the lower forty-eight and beg them to come live where there are oranges all year and an ocean to look at. Cleveland and Chinky have had, between them, maybe three oranges in fifty years, and they would sooner drive down to fish the Tanana River than sit in a pair of plastic chairs and watch the ocean as if it were scenery and not the wild animal they know it to be. When Cleveland dies of old age, Chinky will cut off her long gray braids and carry them to the funeral parlor, to have them laid over him when he is buried.

Chinky will take all the foxglove and monkshood from the flower garden she set behind the All-Purpose, chop the pink, purple, and blue flowers together, and, because she's not sure if she remembers correctly, she chops up the stalks and stamens as well and eats it by handfuls, with a whiskey chaser. The Inuit boy who brings her groceries finds her body, upright on hand-embroidered Chinese silk pillows, blue and pink and purple petals scattered over her nightgown.

Bread of the World

THERE ARE TWO SURPRISES FOR LILLIAN IN PRINCE RUPERT.
Arthur Gilpin is happy, and the new Mrs. Gilpin is a card
shark. She plays Sixty-six, she plays Crazy Eights, which Arthur
calls Swedish Rummy, and he makes Swedish pancakes, lacy and
small as quarters and covered with lingonberries, for Crazy Eights
night. The new Mrs. Gilpin is not much of a cook, as she tells Lillian, but she is a great appreciator, and Mr. Gilpin has turned out to
be a dab hand in the kitchen. Mrs. Gilpin plays Oklahoma Gin and
she plays Rauberskat (and she's glad to have Lillian with them, because you must have three for Rauberskat, which Mrs. Gilpin
prefers above all as her father was one of the founders of the American Skat League and Skat is by way of being her salvation, she says).
Before Lillian goes—after the Gilpins offer her a job as day maid,
after Arthur Gilpin oils her satchel and gives her a pair of beautiful
Austrian hiking boots, close to her size and lined with rabbit fur (the
first Mrs. Gilpin's, he says, and there is no need to show them off to

my bride, I think)—Lorena Gilpin teaches Lillian Napoleon at St. Helena, which is, as she says, "solitaire for people who need it."

It's impossible to steal from these people. Lillian looks over the candlesticks, she casts an eye too often at Arthur's fat wallet, left first on the sideboard, then the kitchen table, then the credenza, left out in a way that is almost insulting in its emphatic belief in Lillian's virtue. At supper one evening, Arthur says he'll take Lillian to the mule train tomorrow; it's tomorrow or another three weeks, and tomorrow would be best. Late that night, he says he must turn in, and he gives his new wife a warm kiss and she squeezes him tight around the waist. Arthur gives Lillian a constrained pat on the shoulder, and Lorena kisses him on the forehead. He looks at her with the question of newlyweds and she shakes her head no with the minutest gesture and he shrugs and goes on upstairs, his heavy footsteps a little reproachful, and the two women look at each other and smile.

"We're old fools," Lorena Gilpin says. "I don't mind a bit. My first husband was handsome as the devil and he had money." She shuffles a deck of thirty-two cards and deals out six apiece for Klaberjass. "Bored me to tears, honey. You know how our mothers used to say, 'Lie on your back and think of England'? I did my multiplication tables and then I did long division, and when he was still going on, like a man sawing wood, I used to say the Lord's Prayer, forward and back, until it was over. My heavens."

Lillian is finding her way through Klaberjass when Lorena Gilpin says, "Arthur told me what you're up to. I had a little girl. Influenza took her." And she says, "There are some boots that were his first wife's, nice and plushy—I think they should fit. You take anything you need. We have some money."

She pushes back in her big armchair, lace antimacassars on both arms and another pinned to the back of the blue brocade, and she gives Lillian's hand a tug. Lillian moves to her and sinks into her lap.

"I do have to go," she says, and thinks that this would be a good time for someone to argue with her.

"I guess you do," Lorena says. "I'm sure you do. Heaven knows what kind of people . . ." She stops and starts again. "Think when you have your little girl in your arms at last, how good that will be."

Lillian does think of that, of Sophie's round, warm arms reaching up to her and of Sophie's pink face and dark eyebrows; her face is sometimes as clear as a photogravure, and sometimes it fades and is suddenly gone, like chalk washed off the sidewalk.

They sit like that for an hour, cards scattered on the parquet table; Lillian's tears run onto Lorena's shirtwaist, just a few tears of Lorena's fall onto Lillian's sleeve. They cry over their daughters and over kindness and over the things love makes you do.

In the morning, Lorena and Arthur Gilpin walk Lillian to the front of the Winslow Hotel and hand her over to the mule train leader.

"This is our daughter," Lorena says, and Arthur Gilpin is surprised but he nods firmly. Lillian kisses them like she is their brave girl, and she touches the beaded reticule Lorena has given her, holding a glass bottle of geranium oil to keep away mosquitoes, two decks of cards (in case someone is all for Spoons or Canasta, Lorena says), five dollars, and a leather box of matches with A.G. burnt into the leather from Arthur, and it is no better or easier than leaving Yaakov. The packer nods and doesn't offer to carry her satchel. Lillian swings it over her back and looks straight ahead. Lorena calls out, "You kiss little Sophie for us," and Lillian walks as tall as she can, for that.

LILLIAN SITS ON TOP OF A MULE, two hundred pounds of goods on either side of her, kegs of nails and wire coil and side blocks propping up her legs like bolsters. Behind her the other mules are carrying books and bacon, board games, a radio that will come to pieces at Telegraph Creek and get put back together, two sewing kits, six cases of rum. They are going north along the Telegraph Trail, eight slow miles a day, and every night someone hands Lillian two corn-meal patties fried in moose fat, or some glistening, gamy bear meat in a biscuit, and every night the men talk about who died (Hank Boss, capsized in Kitselas Canyon; Little Jack Waller, on the Skeena; Gilbert McDonald, ptomaine poisoning up at Yukon Crossing) and who they want to fuck (Lillian Russell, says one of the old men; Bill Morrison's widow at Lower Laberge; the barmaid with big tits at Second Crossing).

Lillian wraps herself tight as a mummy in her two blankets and puts her head on Yitzak Nirenberg's satchel. She hears the men move around the campfire talking and laughing and she hears her name, and one packer says, "She's Constable Gilpin's daughter and Arthur Gilpin is a decent man," and a younger one says, "I don't give a fiddler's fuck whose daughter she is," and Lillian sleeps with a rock in each hand. At three A.M. every day, someone gives her a shake or she hears the snap of the leather on the mules, fifty animals and ten men, and Lillian and the mules are repacked. There's not much con-versation possible, but Lillian hears bits: a claim near Dawson that finally paid off, but so late in the day that the man had to sell it to his half-wit brother-in-law just to settle his debts; which telegraph operators have gone back to the world, vanished with the first signs of spring; the good effects of a vinegar douche if your rubber breaks; the wireless experiment and how it is just a matter of time before radio and telephone do away with the telegraph line altogether. There's a radio tower in Whitehorse, one man says, and the tele-graph poles are rotting all the way to Blackwater. The man riding closest to him says, Fuck that—that's old news—there's tourists coming to Dawson paying forty dollars to walk back to Atlin and shoot caribou. I could do that, the first man says. I could take a bunch of pantywaists to Atlin and put a damn moose in front of them, and the two men nod. They pass a dead mule, skeleton show-ing in back under a gray tail, the head dark and full of flies.

Another night of bear in a biscuit, and Lillian waits and watches for the Athabascan packer and for the cigarette. She wants them both when the sun goes down. He lights his own cigarette with a tall match struck on the sole of his boot and hands her one, and if Lillian were in a position to do more than stay out of everyone's way, she would try to paint him or photograph him, he is that handsome. Reuben Burstein would hire him. He wouldn't like that she was so taken with another man's looks (Reuben had a way of dismissing handsome men by praising their best features extravagantly—"Such a manly jaw," he'd say; "seductive smile," he'd say, laughing a little, leaving it to the admirer to conclude how little these things really mattered), but he would put this man on the stage before a week was out, and Rudolph Valentino would kill himself with envy. The Athabascan hands Lillian her cigarette. That's how she thinks of it, hers. It is a little love; it scorches her throat and raises a hot prickling on her tongue; her lips swell. The smoke goes right to her brain and heart, and stretching her legs and smoking this cigarette are the pleasures of her life.

"Good at the end of the day," the man says.

Lillian nods. His beauty makes her cautious. There might be no reason for caution—he might be kind and loyal, with six children and a wife he cries to leave—but his beauty entitles him to more, and worse, and Lillian thinks that she would be no better than Mrs. Mortimer, trying to hold water in a pair of cupped hands. Lillian pulls at the leaves of a fat sticky plant with glassy reddish clusters.

"Those'll take your finger right off," the man says, and Lillian clasps her hands together like a child. "I'm joking with you. Rosy sundew. It eats bugs. The leaves bloat right up."

"I didn't know," Lillian says. She cannot ask him to stay and let her comb his long black hair, which smells of bear grease. She cannot say, Touch my leg.

"Luck to you," the man says, and walks back to his animal.

Another man yells from his site, "You need some company over there? You lonely?" Lillian calls out very brightly, "No, but thank you for asking," and she gets a few laughs and thinks of Reuben again. He has not been with her very much lately, nor Yaakov, who could well be writing another play by now, and perhaps Reuben is putting it on, perhaps Meyer is starring in it, perhaps the three of them are in the Royale on a Sunday morning, bagels piled high like flannel cakes, steam pluming from samovars, and perhaps they miss her. They are in her heart and she is in theirs and it should be enough just to have been loved, even if the way they loved her now seems to have had something wrong with it, some cramp or crick, but you couldn't say that Reuben hadn't loved her or that Yaakov hadn't. Enough just to be remembered, if they remember her, and Lillian thinks they might, even if Reuben has a new seamstress and Yaakov has a new pupil. There must still be moments, in the costume room as Reuben is sitting in the old brown armchair and the new girl is kneading his thick shoulders the way he likes, or over petits fours at the Royale, when they think of her. But now, as she sits five feet from the campfire, her neck and back tight with the night air, the past is a candle at a great distance: too close to let you quit, too far to comfort you.

The older man who believes she's Arthur Gilpin's daughter squats down beside her and says, "We stop at Echo Creek for a spell and let the tenders take over. It's a short traveling season, girlie."

"You think I should go on my own?" Lillian asks. Again, she thinks.

"He who travels fastest travels alone. Goes for she, too, I guess. I got some buddies up there'll help you out. It's a lot of walking, but if you're in a real hurry . . ."

"I am," she says.

There's no point in saying that she is in a real hurry to sail up the Yukon to the Bering Strait, and walk into Siberia to find a child she has not seen for almost two years but whom she has high hopes of finding in what she thinks may have shaped up to be Stalin's Zionist Paradise. Lillian herself would feel a sort of sorrowful contempt for anyone who said such things.

Guy Gagneaux hates to ask women where they're going and why; the answer is almost always man or child and the likely outcome is obvious enough to make you sick at heart, if you let yourself listen. He gives Lillian a Tlingit knife and his extra pair of shearling gloves and tells her when they get to Echo Creek, all she needs to do is point north, and walk.

THE LIGHT FALLS in narrow green spears through the woods and spreads like a shining stain, a baleful white canopy, sheer and bright, in the open. It is fair hiking in most parts, but the air is black with mosquitoes, some of them big enough that Lillian can see their shadows beside her. In addition to the newborn mosquitoes, lively and high-pitched, there are winter mosquitoes come back from hibernating under the snow, in dead leaves or fallen bark or mossy stumps. They rise up in April, awkward and irritable but dogged, like people who have slept too long. Thousands of them swarm, mating in midair. Their wings whine in her ears like small Furies (Alecto, Megaera, and Tisiphone, and she would have had their names tattooed on her hip, had she known this was coming) and they burrow into her hair and her scalp, into her ears, in the tender place behind her earlobes, beneath her eyelids. She dots the last of the geranium oil where it will do the most good (around her mouth and eyes) and covers all of her skin with mud, even under her shirt and pants, and it does no good. The moment before the mosquito pierces her skin, she can feel its narrow intelligence examining her, feet settling between the fine hairs on her neck or wrist, bracing for the fierce, fast probe and leisurely retreat, and Lillian finds herself shouting at them and crying as she walks.

When she can, Lillian walks to a waltz. She walks to a mazurka for four miles, to a fox-trot for another four. She walks to as much ragtime as she can remember. She sings "Bicycle Built for Two" and "If You Knew Susie" and "The Battle Hymn of the Republic" and sings louder as the summer light fades without ever disappearing. The spaces between the trees will fill in slowly until the woods around her are a spiked gray wall, and Lillian has learned to make herself sleep in the endless, disturbing dusk. She sings the sad, raspy lullabies her mother had sung to her and she'd sung to Sophie: children lost, lovers separated, crops failing—dirges, all of them, and oddly cheering. She sings to Sophie all day. She wakes all night, every time she hears a crackling twig, the feathery slide of a tail over a leaf, the faint splash of something moving in the creek. In the absence of the mosquitoes, her constant companions, the air right around her is very quiet, and the other noises, ten feet, twenty feet, away rend the air.

Lillian is making almost twenty miles a day, although it's hard to keep track. She counts steps when she's too tired to think and forgets the days' final number while she sleeps. She has a scabbed, dime-size blister on her right heel that opens and reopens and two on her left foot that do not open so much as they roll back, one thin layer after another, so that on either side of the arch of her foot is a deep, pink, watery well, and these blisters take as much of her attention as the wild animals, the staggering physical beauty. (She says to herself, a dozen times a day, Remember this. For the rest of her life when she closes her eyes, she finds only three images of the thousand she intended to keep: a line of low purple flowers, sparse and underfed, sprinkled among the fallen trees; green light rippling noisily across the night sky; a pink-and-coral-streaked dawn near Tagish.) She catches two porcupines by dropping her coat over them, managing to club them with her boots, hitting out wildly as they pull themselves into quilled and terrified balls and try to roll away

from death. It is a serious, shaming, and necessary and satisfying
business and she is glad that no one sees her kill them, or wrap her
hands in her bloody coat to avoid their quills or cut their skins off in
a way that is nothing like the elegant undressing she's seen men do;
it is as awkward and uneven as tearing heavy cloth by hand and she
must pull bits of singed skin off the cooked creatures before she can
eat them. She does it and when it makes her sick she drinks water
until it has all passed out of her. Twice she's caught a large, slow-
moving bird lighting on the lower branches or pecking around in the
dirt while she held herself still. She roasted them until they looked
like chicken and she re-created their skeletons, from head to claw,
on either side of her campsite, before she moved on. (The curious
burial customs of the Red Indians, Yaakov had said.) By afternoon,
her socks are wet with blood and pus, and she has a circle of infected
bites on her neck between her shirt collar and her hat, throbbing
with her pulse.

Most of the cabins on the trail are empty. Lillian finds deserted
stations in Stewart, Iskoot, Raspberry, Telegraph Creek, and Shes-
lay. The Overland Telegraph Trail's moment is already past, like the
men on the mule train said, although not everyone knows it yet.
Men and dogs died to make it, private companies stole public
money, the glass batteries cracked, and bluestone water ran all over
the floors and feet of the telegraph operators. The Klondike's great
time had passed. The Telegraph Trail had fifty-five years of use, by
the most generous measuring; by 1935, it was radio and telephone
all the way. The trail had its defenders (old-fashioned men and some
young men, who had a radical nostalgia for things of no use to the
modern world) and they would urge the world to find it useful a little while longer. The trail would have a brief resurrection during
World War II, when Canada was worried about the Pacific arena
and put out a call for operators to work the landline north of Atlin
and south of Hazelton. Quiet, hard-drinking men who lived alone,

May 19, 1926

I Hope We'll Meet on Canaan's Shore

O GODDAMNED SKY, O GODDAMNED SEA, O GODDAMNED AND everlasting snow is what Lillian says to herself as she walks. She could be calling out the Stations of the Cross or naming the circles of hell as she descends. Everything white is her enemy. The sun on the Alaskan snow is bright and terrible; she would be blind by now if not for the scarf wrapped around her head and eyes. She needs to keep looking at the clumps of red berries—the red is a small comfort and it rests her eyes. And the knock-kneed brown moose, a tired group of ten, yards ahead of her for the last three days, comfort her, too. It's like following a pack of grandfathers, their large, weary eyes, red lids sagging, their gray muzzles, puckered as if the world is almost done with them but not quite yet. They smell her when the wind changes, they twist their necks in her direction, but they don't care.

What Lillian can see clearly is her place in the scale of this country, how easily the entire Lower East Side could drop into the cre-

vasses ahead of her. She is a gnat, and what had been her whole
world is no more than a small junk pile, old boots and body parts, an
overturned basket in the middle of the world's thoroughfare. On a
good day, the huge sky, pale as a robin's egg, darkens to a warm
turquoise at noon or one and lowers into pocked and endless gray
before night. Most days, the white sky is no different from the white
land. Sky, sea, snow. The light comes from nowhere, a faint, weary
illumination from behind a dirty screen, a dying candle at some distance. It could be that the world turned upside down while she slept
in a little trough, carved between big rocks; it could be that this
blank, ashy ceiling of sky might really be the icy rut she slept in and
that the slick blue-tinged white spreading out in front of and beneath and behind her might be the sky, not the snow.

Lillian keeps her eyes on the gray boulders ahead to fight off
dizziness. The boulders steady her a little, but they begin to move.
They are elephants, they are houses, they are armored men, they are
dappled horses. She walks through the white field onto a huge plain
that looks like nothing so much as the floor of a vanished sea, brown
and green brush in flattened circles and wild, meandering reefs of
dust-gray pine trees, thin stiff spears yearning up. It is a terrible, dark
ugliness, but for Lillian it has all of the great virtues of home; she
could hardly be more glad if she were walking up the dirt path to her
house in Turov, to her living family, to her found child.

There is a house just ahead. It's a cabin, and there is no smoke
coming from the chimney but it is a cabin, and Lillian prepares to
climb into the world again. She sees her own shadow flying beside
her over the swelling, sticking earth, wavering when her boots burrow wetly into the mud. Her feet pull out of her boots and almost
out of her socks. It seems necessary, it seems suddenly sensible, to
take her feet out of the boots, shed the rough and dirty socks, and
run toward the house barefoot on frozen dirt, and Lillian knows that
there is nothing sensible in that. To run is to die. She will walk in her

boots, with her satchel—she will sashay, by God—Meyer's coat belted around her and her shearling gloves tucked into her cuffs, and she will cross this last mile as she has crossed all the last miles. It is just land now, it is not the Furies of sky and sea and snow. There is nothing to be afraid of. Lillian hears Yaakov setting her straight, *There's plenty to be afraid of, girlie, but don't let it stop you.*

Here is the house, not a half-mile, not a quarter-mile away, and Lillian tells herself to be calm and to be confident (bold, fearless, having no misgivings, she says to herself, and says next, doubtful, uncertain, dubious, and it is a little reassuring, as she walks down to the gray, windowless house in the middle of a brown valley in a wide white sea, expecting to be killed or raped or left as food for the bears, to know at least three good English words for what she is feeling).

A small boy, naked from the waist down, opens the door. His round, tan stomach juts out beneath his shirt and his penis juts out beneath his stomach. He backs away from the door to usher Lillian in. A baby is crying in the arms of another little boy, older than the naked butler. The big brother looks at Lillian and clutches the baby so tightly that her face reddens and she begins to howl in earnest. Then three children are crying and Lillian has not even put down her satchel.

"Are your parents here?"

The children look at her. Lillian clears her throat. It has been two weeks since she has spoken at all. She sets the satchel on the floor and takes off her gloves. She unwraps the thick wool scarf and tucks it into her belt. She looks around the big room for the answer, and she asks again, in Russian, in Yiddish, and in her most American English.

The big brother steps forward and pauses. The baby seems to pause, too. She rolls her shoulders back like a boxer after a fight and wipes her face on her brother's chest. Lillian puts out her arms. The boy must be ready to drop; the baby is almost a toddler and big for her age, and this boy has the wiry, weary look of the eldest child in any place where there's not enough food or light or help. He hands over the baby, who stiffens and then pushes into Lillian's shoulder, putting a fat little hand between her cheek and the rough coat. How bad can it be? the baby seems to think.

"Where is your mother?" Lillian says.

The two boys draw close together. Lillian gives the baby back to the older boy, who seems truly sorry to receive her, and takes off her coat and hangs it on a nail. The boys' eyes widen. They don't mind her wool trousers and high boots, although they have never seen a white lady in pants, but she has a big buck knife right on her belt, in a handsome leather sheath carved in black and red with a Tlingit thunderbird. Their father has one like it, and it might be that this lady (A mother, is what the little boy thinks; he saw how she took Sally right away, saw her look at the cold fireplace, saw her scan the shelves, saw how she looked at his own naked self and that she was concerned but not angry) was sent by him. It might be that she has seen their father and he spoke to her and he has sent her on ahead while he handles the traplines.

Lillian takes the baby back and circles the room with her. The big brother hangs back because he knows what she's looking for and he doesn't want her to find it, not yet. To put her off a little longer, he says, "Sally," and Lillian says, "Sally," and Sally lifts her head and blinks her sea-blue eyes as if to say, You had only to ask.

Lillian points to herself and says, "Lillian." The boys point to themselves, and the older one says, "Ned," and the younger one says, "Billy." Clearly, they are not deaf and not mute, and Lillian thinks they probably speak English at least as well as she does, but something is keeping them from conversation. Lillian thinks, Where is she? Fathers may come and go with the seasons, but mothers stay. There is enough food, tins of milk and hardtack, for another day or two. The floor is swept dirt, and the walls are wood and dirt with some hide patches. There is a chipped cup on the floor, something dark and woody at the base of it.

"Can you change Sally's diaper?" Lillian asks.

Ned nods. He knows she knows he can. Sally would be sick to death from a dirty bottom if Ned had not been changing and washing and drying diapers for the last few days. Ned takes Sally and lays her down on the moose-hide rug. Billy holds Sally's legs apart, which is his job ever since Sally kicked Ned in the jaw. She is not so bad this time, just wet, and there are only a few big red spots on her bottom, and Ned wipes her off with the dry tails of the old diaper. Billy hands Ned the clean diaper, which is stiff as a board from drying outside, and Ned punches it a few times and smacks it against the floor. Sally laughs. Ned beating up her diaper is one of the funniest things she has ever seen and she never tires of it.

Lillian stands on the path from the cabin to the privy, listening to Sally laugh. The mother's body is there, halfway down the path. Lillian can smell her from here, and the mosquitoes are around her like a black cloud. Lillian can hear them from ten feet away. The woman's feet are puffy and bitten and her moccasins have fallen off. They lie right beside her feet as if she has taken them off just in time for her ascension. Her fingertips have been chewed on. The body is swelling under the nightgown, and the boys have put a small blanket over her face and shoulders. Her black hair spills out, half braided, from under it. Lillian doesn't lift the blanket. There is no reason for her to see the damage that the sun and the night and the animals have done to Ned's mother's face, and there is no reason for this woman to be looked on by a stranger. There is no reason for any of this at all.

Ned and Billy and Sally are in the doorway, nothing but a diaper and a shawl on Sally, who is sucking on the ends of the shawl and looking curiously at her mother's body. Her lower lip trembles, and Lillian pushes the three of them back into the house. If Sally calls for her mother and Lillian has to hear that wail of despair, that cry from the center of the soul where all hope has perished, she will have to leave these three children to die in this house, because she is not that strong.

Lillian shuts the door behind them and pats Ned and Billy on the head. They understand that their mother is dead and that there is no bringing her back and they understand Lillian doesn't want the baby to cry. Lillian bounces Sally on her knee and sings to her what she heard the man sing to his daughter on the Great Northern Railway: Trot, trot to Boston. Trot, trot to Lynn. Watch out, baby, or you'll fall in. She opens her legs and lets Sally almost fall through. Even the boys laugh. Trot, trot to Boston. Trot, trot to Dover. Watch out, Sally, or you'll fall over. And Lillian swings Sally way to the right and then way to the left. Billy would like to be bounced, too, and he comes up to Lillian and puts his hand on her shoulder. Lillian does a couple of trot, trots for Billy. She looks at Ned, who shakes his head, and Lillian smiles at him as she would at a grown man.

Lillian puts Sally to bed and asks the boys to sit beside their sister until she falls asleep. Lillian goes out the back, avoiding the dead woman, and climbs up the ladder to the food cache. She finds a jar of honey, three five-pound bags of dried beans, and even two big legs of venison. She brings the beans and the venison and a small bag of flour into the house. She cleans Billy off as best she can, feeds him condensed milk with honey, and wraps him in the shawl. Lillian puts her big coat over him and he falls asleep, holding her shearling glove to his face. It's just Lillian and Ned now. It's very cold in the house.

"Your wood?" Lillian says.

Ned points. There is a small pile of it by the hearth. Tomorrow she can find an ax, she can cut down a tree, she can split wood. She has never used an ax, cut down a tree, or split wood in her life, but there is no help for it. Lillian makes a fire under Ned's supervision and makes some fried dough for them both. Fritters, Ned says. Sure, Lillian says, *knoedlach*. After she finds the ax and chops down the tree and drags it back in pieces to the cabin, after she splits the wood and heats water to wash them all, she will have to bury the mother. Lillian climbs into the bed, putting Sally between her and Billy. Ned climbs up behind her and puts his head on her shoulder and his arm around her waist, as if they have slept together for years.

LILLIAN ALMOST LOSES a hand cutting down a thin pine tree, but she does it. She chops the tree into ragged logs and drags the logs to the splitting block and hacks away, pieces of wood flying so wildly that she yells to the children to go inside so they don't lose an eye. Her hands bleed like Christ on the cross and she apologizes to the dead mother and hopes the bears do not get her tonight, because she can wash the woman's children or bury the woman herself but she cannot do both.

At night, in the big bed, after Lillian has made Billy a pair of trousers out of a man's flannel shirt (the boys won't say what happened to Billy's own pants or how long he was walking around bare-assed), and after Sally has gone to sleep with the other shearling glove, which is now her own dear babydoll, Lillian says to the boys, "We could say a prayer for your mother."

The boys shrug.

"Do you pray?"

They shrug again, and Lillian thinks that she has never sounded so pious or so stupid in her life.

It's not that prayer seems like a bad idea out here. It seems like a good and optimistic idea, but Lillian does not believe in anything like God. She's petitioned particular gods lately (the god of edible red berries, the god of slow-moving streams), but she doesn't address

or hope to be heard by the Creator of the Universe. Lillian believes
in luck and hunger (and greed, which is really just the rich man's
hunger—she doesn't even mind anymore; that people are ruled by
their wants seems a reliable truth). She believes in fear as a motiva-
tor and she believes in curiosity (hers should have shrunk to nothing
by now but feeds on something Lillian cannot make sense of) and
she believes in will. It is so frail and delicate at night that she can't
even imagine the next morning, but it is so wide and binding by the
middle of the next day that she cannot even remember the terrible
night. It is as if she gives birth every day.

And the mighty kingdoms she has passed through, the ceaseless
white, the endless dark, swallowed up everything for weeks but spit
back Ned and Billy and Sally, and as a kindness or an afterthought,
Lillian as well. Tossed her up the path to the cold cabin, to children
who would have died, first Sally, gone in a minute one sunny day, then
Ned, neck broken trying to save Billy, fallen into the ravine looking
for Sally. And Billy under a pine tree for two days and two nights,
back broken, as the snow covered him. All three of them dead,
plucked out of the world twelve days after their mother ate a very bad
piece of meat. But here is Lillian and the four of them are safe in bed,
and not cold, and not hungry. We live and we love the world, Lillian
thinks, and we kid ourselves that the world loves us back.

"Boys," she says. They will pray, no matter what any of them believes.

She says the Sh'ma Koleinu in Hebrew, stammering a little over
her father's phrasing, and she says in English, "Hear our voice, Lord
our God, pity us, save us, accept our prayer with compassion and
kindness." She goes on to the next piece that she can manage to
translate. "Do not abandon us, Lord our God, do not be far from
us." Oh, do not be far from me, she thinks, and do not concern yourself with my lack of belief. "For You we wait, our God; You, O Lord,
will answer."

Billy lies with his right leg thrust over Lillian's waist, his face on Lillian's breast, sucking his thumb. Ned props himself up on one elbow and looks at Lillian directly. He understands that they are appealing to God, that she is asking someone they can't see and have never seen to come and help them before Lillian falls down herself and dies like his mother. Ned looks at Lillian and smiles grimly. He nestles beside her, his left leg over her legs, his left arm around her waist, pressed against his brother's shoulder, and Lillian breathes deeply between them.

IT COULD HAVE HAPPENED that the children's father would be the man Lillian had just begun to imagine, a man she hoped to dream of after another night of sleep and food, handsome as a movie star, but Athabascan and quietly desirous. Lillian lies on the bed thinking of Reuben's hands on her, and she stirs and sees pink velvet chairs and smells everything she ate the night of her dinner with Meyer at Ye Olde Chop House and she could cry for the creamed spinach and the ice cream coupe and she can feel the furry edge of the pink velvet as it pressed up beneath the thin fabric of her dress that night, caressing the backs of her thighs, where Sally's foot and patched homespun are now.

In the event, Mr. Mason is not handsome. He's able-bodied and mild in his grief, and grateful. He asks Lillian's help, he says he has no right to ask more of her but he does, and Lillian thinks that she's the same way—who isn't—we're all like cats going back to the ones who put out the milk. She's obligated to help Mr. Mason because she's done it before, because she's led him to expect it, because she has given him hope and therefore she owes him everything. They wrap the stinking corpse of Mrs. Mason in canvas and bury her on the slope to the left of the privy, Mr. Mason and Lillian digging together and in shifts for six hours. Mr. Mason says, "He maketh me

Our Brief Life

I T IS THE WARMEST SUNDAY IN JUNE SO FAR, THE SUN JUST BE-
ginning to dip. At the moment that the sun is brightest behind
her, and the shadow deepest ahead, Lillian comes over the crest and
stands not a hundred yards from the porch of a lopsided cabin.
Meyer's coat flaps at her ankles, its shoulders hang down around her
elbows, and she has Mr. Mason's iron crowbar slung like a quiver behind her. She has a bedroll on her back and she still carries Yitzak
Nirenberg's satchel, with grass woven through the handles. She
doesn't see a soul; it's possible that this cabin is abandoned, too,
which would not be the worst thing. She could use a bath, she could
use some decent food, she could use several days' rest; all of the
things she could use lie on the other side of that cabin door.

It's been easier, lately, to be alone, talking to Sophie and Yaakov,
managing the ins and outs of loneliness (soleness, she remembers,
also singleness, solitude—which implies something special and even
pleasant—and lonesomeness, which is the right, mournful, Western

word for what she feels), and when she does find a telegraph operator in residence, ready to feed her and house her for as long as she
would like to stay (and some of them seem happy to do it, most particularly the ones with native wives who come after dark and leave in
the morning, before Lillian is up, placing a little beaded bracelet or
a cupful of birch-bark poultice on the side of her bedding), she stays
a little longer. Some others make it clear that she can stay one or two
nights but that the cabin is too small and they have chosen to be
alone for very good reasons and Lillian does not have to stay even
one night with those men to know what the reasons are. When Lillian is almost at the front step, there is the creak of a rocking chair
and a shotgun gleams darkly in the shadow of the porch. Lillian
lowers her satchel slowly, so she can raise her hands as she's seen
criminals do in the movies, and she knocks her hat to the ground.
Her hair comes down and she pushes it behind her ears. It is embarrassing to have anyone, even a man with a gun and a bloodstained
undershirt, see how dirty her hair is.

John Bishop is in exile; Refuge Cabin Number Nine is his Elba.
Every morning unveils more sadness; every night he sits on the
porch and looks in the direction of home. Messages come and he
sends them out and in nine months there has been nothing particularly meant for him, Dick Bauer's recipes, Ben Benson's fantasies,
and, two days ago, the news that a woman is coming.

He watches the woman put the bag down. The fine hairs on her
neck are lit gold from the sun, her neck is ringed with dirt and
tanned between the big coat collar and her shirt. Don't move, he says
to her, and keeps his shotgun on her chest. The best thing, the smart
thing, might be to drop her where she stands and never have to
know her at all.

"I am not bearing arms," Lillian says. She keeps her hands up.

She's not bearing arms, she sounds foreign (German or Russian
was Dick's best bet but Dick had also thought she might be a Com-

munist spy) and scared to death. There's no reason to keep the shot-gun turned on her except that he can and it puts off the moment he has to speak to her. She's listing so badly to the right now, almost kneeling on her satchel, she must have limped the last ten miles. Shiny white nits cling to her scalp, climbing the strands of her hair. It seems altogether unfair to ask for, and just plain foolish to expect, some conversation or a decent game of checkers from a woman in such bad shape. They could have played gin rummy or even chess, if she knew how, and if that part didn't go too badly, or even if it did but they had laughed it off, he had imagined asking her to just lie down with him for the evening, before she went on her way. He had imagined a clean, blond, pretty woman wearing a trim jacket, and maybe a split skirt flaring above her polished cordovan boots as if she'd come down for a day's hike. He had imagined a few stalks of fireweed dressing her hair, a dimple, ruffled underthings, some incli-nation to please, or be pleased.

John Bishop lays the gun down carefully, making a show of it; he points the muzzle toward the cabin and folds his arms. Lillian takes this to mean she can put her hands down. She moves to pick up her satchel, her coat billows behind her like a stiff, dark sail, and as she tries to get a better look at him, she stumbles (her bad knee, her stiff ankle) and catches herself on the porch rail. He doesn't make a move to help her.

He does say, "You could use a bath, I expect," and it is an offer, without being an invitation.

Lillian says, "I would be grateful."

"John Bishop." He puts his hand to the brim of his hat.

"Lillian Leyb," Lillian says and she ducks her head as she's seen women do in the West. It is the very last trace of a curtsy. The for-mality strikes them both but there's no smiling at it; people up here have been known to kill each other over a dropped phrase or the fail-ure to return a pie plate.

"Would you care to come in," John Bishop says, as if she might prefer to continue on and he would not wish to keep her.

Lillian contemplates the lowering sky, the wilderness stretching out in every direction. She drops her satchel and her bedroll, sits down, and lays the crowbar across her lap.

"I would," Lillian says and she sits for another minute so that she can walk in; her legs have collapsed right under her.

Refuge Cabin Number Nine is like every other cabin she has been in. Double logs on the wall, mud chinking, a few pots and pans hanging from the rafters, clothes hung on nails, and pine plank shelving. Lillian sits in the willow chair, not moving much, and John Bishop leaves his jacket on a nail and makes four trips to the river with a big bucket. Lillian lays her things out around her in a neat line, for comfort as much as for order. She folds up her coat. She lays the crowbar on top of the coat, puts the satchel beside it, and crushes her hat into the satchel.

"I wouldn't do that," he says. "You got lice."

"I know."

You can see the lice easily, tumbling like acrobats across the crown of the hat, climbing up the hairs caught on the inside ribbon. Lillian has seen them every day for the last five days and lived with it and she thinks that a different kind of man might not have called attention to it and John Bishop thinks that, too. He thinks that he's been away from people so long, he can't talk decently to another person. Lillian turns her face away and swallows. She is not going to be embarrassed out of her rest and her bath and her dinner.

"It's a fine hat," he says and he takes it, two fingers on the edge of the brim, and he carries it outside and sets it in the sunshine, on top of a split log a few feet away from the porch.

"It looks good there," he says when he comes back inside.

"It's all right," Lillian says and John Bishop thinks that he has lost his mind.

As bad as the lice are, her feet are worse, and there is no hiding them. Her blisters weep pink, red, and yellow. The bones of her feet have been sinking inside her skin for the last two days. Even after tearing her last shirt in half and swaddling each foot like you would a baby, the blisters have soaked the muslin like wet mouths. It is terrible to watch her pull her boots off, to see the wool sock stick to the suppurating skin, and to hear her gasp when she does it. He heats the water in the fireplace and pours it into the small copper tub he washes his clothes in and uses to catch blood when he's dressing the animals he traps and soaks their skins in. He puts a handful of mint in the copper tub, to distract from its other uses and for whatever healing mint can do for her. Her ankles are bruised blue, her feet are grayish white where they are not streaked red with infection, and spotted near black with scabs. They smell like rotting meat, which they are. Her blisters are infected, her bites are infected, her sweat is rank and dark, and if she prefers not to speak of it, he prefers that, too.

"I'm sorry," Lillian says.

"Just get in the tub," he says. "I've seen worse. Hell, I've been worse."

Her body is a map of pain, each mark tells its story clearly, and John looks at them all and away, busying himself with a stew while she bathes. He peels onions and potatoes and he shoves two skinned rabbits to the side with his elbow. Lillian watches him over her shoulder while she is squeezing tepid water from a big sponge and wonders how anyone can look on those skinned animals without seeing slaughter and dead children and then thinks that if she hadn't seen humans laid out like meat, she wouldn't be likely to trouble herself over rabbit stew. There is no reason to criticize the man for making dinner.

She is surprised to hear herself say, "Those rabbits look like dead people. Dead children," she adds, as if this will clear things up.

John looks at the slick, neat ivory-and-pink bodies and nods.

Lillian says, "I'm a Jew," and she thinks, I must be out of my mind.

He had thought she might be a Jew, not that he's known many—one good boxer and his pretty, wild sister had said they were Jews, but they had also said they were the illegitimate children of Harry Houdini and he had not pursued it with them.

"Jewish. You're far from home."

Lillian opens her mouth to say that, on the contrary, Jews are found from China to everywhere else, but really, she is far from home.

"You people sure do land in the skillet."

This is either the kind of not-unfriendly remark Lillian has gotten used to in the West (in its darker versions, You people sure do have all the money; You people sure do stick together) or just a statement of fact and so observably true in this world that no Jew anywhere would dream of arguing the point.

"Yes, we do," Lillian says and she does not say, And just what do you make of those skillets, mister?

Lillian starts to lose her footing. She rights herself and she calls out, I'm fine, I'm fine, as if he is not seven feet away, close enough to see the water run out from the sponge down the bumps of her spine, over her ass, speckled with bug bites, and down her handsome legs. Without saying anything more, so they can both pretend he's not in the room, he lays a large square of linen behind her and a pair of Little Jack Waller's pants, left behind after his drowning. Lillian steps out of the tub, her wet feet by his boots, dirty water dripping off her.

John brings a stool, a copper tub, and another linen square outside and Lillian follows him. He pours warm grease, and then cool vinegar, over her hair for the nits and chases them out with a steel comb, and she lies with her head back against the edge of the copper tub and he rolls up another cloth and puts it under her neck, as if she is the child and he is the mother.

.   .   .

LILLIAN SITS IN A PAIR of men's long johns, with her feet in a tub of green and gray and violet water (John Bishop has thrown in every dried herb and bud he can find), sipping hot rum. It's the point in the evening when she should ask him something about himself, for politeness' sake, and she cannot think how to frame what she really wants to know.

John Bishop rolls his mug in his hands and says: "You know, well, you might not know—I don't imagine you've been in too many—bar fights happen fast. A bar fight is not ten rounds; hell, a bar fight is two minutes. You're sitting there, minding your own business as well as you can, there's men three-deep at the bar—it's a popular place. It's Friday night, everybody who gets paid has got paid, and we're all enjoying ourselves at the Golden Swan. I have my beer; it's not my first beer of the evening and I am with the girl I'm going to marry. . . ."

This is the kind of thing Lillian had wanted to ask about and as soon as he mentions her, Lillian is sorry.

"And the Golden Swan is her favorite place because no one from the force drinks there—I was a cop—and the man on my right leans in to admire her and he leans in a little too close and he says something I don't care for; I'm not going to repeat it. . . ."

Later, he does tell her what the man said and Lillian says, "You fought over that?" and she puts her hand on his chest, as if to undo it.

"And, what's too bad, it's the kind of thing I don't believe a man can ignore. So I stand up, just to indicate that he needs to back off, that that would be a good idea, and he puts his head down, like he's ashamed of himself and finding the right words to apologize, and the sonofabitch hits me so hard, right here"—and he puts Lillian's hand on his sternum—"I'm down on the ground gasping. It's like a horse kicked me. And he doesn't touch me while I'm down there, gasping like a fish. He says—and he's so English, I can hardly make out what he's saying—'Marquis of Queensbury,' he says. 'You've got ten seconds to pull yourself up.' I get up. I can't stay on the floor all night, although I would rather, and he looks joyful, like I am a gift of some kind—his eyes are black with the beating he's gonna give me and I think, My brother can have my old shotgun and my service revolver, my mother will get my last week's wages, and I will never make captain. I am up on one knee and the Englishman throws beer in my eyes and sweeps me down again and I get up one more time, staggering like a drunk, because I have to get up and I hit him as hard as I have ever hit anyone, a hook to the left temple and he goes back a little, not a lot—the man has a hard head and a neck like steel cable. I hit him again while I can and he shakes it off and comes toward me, with huge hands, knuckles big as walnuts. I hit him one more time—at least I've done what I can—and he trips, don't you know, his foot catches on the brass rail and he hits his hard head on the edge of a packing crate the boys hadn't finished unloading, and the man doesn't get up. He just lays on the floor. He's pale, there is some blood coming from his ear, but not so bad. I seen worse than that—I was bleeding worse than that myself. And my girl is crying and she says to me, 'John, my God, you killed him,' and I say, 'Of course I didn't kill him—the guy's an ox—wait a minute.' And he doesn't stir. I figure we should go, anyway, before the guy gets up and clobbers me—he has that Jack Dempsey look about him, and brawling in a bar is not what the brass likes. We leave—people step out of our way like I'm a dangerous man, which is a laugh.

"He was dead by the time they got to the hospital. Cause of death: the rupture, by force, of blood vessels in the brain. In the early morning, the bartender sends his nephew to me, to bring me the news.

"The brain," John Bishop says, "is like a bowl of jelly in a box, which is the skull. You hit someone hard, the skull stops moving but the brain keeps moving for a while, back and forth or side to side, from whichever way the punch came. Contrecoup, they call it. Against the blow."

He puts his hand on top of Lillian's head and shakes it, just a little bit.

"So, I am lying in bed in my brother's house; he's had his own troubles, some rum-running, some trafficking, which is how he got the house, but he's on the straight and narrow now, he's a good man, he always was a good man. He's got a wife, a nice girl, thick as a brick but all heart, he's got a baby on the way. I'm not alone in the bed, as you can probably figure—my girl is frightened for me and our future—and the bartender's nephew says, 'Tibby Kunish is dead, and everyone saw you knock him down.' The kid says, 'My uncle said you better blow.' And the kid hands me ten bucks and I take it. I have nowhere to put it, standing there in my shorts, but the kid is looking at my girl—Alice is her name—in my bed, probably the first time he's seen a woman with nothing more than a sheet on her and he says to me, still not taking his eyes off Alice for a minute in case the sheet drops, he says, 'You killed him with one punch, mister—I saw it.' And Alice says, 'That's murder, my God.' While I'm dressing, and packing my revolver, I say, 'Alice, sweetheart, I don't want to leave but I have to—it's manslaughter at the very least and I shouldn't have hit him.'

"I had some trouble before that," he says, and Lillian pours them both a little more rum.

"I say to the kid, 'Tell your uncle I'm sorry—it was an accident.' And the kid takes off. I'll go to Mexico for a little while, is what I say to Alice, wanting to see how she feels about that. She lies back down in the bed, crying a little, and pulls the blanket up, which could be an invitation, like she's keeping the bed warm for me but it's also, you can see, my answer to whether or not she wants to come with me," and Lillian can see. "And we have the hero's farewell, if you know what I mean." And Lillian does.

"And I get dressed, and take a suitcase and my brother's bedroll from when we used to camp in the Sierras. I come back to my room for one more kiss from Alice and she's gone like she was never there and so I beat it and I hear there are jobs in the Yukon, so I come up here, which is a place, you must have noticed, where people don't inquire too much about the past."

"I have noticed," Lillian says, and pushes the rabbit bones into the center of her plate.

"And you. What's your story?"

Lillian empties the tub off the side of the porch and refills it and washes the dinner dishes. She wouldn't mind if he knew but she can't bring herself to say Sophie's name out in the open anymore; at Hazelton, they had all suffered—missing and dead children were as commonplace and terrible as toothaches. Out in the world, she could become like the poor women walking down Essex Street at suppertime, holding up pictures of their husbands to anyone who would look. Have you seen my Moishe? they said, and no one had the heart to tell them the truth, that after five years, it didn't matter if anyone'd seen Moishe or not. In California or just six blocks away, with a new wife and a new baby, the man was as gone as gone could be.

Surely, somewhere in the back of Bulfinch, in a part Lillian had not gotten to, there is an obscure (abstruse, arcane, shadowy, and even hidden) version of Proserpine in the Underworld in which a tired Jewish Ceres schleps through the outskirts of Tartarus, an ugly village of tired whores who must double as laundresses and barbers, a couple of saloons, a nearly empty five-and-dime, and people too poor to pull up stakes. In this version, Ceres looks all over town for her Proserpine, who crossed the River Cyane in a pretty sailboat with Pluto, having had the good sense to come to an understanding with the king early on. Pluto and Proserpine picnic in a charming park, twinkling lights overhead and handsome wide benches like the ones in Central Park. When Ceres comes, tripping a little on her hem as she walks through the soft grass, muttering and trying to yank Proserpine to her feet so they can start the long trip home to

Enna and daylight (which has lost much of its luster, now that Proserpine is queen of all she surveys), the girl does not jump up at the sight of her mother, but takes her time handing out the sandwiches and pours cups of sweetened tea for the three of them. She lays a nicely ironed napkin in her lap and another in the lap of her new husband, the king. Proserpine does not eat the pomegranate seeds by mistake, or in a moment of desperate hunger, or fright, or misunderstanding. She takes the pomegranate slice out of her husband's dark and glittering hand and pulls the seeds into her open, laughing mouth; she eats only six seeds because her mother knocks it out of her hand before she can swallow the whole sparkling red cluster.

"We have to get home," Ceres says.

"I am home," her daughter says.

"ANOTHER TIME," Lillian says to John.

"Okay," he says. "Another time."

AT MIDNIGHT, Lillian feels him before she sees him, a darker shape in a dark room, his body blocking the faint moonlight. Lillian folds herself up, slowly, arms on chest, her thighs pressed together, and she tries to pace her breath to his (the same when she'd come upon a fox near Cabin Number Five in Atlin; it had stood, taut and ears pricking, inches away from her, and she'd been too tired to back up a half-mile, as you are supposed to do when you run into an animal with teeth and claws; she and the fox watched each other until the fox yawned, black gums and white teeth, and walked away, tail switching). Lillian lies still. She pretends to sleep, and under the warmth of the blanket, next to her unmoving and unsure host and because she cannot find her way in the dark, she falls asleep.

If she opens her eyes, if she looks in any way glad to see him beside her, John Bishop plans to at least take Lillian's hand and run his thumb over the smooth, round part of her palm. He'll lift the quilt just a little so there is not too much cold air above her and she'll slide over a bit to make room for him on the narrow bed. He'll lie down beside her and she might put her head on his shoulder, and let the weight of her breasts fall on his chest, her bad knee resting on his leg. Lillian doesn't open her eyes. He pushes her damp, oiled hair off the small sunburnt vee at the base of her neck, and she does seem to turn a little in his direction—it seems as if she's smiling in her sleep—but nothing more than that. He goes back to his bedroll on the other side of the room.

SUNLIGHT FLOODS THE ROOM and Lillian is ready, dressed and waiting for it. She steps over John Bishop, sleeping flat on his stomach, outstretched like a bearskin rug, and she moves lightly across the cold wood floor for her satchel, her coat, the new pair of pants from the late Jack Waller, and Helen Gilpin's boots, like a thief. The man has washed her socks, her shirt, the rags she wrapped around her feet, and hung them, almost clean, damp still and mint-scented, on the rough edges of the fireplace. It seems impossible to leave a man who would do that but it will be harder tomorrow, and harder the next day, and still she'll have to be going, and sooner, not later. Her hat is still sitting on the log near the porch, where he put it when he was so sorry that he'd hurt her feelings. It's wet with dew and she should take it, she knows, but there is a quick bite of pleasure in leaving something behind, in the thought that he'll see it and think of her.

Lillian walks for twenty minutes and not at her usual pace; she composes as she walks. (Miss Eriksen said: Greet with the Salutation, Explain in the Body, Close with Civility. Lillian has a sudden longing for Miss Eriksen. Each time she entered the classroom, there was the same list on the blackboard: THE NOUN (THE THING), THE

VERB (THE ACTION), THE ADJECTIVE (THE KIND OF THING), and
THE ADVERB (HOW THE THING IS DONE).

Every time Lillian went to the English class for adults (Miss
Eriksen's English was to Judith's as Judith's was to Lillian's; it was
white satin, not a bump or tear or bulging thread in it), Lillian
passed the Fishbein family and Mrs. Arbitman on the stoop.

Every time, the Fishbein boy blinked at Lillian and bawled like
a goat, "Ma, Ma, Ma," yanking on his mother's dress until the hem
was almost down over her slippers, and then Mrs. Fishbein's great
arm would come up, blocking the sun.

"Ma," Louie said, "why is there air?" Or "Why is the stove hot?"

"Hot?" Ada Fishbein said. "I'll give you hot. It's hot because
there's a fire inside. It's hot to cook the food, and if you touch even
the door it will cook you like a chicken. It could burn up a little boy,
that fire, jump out, the flames, and burn you to a crisp."

She lifted her skirt to her thigh (she did this when the subject of
stoves or children or tenement conditions came up), and she showed
her son and Mrs. Arbitman and Lillian a large webbed triangle, dark
red and wide as an iron, where she was burned. They'd all seen it before; it was her treasure. As Mrs. Arbitman had her husband's death
certificate and Frieda had her one blue eye and one brown and her
boarders, Mrs. Fishbein had her terrible scar.

Lillian began to walk past the terrible Fishbeins and the relentless Mrs. Arbitman when the social worker came up the stoop, carrying clothes for the Grossmans. The social worker particularly
liked the Grossmans because they were so grateful. They thanked
the social worker when she came up the stairs, they thanked her
when she took the clothes out of the bag and when she handed out
the clothes and when she went back down the stairs, and when she
walked away from the building, Mrs. Grossman yelled out the window, "Thank you, thank you, God bless you, lady." And Ada Fishbein and Mrs. Arbitman rolled their eyes.

At the stoop, the social worker said to Mrs. Fishbein, still waving her arm over Louie like the wrath of God, "I think you are frightening your son, ma'am." Louie buried his face in his mother's leg, his hand covering the scar, not from shame, and certainly not from fear. His mother's whole body was a comfort to him, her fat white arms, strong as a man's, her cracked, dirty feet, her fierce Ukrainian eyes. Everything she had, everything she was, was his. Louie moved his hand up to his mother's neck and petted her chest. Mrs. Arbitman laughed.

"Very frightened boy," she said.

The social worker gathered her little red jacket around her (it was very like Judith's, and Lillian had meant to tell Judith; it would have pleased her). She opened her mouth to make a smart answer and closed it, overmatched.

Mrs. Fishbein said she had two children die in a fire because of no heat and they turned the stove on and the building burned and them in it, and when this lady became the mother of dead children she could tell Mrs. Fishbein what was what.

The social worker hurried away, pink as sunset, and it was a great day for Mrs. Fishbein; she told the story to everyone for months to come, how she told off Pearl Grossman's social worker. Lillian thinks she must be telling it still and standing on the rise; she misses Ada Fishbein and her son and her friend Mrs. Arbitman and Miss Eriksen, in her pale-blue shirtwaist, as if they were her dearest friends.

DEAR JOHN, Thank you for the rabbit stew and for your kindness. I have left my hat behind, as you will see. You may want to burn it. Thank you again. Sincerely, Lillian Leyb.

Brevity and grace, Miss Eriksen said, and we do not wish to presume on mere acquaintance.

Dear John Bishop, Thank you for your gracious friendliness. I appreciate your hospitality and your fine stew. Yours truly, Lillian Leyb. (Maybe she won't mention the hat.)

Dear John, Thank you for your generous hospitality. The bed was very comfortable. You may burn the hat. Your grateful guest, Lillian Leyb. (Maybe there's no reason to mention the rabbits.)

She thinks of girls in mythology, in love with their fathers' enemies, their brothers' rivals, in love with men who don't even speak their language or worship their gods. She makes herself go as far as the next stand of spruce, then a little farther, until she can't see the top of the crest even when she stands on a boulder to look back and up the muddy hill.

There must be a laundry list of mistakes like this, opening the box that must not be opened, looking over their shoulders when looking is the one thing they must not do, Psyche burning Cupid with the lamp's hot oil, because she needs to see who it is that could love her so. Lillian turns around.

SHE WALKS PAST HER HAT and its city of lice, still on the split log. She can walk in quietly and leave the best of the thank-you notes on the brown paper he keeps near the jar of beans (in which he has stuck several pencils), and she pictures herself doing just that as she opens the door and it creaks harshly and John Bishop, blond hair loose to his shoulders, sits up on one elbow, long and narrow and bare-chested underneath the blanket.

"You missed me," he says and he smiles as if this is an old joke between married people, as if they've been parting and returning to each other hundreds of times over the years, and have come to know, the hard way, that the measure of the love is not how many partings you go through but that there is always one more reunion.

"I guess I did," Lillian says. There's no reason to mention the thank-you notes or how far she had gotten down the trail, because she did miss him, and surely, as she is already almost departed, and there can be no reason (rationale, explanation, stated cause, and also the why and wherefore) to believe that she missed him terribly in just an hour, it can't hurt to tell him the truth.

Lillian drops her satchel and her coat and her bedroll and she lays her crowbar on top of it all. She puts her boots next to his, facing the same way and she stands over him.

"You could come a little bit closer," he says.

Lillian gets under the blanket next to him, in her wool pants and grass-stained shirt and puts out a hand to find a comfortable resting spot and finds the smooth skin of his hip. She pulls her hand away.

"I'm sorry," John says. "I can put something on."

Lillian shakes her head and lies down beside him. They clasp hands and lie there, faceup and frozen, like consorts on an Etruscan tomb until, very cautiously, John puts his hand on her thigh. Lillian winces.

"Oh, my. I remember that bruise. It looked like the map of Africa, down to here," and he runs his forefinger down her leg. "I saw when you were having your bath."

"I know," Lillian says and she does know—his dark eyes had been warm on her back. She'd gotten gooseflesh time and again, standing in that sponge bath, and she'd thought, Look if you want to, because who would want to. And then he did and what he saw didn't seem to put him off. And here they are.

Lillian pulls her shirt up over her head and kicks her pants and belt to the bottom of the blanket.

"Thank you," John says.

If it was dark, Lillian might have opened her legs and closed her eyes and John might have lifted himself up and over her, and entered her, and they would have done only what they needed to, and done it so fast as to leave no trace that mattered. If it was dark, they might have found a suitable and blameless place to hide. But in the morning everything can, and must, be seen. Daylight takes us; it peels us like fruit. Their two bodies are rough and tanned along the arms and neck, shy white everywhere else, and they are marked by travel and trouble all over, like people twice their age. There are signs of misjudgment and misfortune: blackened toes, nails half gone, festering sores, her circle of bug bites, purple with white-pricked centers, his two blackened scabs of frostbite, thick, coal-like ovals cracked with red, winking slits, a barbed-wire scar, still livid, circling his wrist; lilac, mauve, and purple chafings under her arms.

LILLIAN PUTS HER FINGERS on the deep zigzag of his collarbone, broken and never set, on the line of pockmarks at his jaw, on the tiny dark nipples circled with brown hair, on his darkly furred stomach; she lowers her face to attend to it all and John pulls her up.

"Kiss me," he says, a little harshly.

He doesn't kiss her to make a show of tenderness, where there might be an actual lack, or to lighten the moment or to assure her of some sweet understanding between them that might or might not last until tomorrow, but it's still too much for Lillian and she kisses him on the forehead, awkwardly, as if he's a friend of a friend. She presses her cheek next to his and looks at the wall. They lie like this, close but unable to see each other, her breasts pressed against his sharp ribs, her hips against his, grinding a little, entwined like unborn twins.

"I think I'm not a romantic," Lillian says.

"Maybe not," John says. "So far, I can't argue with you. How would you know?"

How would she know? Lillian moves her hand tenderly along his neck until she comes to the charred circle of frostbite, which has no feeling except at the edges, where it joins his living flesh. She runs her finger around the edge delicately.

"Ugly thing," John says. "Watch it."

Lillian lifts her hand and shifts her weight away from him in apology. No, no, he whispers. I want you closer. She wraps her arms around his chest, the blue veins snaking under the skin, through the muscle and bone. Closer, he says. Come on.

Lillian wraps her legs around his waist. His hands are in her hair ("Nice and clean," he says. "I could open a business"). Her right hand cups his shoulder blade like a resting wing and she runs her left hand down his spine and presses hard at the small of his back, until he curves into her. Closer, she says. Kiss me.

THEY HAVE LAIN ON THE FLOOR so long, the room has grown dark, and now seems a good time to tell the story of Sophie, winnowed down to the essentials.

Lillian tells him as quickly as she can and he knows enough not to try to get more, or different. And he listens without moving his hand from between her breasts.

He says, "I'll come with you. Two would be better than one."

He'll come with her. Lillian gets up to boil water for their tea and he watches her measure and pour with the sharp moves of a woman offended. For all his official helpfulness, as a cop, as a good influence in the family, he's a million miles from home in the back ass of nowhere, and his black-sheep brother is the man of the family now. Alice has gone on to a more suitable husband, and who can blame her, and a good part of his day is spent sending telegrams that seem less urgent than he'd imagined (healthy babies, long-awaited deaths, business deals gone sour) and swapping recipes with other misfits. He grows a few vegetables and eats the animals he catches, none of which he's ashamed of, but none of it is much to the wider world and clearly none of it can be offered up to Lillian Leyb.

There's nothing about him, not his previous engagement to Alice, not his accidental killing of Tibby Kunish, not his temporary occupation as telegraph operator, that makes him unsuitable in Lillian's eyes. She just doesn't really hear him. He says again that he'll come with her, he says that it won't be easy. He stretches out an arm to show how they will go along the Yukon and manage the Deadman's Corner between them, and she shakes her head, as if a gnat has flown in between them. Sometimes it's the case that when you hear the thing you have most wanted to hear, you cannot take it in. Hope is everyone's mirage and everyone who comes upon that green and grassy spot, the swaying date palms and the bubbling blue pool, is temporarily taken in, even people who have been there before and even when, upon closer inspection, the oasis is nothing but a reef of sand; even with grains of sand blowing lightly across our faces, we find ourselves standing on soft grass of a tenacious, unreasonable green.

It is several hours before Lillian hears him.

"Oh," she says and she puts her head on his chest and cries and John cries, too. They are both the kind of people who wipe their tears quickly. He puts his wet hand on her wet face.

"Tell me," he says.

She tells him while they make love. She says his name and Sophie's after, as if she is introducing them. He holds her up against a tree, the bark pressing into her bare skin and she tells him every clever, darling thing Sophie ever did until the sky begins to darken. When they have to eat, they cook, and when they are sitting naked on the big Pendleton blanket, eating blintzes, Lillian lights a cigarette and takes out a deck of cards. John cracks his knuckles. They play Crazy Eights.

LILLIAN OFFERED TO CHECK the seine traps in the river while John worked and she's taken a shortcut back up the hill, coming out of a thicket of brush and pine to an afternoon sky that is much darker than it should be for June. Now she's almost lost; she moves quickly, hoping that what's in the air is the fear of snow coming but not snow itself. There's nothing to do but go back to the river and retrace her steps until she's on the right path again. And then she is, giddy with the feeling of undeserved and unlikely triumph that people with no sense of direction are prone to when they have guessed right; when two small snowflakes land on Lillian's face, she doesn't see or feel the dozen coming to rest in her hair. A June snow is the briefest flurry of small flakes melting as they fall, leaving a slick muddy glaze on the ground, unless the sun dries it before nightfall. The snow comes down in a fat and furious wave, cutting up and around her, falling so fast and thick, it drapes over the bushes and brush like wet laundry, piling around Lillian's ankles. The snow should come to nothing—it should melt away in an hour. But this particular snow is not a spring squall—it is a storm people from Nakeena to Dawson will talk about for years: frozen falling trees, birds dead on the branches in icy shrouds, hours of winter darkness in the middle of a June afternoon. The snow fills the sky entirely and it's impossible to go forward, walking into nothing, and it's terrifying to stop and look at a world that's lost its shape and shadow. Lillian finds a dryish spot beneath a pair of fallen spruce and balls herself up as tightly as the porcupines and she thinks, Do not come look for me.

When the snow does stop, late at night, the sky brightens and the world around Lillian gleams like glass. Moonlight spreads silver all over the hills, on each jeweled leaf, on the shining tree trunks themselves, everything blazing like a marquee.

Under the snow, Lillian's landmarks are no use to her. Every pine grove and stand of spruce seems the way to John's cabin, but they are as unknown as they are familiar, everything seeming changed or uprooted under the snow.

"I'm back," Lillian says as she walks through the door, and she is crying before she takes off her coat. In twelve hours, everything in the room has turned its back on her: John's jacket, the darkening rabbit skins, the crock of soaking beans. She looks for a note and finds it tucked into her cleaned hat, which smells of cider vinegar.

I HAVE GONE OUT TO FIND YOU. STAY HERE UNTIL I RETURN. JOHN BISHOP.

Lillian sits on the porch for twenty-four hours, in John's rocking chair, until it is Sunday night. She listens to the bright sound of the river rising, spreading up and onto the banks. Lillian walks off sixteen quadrants in a square mile around the cabin, careful as a surveyor, from farthest to closest, and there's no sign of John Bishop. Each day, she walks off a bigger square, tying pieces of blue cloth to different trees. At night she rolls a blanket and sleeps with her arms around it. She drinks all of John's rum and it occurs to her, really for the first time, what hard liquor is for.

The woods are clear of anything that looks like a body, a boot, a dragged carcass, and Lillian stays on for another twenty-one days, until there is almost no food. John would tell her to go, and Sophie, because she is only four, would tell her to come. And Aunt Mariam would say, This place is cursed for you now, and it may be that there is simply no place that is not.

In the last true part of Alaskan summer, she pins a note to the cabin door. It stays there, fading but legible, for two more weeks: JOHN BISHOP LOST IN SNOWSTORM, JUNE 18, 1926. PLEASE SEARCH FOR HIM—LILLIAN LEYB, BOUND FOR DAWSON, JULY 11, 1926. She leaves another note in the bean jar and trusts that if he returns, he'll find it and read that she loves him. She nails a third note on the biggest spruce with the Queen of Hearts over it and the note and the playing card blow off the tree before she is three miles up the trail. She makes her way to Dawson, posting notes every ten miles and envying the dead.

·   ·   ·

IN 1926, DAWSON CITY is no longer the Paris of the North, if it ever was. You could have called it that for a few years in the late 1800s, but only if Paris means a lot of French-speaking Belgian whores; François and Moïse Mercier, a pair of *coureurs de bois* representing the Alaska Commercial Company's interests, before they moved on to Fort Yukon; Josephine's French Laundry; and a handful of pimps, all of them actually born in Paris.

Lillian arrives by steamboat. The trip up the Yukon to Dawson is not much more than a weeklong drive up Canal Street on a Saturday morning, with scows and barges, paddlewheels dressed up for tourists and beating the water, rafts loaded with firewood, all vying and chivying, slowing at invisible signals, pulling up to the banks in the face of greater horsepower and its eddying consequences, and men yelling like city drivers (Get out of here, you blind, worthless sonofabitch! What you think I got here, you can't see these logs?) and helping one another when something goes wrong (a cow falls in the river, water pours over the wheelhouse and knocks some young boy overboard).

Lillian hears John behind her. She sees him in every other man that passes by, she smells his tobacco, she feels his hand on the back of her neck. The owner of the Cozy Lunch Room lets her pin a note to the back door and says, If you need a place to stay, there's one, and Lillian crosses the backyard to a boardinghouse. In its parlor are four schoolteachers, a middle-aged lady and three women Lillian's age, celebrating the end of the term, two of them getting ready to go home to Vancouver. Is she a teacher, they ask, and Lillian says no. Is she meeting up with a fiancé, then? Lillian shakes her head no, as there's no room here for the story of John Bishop. Chinese tea is poured in heavy white mugs, almond cookies are passed around, and some looks exchanged among the schoolteachers. Is she there, by any chance, to meet a gentleman—they just want to know—and Lillian says no again. The youngest schoolteacher, with wavy brown hair and bright-green eyes, says, Because you know what they say if you're a girl up here: the odds are good but the goods are odd, and I swear it's so.

They offer Lillian more tea and the older woman brings out small iced cakes she's brought over from Cozy's.

"I am looking for a boat," Lillian says.

The middle-aged woman says, "There's a boatyard where Harper dead-ends First Avenue—you can ask for Mr. Henry."

The young schoolteacher with the wavy brown hair says, "Mr. Henry is Miss Yardley's intended." Miss Yardley, the middle-aged woman, nods gravely and shows Lillian her engagement ring and she passes the cake plate again.

She pats Lillian's hand and Lillian cannot help but think that the gears of her life, which usually have a stick caught in them, which have brought her to this place heartsick twice over, are now meshing like a watch's oiled insides.

At the Dawson boatyard, a short man with a big mustache says, "Bill Henry's out drunk. What can I do you for?" and when Lillian tells him only that she wishes to go up the Yukon River and make her way from Little to Big Diomede and into Siberia, he takes a long pull on his beer and studies her, not even pretending not to. He laughs unpleasantly. Lillian takes out two of her maps and the man brushes them away.

"You'd need a damn sturdy boat and an outboard motor," the man says. "And a crew. And still you'd be crazy."

And before Lillian can say, I can buy an outboard motor, a younger man, thin and angry, folds his arms and says, "We don't got any—we won't until October, and then it's all ice and no good to you. I'm thinking next spring."

The men settle themselves on the barrels and light their pipes.

Now that it is clear to everyone that they won't be selling her anything, that she'll go home empty-handed, and that they might be
seeing her around town all winter, and one of them might find himself wanting to court her come October, the man with the mustache
says pleasantly, "We're on the list for an Evinrude—that's a good
motor."

SHE COULD SETTLE IN DAWSON—people do, some eight thousand
of them, in the neat dollhouses on Duke and Albert or the shabby
mansions on Princess and Queen. There are signs all over, showing
that there used to be a flourishing township: two hospitals, Shriners,
the Flora Dora Dance Hall, the Yukon College of Physicians and
Surgeons, four churches, and sixty-three restaurants. What is left
since the fire of 1899 are lopsided buildings trussed with metal, a
handful of cafés and more cigar stores (which double as whore-
houses), and three dry-goods shops (Mac's Groceries, Arctic Sun-
dries, and Margie's Five Cent Store). And then, right there, nailed
square above the door, ISAAC ROSEN, FINE TAILORING, ALTERATIONS
FOR ALL OCCASIONS.

Isaac Rosen sounds like a widower, the kind with a pretty,
plump, black-eyed daughter around eight, her dark-brown hair
pulled tightly to one side with a cluster of white bows. Isaac Rosen
sounds like Opportunity. Lillian tries to picture the Rosen girl and
Sophie playing in the parlor while Lillian makes dinner and she sees
Isaac Rosen, thinning brown hair and gold-rimmed spectacles,
reading the newspaper. He moves his feet to make room for the girls
playing on the floor. He looks a bit like Yaakov, and Sophie runs a
wooden carriage around his chair. Lillian is almost bored by her own
tears; they fall at nothing now since John. She keeps walking.

At the corner of Princess and Front streets, behind an old man
and a young boy, Lillian sees her boat, sitting on a pair of iron run-

ners. It is wide and deep and misshapen, more like a seventeen-foot pumpkin with the top cut off than a barge. Lillian runs her hand along the rail.

"She has grip in the water—no rolling." The man is old and a little drunk and possibly Norwegian, with icy blue eyes and seamed red skin. "See her afloat, you might think she's nothing much, but she goes deep—she won't throw you."

"Good," says Lillian.

"It's not a scow. Why, you could handle it yourself, young lady."

The son or grandson, small but game, probably the only one in the family who still talks to the old man, says, "We could use the cash." The old man nods and says, "That is no lie but she's a good boat," and Lillian says, "I'm sure it is."

"Business or pleasure," the man asks, although the boat doesn't look like it could provide either.

"I am going up the Yukon, across the Bering Strait, past the Diomede Islands, and on to Siberia."

The little boy laughs. The old man slaps the back of his head and spits.

"Fifty-three miles," he says. "It's been done. I got a friend killed a bowhead whale out there. Still got the teeth."

"Oh, good," Lillian says and she sees herself exactly as they see her: doomed, foolish, and peculiar.

"Three weeks," the man says and he steadies himself on the boy's shoulders. "She'll be ready."

"Fine."

This must be where she was headed all along.

JOHN BISHOP BROKE both of his legs. He knew it the minute he fell down the incline, ass over teakettle, and felt his feet lock under a cross of heavy pine branches. They're not the worst breaks and there is no bone showing through the skin, which would have undone him, but his feet are stuck in the mud and branches and sliding rocks, useless as flippers. He will probably die wedged under a reef of pine, never see Lillian or his mother (she will have buried two boys now, his little brother gone with the croup in 1912). Alice will probably sing at the funeral, proud as she is of her singing voice, and it is good to know, before he dies, that Alice didn't do anything like break his heart, which is what he had been thinking this past year. She chipped it just so, like undercutting stone to get the right angle, and Lillian came along and took off the top. If she's not dead, Lillian must be worried sick.

He wakes up looking at strips of birch bark. He is lying in a canoe, lucid and not uncomfortable except when he twists his torso a little to see what part of the river they're on. When he shifts to see over the strips of bark, he finds two kinds of pain, a flash of lightning inside his tibia, a red-hot web over his anklebone. Two men are paddling the canoe, which is built for two small men and a load of fish. Neither of them speaks to him when he tries to sit up; the man behind him puts a hand on his shoulder, to press him down and steady the canoe. They are Tr'ondeck Hwech'in, the Han people of the First Nation, known to the telegraph operators as the People of the River. The telegraph operators are known to them as men without women and they are bringing this man back to their village the way a child brings home a stray dog, in a rush of kindness and curiosity.

In the month John Bishop spends in the Twelve Mile village, he is always the stray dog. When someone really needs a hand, when even a white, crippled hand is better than nothing, they invite him to help. Women leave his meals on the porch. For two weeks, they carry him to his chores. He helps caulk another man's birch canoe, chewing wads of spruce pitch with the women and plugging small seams on the frame; he helps Walter Isaacs put an outboard motor on his boat. When the men go for grayling and whitefish, they don't invite John, because of his color and his condition. He hangs fish to dry and studies the women's birch baskets, which seem as sturdy as rubber; he throws dried salmon to the dogs and sits on the ground to sort potatoes for Jerry Woods. At night, Lillian finds him in the woods, or he finds her in Dawson, and waking up is the only thing he cannot bear.

There are ten houses in Twelve Mile. The water is clean and the Han give John the cabin of an old couple who died of the flu just two months ago. As soon as he knows who speaks English, he asks for a pencil, he asks for paper, he asks if anyone is going to Dawson. The Han go to Dawson all the time—everyone says they are the Jews of the Yukon: they trade, they bring in furs and tons of caribou meat and the mitts and parkas their women make; they take out guns and canvas and tea. There are the Anglican boarding schools, waiting to snatch their children in Dawson, and the Royal Canadian Mounted Police enforcing new laws, hunting licenses and fishing licenses costing a hundred dollars. No one in Twelve Mile is inclined to go into town just now, with their illegal catch. In winter, one of John's rescuers says, white people'll be happy to see the meat. Jerry Woods makes John a pair of crutches with moose-hide pads. He walks every day, a little farther each time, and two small boys walk behind, pretending their pine branches are crutches. Soon, Jerry says, I'll be making you a cane, and John thanks him for the thought.

"You got a woman," Jerry Woods says.

"I do. Probably gone to Dawson."

Jerry says, "Dawson's not far. I might be making a run over there. I like the nightlife."

He winks at John, who winks back, thinking that whatever this man might want or need or choose to do under cover of night, he will do it with him, if it gets him to Dawson.

. . .

THE OLD MAN AND HIS SON let Lillian help in their scrubby vegetable garden and make them dinner on their two-burner stove. The little boy never mentions a mother or a father or school, or any life except helping this old drunk prepare Lillian's boat. They spend some of her money on repairs and three weeks later to the day, they rub fish oil on the iron runners so they shine and stink. Lillian puts the last of her notes for John Bishop at the entrance to the boatyard. They hook a chain through the prow and push the boat into the water, snub nose first, splashing the deck. And there is Lillian, heading north to go south, as one must on the Yukon River. The mustachioed man from the real boatyard contributed a coil of rope, a sack of flour ("Since you're hellbent on going," he said), and a heavy, waxed canvas life preserver from his father's ship, the *Lindeman,* which sank in the White Horse Rapids twenty-five years ago.

Torbjörn Jensen and the little boy, Oyvind, wave their hands and Lillian waves back, one hand on the sweep, her satchel between her feet. The men shake their heads as one when they lose sight of her.

THE YUKON RIVER IS A WIDE, calm flow of dark-brown water, mild as chocolate milk, but the current is against Lillian. The river pulls the wrong way and the few men walking along the banks can keep up with her. She has the small, glossy map of the Bering Strait that Yaakov stole from the New York Public Library and she has Torbjörn Jensen's pencil sketch, showing that she will come out near St. Michael, sail across the narrow and traversable Bering Strait to Chukot, where she will meet Indians who are just like the Han and the Athabascan but happen to be Russian, according to Mr. Jensen.

There are endless bends in the river and the boat seems drawn to the banks even as Lillian pulls it, like a mule, toward the river's center. Young trees along the river's edge bend down to the water and bunches of them seem to grow facedown in it, their branches waving like women in distress. The oar is useless; the boat bounces from the banks to midstream and back and as it begins to settle again, there is some eddying, which Mr. Jensen has prepared Lillian for (Stay away from what you can't beat, he said. Don't be fooled by the calm, and Lillian thinks that all advice is like Mr. Jensen's: true enough and useless as tits on a bull, another expression she's learned from him).

Lillian's ship is shoved from behind, and she hits a rock twice, the current pressing the side of the boat firmly up onto the rock, which had seemed like a turtle twenty feet away and now seems like a humpback whale, implacable and fierce, as if she is in its way. Lillian moves the sweep, she guides the ship away from the treacherous rock and is midstream again but listing, water spitting up from a whirling pool, splashing up and over the deck. In the slow motion of all accidents, Lillian is waist-deep in cold water, her satchel is five, then ten, then thirty feet downstream, as is her sack of flour, her salted caribou meat, her sealed carton of cigarettes, her maps. Right below the two inches of sun-warmed water, the river is the cold, thick thing that it is. Lillian kicks her legs hard; she can feel them tighten and slow, her heart beats in her ears and she chips a tooth on a metal edge as the boat slides past her. It comes to lie sideways on a sandbar, like a horse sleeping in a field.

Her clothes are plastered to her skin, cold water running from her head to her boots, pooling in the wet rabbit fur around her ankles. Lillian takes off her blouse, tearing off all the buttons, and wrings it out and puts it back on, leaving it unbuttoned to speed the drying. Gasping with cold, she wrings out the sleeves of Meyer's overcoat and then twists the heavy fabric from shoulder to hem, until she has gotten as much water out of it as she can. She empties the pockets, in which she has, inevitably, her clip of safety pins and Snooky's waterlogged gold watch and the chain, but not the cherrywood cross Mary Hornsmith gave her. She has less now than she did when she walked through Ellis Island with Frieda's address pinned to her blouse. She's gone five miles from Dawson.

EVERYTHING RAISELE HAD SAID WAS TRUE: the Pinskys found Sophie crying on the steps of the chicken coop; they put a quilt in the bottom of the wheelbarrow and covered Sophie with rags, so she would not excite any interest. They headed east (Lev Pinsky said, Everyone's going west. By the time we get wherever we're going, people will be closing their doors to Jews; they'll be sick of us—and he was not wrong). Mariam had been truly mistaken—she did think she'd seen little Sophie's ribbons floating in the Pripiat, as she would see her dead relatives floating, and sitting in cafés, tilling fields in Turov, and occasionally walking naked on the streets of Vilna, for the rest of her life.

The Pinskys made their way to Tikhonaia, the Zionist Paradise, which had no drinkable water, swamps on every side, and barracks for the families not lucky enough to get a moss house, dug into the side of a hill and very much like the winter villages of the Han, but not as nice. Tikhonaia was renamed Birobidzhan. Signs were posted everywhere to remind the settlers where they were, and Birobidzhan got its own lottery, to raise money for sewers, farming equipment, and public lighting; it got the Kaganovich Jewish Theater, and it got its own newspaper, in which the writers were free to express contempt for all things Jewish, and enthusiasm for all things Soviet, in Yiddish, no less. Birobidzhan was declared the capital of the Jewish Autonomous Region. As M. I. Kalinin put it in one of his barnstorming tours of the region, "You people are the colonizers of a free, rich land, people with big fists and strong teeth."

Lev Pinsky wasn't fooled. He saw accountants, tailors, bookkeepers, and tinsmiths face-to-face with musk oxen and ancient plows, four thousand Korean residents who were as puzzled as the Jews. He noted the proximity to the borders of hostile nations. He waited for another day's outbreak of confusion, another train dumping Jews onto a patch of dirt and pulling away as women and children cried in disbelief at the wreckage surrounding them. He saw what was called for and he exerted himself. He broke the neck of a low-level railroad employee and took his papers, and shoved the body into an empty hut. At night, behind the barracks, he said to Rivka and little Sophie (who will never know that she is adopted, who will remember Lillian as the smiling, dark-haired cousin who gave her a blue wool scarf), "We are the Bugayenkos now and we are going to Vladivostock."

Sophie is the heart of Rivka Pinsky's life; she is her mother's jewel, hidden and undeserved. She grows up as Tatiana Bugayenko, an atheist, a Red Pioneer, when her father thinks the time is right, and it is Lev's eye for the brass ring, his heartless opportunism, that saves their lives. It gives Sophie the chance to be first in her class in Vladivostock, picnicking in the botanical gardens with good-looking gentile boys who are only a little intimidated by her intelligence. Lev's is the best kind of opportunism; it makes him say to Sophie, Go to the university, and when she expresses some doubt in the fall of 1939 that an eighteen-year-old girl can or should go to the state university of Leningrad, Rivka says, There is nothing you can't do, my darling, and Lev says, Go for me and study science—it's hard to debate science, and she goes. He is not quite right about the safety of science, but it proves safer than philosophy or poetry or journalism. A poem by Tatiana Bugayenko surfaces in the early 1960s and is very popular among young people, in which the poet thanks her father for telling her the truth about the university. Sophie reads and writes poetry, she translates some Mallarmé into Russian; she marries another scientist and they have no children but they have three nephews whom they spoil. They live in relative comfort and they betray no one. They retire to Vladivostock and sit on a small cement terrace, with two curvy, wrought-iron chairs and a small bistro table. They have tea every day at four o'clock, which is her husband's favorite English custom. They watch the sea.

THE SPRUCE IS THICK in front of Lillian, and past that she can see the luminous birch trees and beyond the stand of birches there is some movement, a flash of soft brown, an animal. John Bishop is walking. He doesn't have the handsome, swinging gait he did and it is not the fault of his bear-head cane. ("There's a hitch in my giddyap" is what he says about it.) His awkward, determined walk comes to be how Lillian finds him in crowds. His walk and his long blond hair, and even when it goes gray, it seems to her that there is always some gold in it and that she can find him as long as there is light.

Lillian will sail the Yukon two more times, in a better boat and with John, and they will get farther each time, but never near far enough. They sell the boat and have two children and when her daughter climbs into her lap and says, Tell me when you were a little girl, Mama, Lillian says, Oh, *shainele punim,* it was such a long time ago, who remembers? And she brings out her illustrated Shakespeare, so they can act out the three witches or the balcony scene.

When they are old people, when Lillian has stopped teaching English to the children of Skagway, she packs up her classroom and brings home her seven dictionaries, her thesaurus, her copy of Bulfinch, the collected works of William Shakespeare, and two shelves full of other poets. (She does read the Russian poets, in the original, Anna Akhmatova and Mandelshtam, but she doesn't come across the poems of Tatiana Bugayenko, and even if she had—.) When there is a warm, bright afternoon, she walks over to the river; she sits with a blanket and a book; she reads to Sophie.

John retires as police captain, after twenty-five years, and retires again as sheriff. Their son and their daughter move away and John and Lillian visit the children and grandchildren every winter, until even that is too difficult. They make one last trip to California. They are strolling slowly, like tourists, like old people for whom a trip to San Francisco's Fisherman's Wharf is an adventure, and their hands loosen. They are pulled apart by the crowd, by sightseers and grifters, by people handing out sample chocolates and directions to restaurants, by small girls in blue hair ribbons sitting on their young fathers' handsome, wide shoulders. Lillian looks for John, she looks right and left for his bear-head cane and shining hair, and her daughter says, "It's all right, Ma, we'll find him."

Lillian pushes her away as if she has never heard such cruel, useless nonsense and walks into the crowd. John looks from face to face for Lillian's big eyes, he looks for a small, straight back and a gray braid and sees none. Lillian comes up behind him. She puts her hands in his pockets. They hold each other in the shifting crowd and she says, into his chest, "I thought I had lost you." They are standing, wet-faced and smiling, with their arms around each other when their daughter comes upon them. Her father says to her mother, You couldn't if you tried.

LILLIAN DRIES HER FACE and hands on the birch leaves. She takes off her wet boots and stands, barefoot, in a drift of dead leaves. She presses her face against a tree until she can feel the bark marking her cheek. She has thought before that she couldn't bear it, that despair would drop her where she stood, but she was wrong. It was terrible, but nothing to this, and she puts both arms in front of her, like a swimmer, parting the low branches, to find a place to lie down. The light in the woods is a thick, wavering green. She hears the drumming of a woodpecker above her head and the leaves rustle toward her. It is John's hand she sees first.

Author's Note

This is a work of fiction, from beginning to end. To the best of my ability, I have worked from the particulars and facts of geography, chronology, and customs of the past. I have also moved things and people, adjusted and reconfigured both, when it suited the story.

Acknowledgments

I am blessed, as I have been from the beginning, in my Random House editor, Kate Medina, an icon of literate and wide-ranging intelligence, civility, and elegant strength, and in my agent, Phyllis Wender, undaunted, wily champion, knowledgeable scout, and inestimable home port. I am grateful to the Bogliasco Foundation, the Yaddo Foundation, the MacDowell Colony, and Gil Kelman's Stone Cottage, as much of this book was written in those places.

I have made great use of a number of books, loaned by libraries from Anchorage's Municipal Libraries and the Rasmussen Library at the University of Alaska, Fairbanks, to Yale's Sterling Memorial Library and my own Durham Public Library, and must particularly mention Bill Miller's *Wires in the Wilderness;* Cassandra Pybus's *The Woman Who Walked to Russia;* Charlene Porsild's *Gamblers and Dreamers;* Robert Weinberg's *Stalin's Forgotten Zion* (about which I would have known nothing if not for Andrew Gould); and *What a Life!,* by Pesach'ke Burstein with Lillian Lux Burstein, as useful and intriguing sources. I must also thank Mark Slobin for his generous and endless knowledge of music in general and Yiddishkeit in particular and the students and English-department faculty of the University of Alaska campuses in Anchorage, Homer, and Fairbanks, who made me welcome, looked after me when I was sick, and helped me know what remains of that beautiful wilderness.

240 *Acknowledgments*

Joy Johannessen continues to be the archangel of editors. She is unerring, unswerving, attentive to a laserlike degree, and always, always devoted to the writer, the sentence, and the best possible book.

My friend Malcolm Keith, who guided and judged so much of my work, is with me only in memory now, but my other friends and dear readers Kay Ariel and Bob Bledsoe have stood and sat and walked and talked with me, late at night and early in the morning, with heart and soul and no shortage of intelligent criticism. My friend Richard McCann came in at the eleventh hour with the clarity, brilliant wit, and patient insight that the eleventh hour seems to require.

My assistant and friend, Blake Gilpin, is a rock when a rock is needed, a pal and a sounding board, a fine musician, a fine writer, and the gold standard for amanuenses everywhere.

And I must thank Brian Ameche for keeping me and Lillian company on the last leg of our journey, through such difficult terrain.